For my husband, J.B.; my biggest fan, my strongest supporter, my inspiration. I love you, CAG

About The Author

Residing amidst the picturesque mountains of Pennsylvania, Cyn's creativity flourishes as she weaves tales of love and mirth. With her beloved spouse by her side, she has raised four handsome sons. When not penning down her thoughts, Cyn works in her field of study: Art/Interior Design.

Table of Contents

Chapter One

Philadelphia, Pennsylvania, 1800

The heavy winds caused a cacophony of sounds as shutters banged against building walls, tarps flapped against wagons, and branches and hats blew down the sidewalk and street. Tiny dust tornadoes swirled around, picking up leaves and debris along their path and pushing them under porches and benches.

When a deafening whack sounded against Natalie Wakefield's building, she shot straight out of her chair and hustled to the front of the shop. There, hanging by one chain, blowing back and forth and occasionally crashing into the building, was her ornate shop sign: *Natalie Wakefield, Couturiere of Fine Fashion.*

Before she had time to react, another strong gust returned and swung the sign against the building, barely missing the display window. Distraught, Natalie rushed down the hall to grab her cloak. She was frantic that the wind might damage her property any minute, and she agonized over how to remedy the threatening situation.

When Natalie returned to the front, she saw a man reaching for the sign. His coat collar stood up, and his hat was pulled low, shading his face. He held the free end of the sign in one hand while he unhooked the chain of the secured end with his other. Relief washed over her as she watched him successfully lower it from the bracket. She hustled to the portal to welcome him inside.

"I can't thank you enough. Please, come in," she offered, swinging the door wide.

As soon as he cleared the threshold, Natalie slammed the door shut against the wind while the man moved to the far corner of the shop to prop the sign against the wall out of harm's way. He removed his hat and turned around to face her.

"Ben, it's you! I did not recognize you," Natalie sang with a pleasant surprise. "Please, take off your coat. I will make you a hot cup of tea,"

"No, thank you," he answered. "I appreciate that, madam, but I have some pressing business and can't stay."

"Oh . . . yes, of course. I know you are a busy man," she replied, disappointment shading her voice.

"I delivered a cabinet across the street and saw your broken sign. I thought I would take it off the bracket before it damaged your building."

"I am so thankful you saw that, Ben. I was not sure what to do. My first thought was Stanley Musser. I know he is always willing to help me."

Natalie knew Ben was not fond of Stanley Musser, so she deliberately threw out the bait to see his reaction. Ben had often commented that she better be careful with what she asked of Stanley because he had "other things" on his mind where she was concerned. And perhaps Ben was right about Stanley's dishonorable intentions, but as far as Natalie was concerned, Stanley Musser was of no interest to her except to make Ben jealous.

Ben stood by the window with his back to her. "If this wind dies down, I'll try to return later today and get it back up for you."

Natalie's heart soared. "Perhaps you will stay for dinner then? My way of payment for all you do," she suggested, moving closer.

Ben turned to face her, his gaze sweeping from the top of her auburn curls down to her shod feet, returning until their eyes met.

"You do not owe me, Natalie. We are friends who help each other. I'm sure the future holds some favor I'll need to ask of you."

"I hope so, Ben," she breathed.

He stared at her disappointed expression for a long moment, then slapped the side of his leg in resignation. "Listen, I'll try to get back early enough to fix that sign and share dinner."

She reached out, placed her hand on his arm, and smiled delightedly. "Really? Oh, Ben, that is wonderful, simply wonderful," she repeated, unable to contain her excitement.

He glanced down at her hand on his arm with drawn brows, politely nodded, and walked out the door.

When Ben departed, Natalie returned to her apartment to organize her meal. She hung her cloak on the hook, paused before the standing mirror, smoothed her coiffure, and adjusted the locket around her neck. Staring at her reflection, she pondered why Ben Walters had never made an intimate approach. Granted, she wasn't sixteen anymore, but her skin and eyes were smooth, and she knew her figure captured a man's attention. In addition, she was single, successful, and possessed a goodly number of female talents. She could cook, sew, keep a tidy house, grow a decent garden, and run a thriving dress shop

3

without skipping a beat. Natalie thought she was quite a catch and could not understand his reticence.

Often, she detected a burning light of desire in Ben's eyes when he looked at her, but he always turned away with a frail excuse that something else was calling him to duty. It frustrated her beyond reason. She needed to uncover what held him back and was determined not to give up until then. He was entirely too important to her.

Her workload was lighter than usual today, offering her a few hours to devote to the evening ahead. Tonight was the night. She was not going to let his excuses stand in the way again. No sir-eee. She would show him she could stir more than a pot this time!

There was no dinner guest Natalie enjoyed more than Ben Walters. He flattered her culinary skills by accepting a hefty second serving of everything and ended each meal with a large portion of dessert and a hot cup of coffee. One wouldn't know it by his physique, though. His strong, six-foot frame walked with a purposeful gait and a confident air. His arms, defined with boulder-like muscles, swung from shoulders broad and straight, and his lust for life sounded in the deep timbre of his laughter and showed in the sparkle that shot from his beautiful blue eyes. In Natalie's opinion, Ben Walters was the epitome of perfection.

"You are a very talented woman, Natalie," Ben complimented after finishing the last bite of pie.

"Well, Ben, I have worked a needle since I've been six years old and have had plenty of practice."

He nodded in agreement. "But it's not only your sewing talents I'm referring to, madam. That meal was fit for a king."

Natalie's heart skipped a beat as she watched his hand pat his tight abdomen. She loved those hands. Strong work-worn hands. Competent hands. Hands that turned raw wood into fine furniture that felt as smooth as a newborn baby's bottom. She wished to feel those hands on her body someday, stroking her with the tender caresses she longed for. Her heart beat out a rapid rhythm with the mere thought of it.

This evening had turned out well. Ben had relaxed throughout dinner and generously contributed to their conversation. They had shared concerns over city politics, highlights, and grievances with their recent business transactions. He had even gifted Natalie with a hearty chuckle when she dramatized some of her clients' bizarre requests. But more so, Natalie had noticed Ben's interest in her swaying skirts each time she rose from the table to retrieve a needed item. His gaze had followed her every move with interest, which pleased her immensely. In fact, at one point, when she was recounting a tender story, he had even reached across the table and squeezed her hand with affection.

The evening seemed perfect.

That was until, without warning, his mood shifted, and he suddenly stood up and carried his empty dessert plate to the sink in a signal of farewell.

Natalie was flummoxed. One minute they were laughing, sharing, and *touching,* and the next minute, he was leaving! Why?

"You are a generous woman, Natalie, but I should call it a night. I'll bring wood in for you." And just like that, Ben exited the kitchen.

Natalie's spirits plummeted. She nervously moved to the hutch and filled a bag with her freshly baked cookies for Ben's ride home while fretting over what she could do next to hold him. She hated the goodbyes and promised herself that this evening would end differently come hell or high water. He had never ended their evenings with an invitation to the theater, a Sunday afternoon ride in the country, and *never* a kiss good night! Nothing! By darn, she wanted more from their relationship, and she was at the end of her rope with how best to make that happen.

"There you go," he stated when he returned, dropping an armful of wood into the rack and brushing the debris from his shirt.

Natalie moved closer. "Thank you for fixing my sign, Ben," she purred.

"And thank *you* for a fine evening," he added as he squeezed her shoulders and brushed past to retrieve his outerwear.

Oh, that made her mad. Her hands drew into tight fists; her expression turned thunderous. She had given him plenty of time, enough invitations, and a handful of opportunities to kiss her, yet for the past two years, he had fooled with her heart, teased her with endearments, winked at her while giving her a manly head-to-toe appreciative inspection and all without an ounce of physical contact. Tonight, she was determined to put it to an end. He had taken this thing too far!

"Just a minute, Benjamin Walters," she bit out in a tone that stopped him dead in his tracks. "I need to know exactly what is going on between us. I am embarrassed to bring this up, but if it's left to "*YOU*," I'll wait until Hell freezes!"

Ben's brow creased at her tone and choice of words.

"And don't look at me like that," she scolded. I mean to have this out! It has been two blasted years of pussyfooting around. You come to dinner, we stretch it out for two or three hours, hash over everything from church to politics, and then you bid me a brotherly goodbye!"

Ben's gaze swept over her with a slow and thorough inspection.

Natalie wiggled her shoulders and pursed her lips.

"What kind of goodbye did you expect?" Ben said in a low daring tone, standing a hair's breadth away from her.

"A manly goodbye," she fearlessly returned, pushing her chin up to face him directly. "You are a coward, Benjamin Walters! No, excuse me; perhaps the word is amateur!"

But before Natalie got another word out, Ben yanked her close, gripped her head, and pulled her to his lips, giving her exactly what she had been begging for.

Natalie's arms wrapped around him instantly, surrendering to the kiss, while her fingers pressed along the strong column of his backbone. A fervent growl sounded from deep in his chest as the kiss intensified. Their lips parted, and at the first touch of their tongues, Natalie realized Ben's desires were stoked and encouraged to journey down a bolder path. His hand slid low, applying gentle pressure on her derriere, drawing their bodies closer, while his other hand slid up her rib cage and caressed the side of her breast. Natalie was in heaven. His hands were finally on her; they felt exactly as she had dreamed.

But just like that, when she thought she had finally won the battle, Ben grasped her upper arms and set her from him, ending the magical moment.

His chest expanded with an intake of breath. His expression was stormy. His words were threatening.

"Judge me now, Miss Wakefield."

Natalie's heart pounded with excitement. She felt delightfully lightheaded, taking no notice of his aggravation. She wanted to answer him with, "*the best kisser I've ever known,*" but before she could form the words, he jerked up his coat collar, took a long sweeping gaze of her from head to toe, then marched out the door into the cool night air.

His exit snapped her out of her dreamlike state. Ben hadn't cleared the porch steps when Natalie's voice frantically called out to him.

"Ben! Wait!"

Ben stopped, squeezed his eyes shut, and sucked in an exasperated breath of air before turning toward her.

"You forgot your goodies," she cried, rushing forward with the sack of cookies.

He reached for the bag, an exasperated expression covering his face. "Get in. It's cold out here," he ordered. Ben turned away, missing the kiss goodbye Natalie blew from her fingertips.

#

Chapter Two

When Natalie gazed out her bedroom window the following morning, she realized the sun had never shone brighter. It reflected off the frost-covered October landscape, casting prisms of light from the crystal-covered leaves. Winter would soon rush in with a frigid blast, but the fire burning inside her promised a long-awaited comfort for the cold months ahead.

Ben Walters! What a man!

To think she called him an amateur! The sheer memory of the kiss they had shared the night before had her body tingling from head to toe, reassuring her that Ben Walters was no upstart in the love department. She squeezed her pillow, emitting a sigh of pure pleasure. His kiss was perfect, a delicious memory to savor repeatedly.

Natalie's day presented a full schedule of demanding clientele, and she knew lying abed with a headful of dreams was impossible. So, reluctantly, she slipped from the cozy covers, drew on a warm robe, and padded to the kitchen to start her day. She felt an extra surge of energy this morning. There was a bounce in her step, a song in her voice, and an excited pounding in her heart. She nearly waltzed to the hutch that housed her teacup, lifted it from the shelf with a wrist swing (pinky extended), and placed it on the table as if she were fit to serve tea to the Queen of England. One kiss from Ben and her spirits had been lifted higher than the clouds. Natalie believed little could spoil her day, week, and future with the man of her dreams. Life was good.

Three mornings later, Estelle Wilcox walked into the couturiere's shop. Then Natalie's euphoric mood over the past seventy-two hours met a swift death.

Estelle's incessant gossiping ground Natalie to a hard edge. Upon the first hello, Estelle spouted negativities about someone or something, and her chatter didn't stop until she departed. It went without saying that a fitting with Estelle Wilcox was equal to the pain of a sharp blade across her wrist.

"Yoo-Hoo! Natalie! Estelle, here!"

Natalie squeezed her eyes shut, ground her teeth, and took a fortifying breath before she laid her fabric on the tabletop and moved into the shop.

"Good morning, Estelle," she greeted with measured patience.

"My, there's an autumn nip in the air. Winter is just around the corner," Estelle chirped. She shrugged from her drab cloak and blew lightly on her hands, turning toward the waiting couturière. "Natalie, what an absolutely gorgeous shade on you. I would love to wear something so bright."

"You're comfortable with more subtle shades, Estelle," Natalie drolly reminded her.

Natalie always offered the customer her professional opinion, and, in her estimation, Estelle's best colors were gray, brown, and black. Those colors matched the dark mood she was forced into in Estelle's company. Most of all, Natalie couldn't picture Estelle in vibrant shades. Her offensive personality needed little else to draw the attention of others.

"You're right. Actually, you're always right in matters of apparel," Estelle agreed, turning to the movement outside Natalie's front window. "Would you look at that? She is sweeping her front stoop again when there's simply nothing to sweep! Really, Natalie, doesn't that bother you?"

Without looking, Natalie knew Estelle was speaking of her dear, sweet neighbor, Beatrice Nagel. Beatrice's broom and dust cloth saw many hours of use in a day but bother Natalie . . . no!

"Don't you know that cleanliness is next to Godliness, Estelle," Natalie stated in defense of her kind neighbor.

"You are too kind, Natalie. I rather think she's fanatical!" Estelle harrumphed while moving to a table of accessories. "A pity she has nothing more substantial to do with her day," Estelle said, waving her hand dismissingly toward the neighbor. "Oh well, so be it. Anyway, Natalie, I must warn you of some findings I have uncovered. I should have stopped to inform you immediately, but I had too much on my schedule and ran out of time. You see, Gertrude and I were outside the hotel on Monday when a coach bearing a family crest pulled up." Estelle turned toward Natalie and whispered the rest behind a hand, "We deliberately killed time until the occupants alighted. In this town, you never know what sort of important people will show."

Natalie rolled her eyes as she moved toward the fitting room. "Shall we take a look at your gown?" she suggested, trying to divert the conversation and move the fitting along as quickly as possible.

"Surely," Estelle answered, following the couturiere down the hall.

When they entered the fitting room, Estelle's gaze fell upon her gown displayed on the form, and she let out a long, satisfying sigh. It was made of soft brown fabric tailored in simple lines meant to drape

Estelle's form ultra-conservatively. Its high neck and cuffs were trimmed in lace, and the waist was enhanced with pleated taffeta of the same color.

"Natalie, it is simply beautiful!" she crowed.

Natalie forced a smile. "Glad you like it. Let me help you slip this on."

As soon as the gown was in place, Natalie grabbed the pincushion and went to work.

"Lift your arm, please," Natalie ordered.

Estelle obliged, rolling immediately into the gossip she needed to pass along.

"As I was saying. . . the driver assisted two fair-haired ladies from the conveyance. There were NO male escorts in the party, and believe me, my mind raced. Well, you know Gertrude, she always beats me to the details. She heard the pair was a wealthy mother and daughter from Massachusetts: Olivia and Hope Dansbury. And this is the part you won't believe! My word, Natalie, would you hurry along? The blood is rushing from my fingers to the base of my neck!" Estelle rolled her head around in dramatic discomfort, stopping to gaze at Natalie over her shoulder. "This is the perfect opportunity to fill you in on this news, my dear, here in the privacy of your shop. And I'm especially happy I can tell you this before you hear it from someone less sensitive."

That declaration nearly made Natalie scream! Sensitivity was *never* something Estelle practiced. Estelle's goal was always to be first with the news, good or bad, no matter whom she hurt.

"Natalie, this woman Olivia Dansbury is not just someone passing through. No, ma'am, she is not! Olivia Dansbury is Ben Walters' old flame, and she's back to rekindle the fire."

In that very instant, Natalie's pin punctured the old crow's skin.

Ouch!" Estelle slapped the palm of her hand to her underarm and glared at the dressmaker.

"Sorry, Estelle, I didn't know I was so close."

Natalie's fingers drew into tight fists. Estelle's details from yesterday's sighting at the hotel hit Natalie like a veritable slap. She felt her stomach roll over in rebellion as unbearable images of Ben with another woman flashed through her mind.

"It didn't take Ben long to discover she was in town either," Estelle continued as she rubbed her underarm. "He took her to dinner at the *Steven Matthews* and, according to Sarah Burkett, Ben looked much taken with her."

Natalie felt excruciating pain. In the past two years of close friendship with Ben, he had never once suggested that she join him for dinner at the *Steven Matthews Hotel.*

"Good heavens, Natalie. You pinned me well!" Estelle complained. "No more details until you put those bloodthirsty things away."

"Enough!" Natalie cried out. Estelle had gone too far, and Natalie refused to tolerate one more word from her.

"I'll tell you what, Estelle," Natalie bit out, punctuating each word by flicking the wrist of her hand that held the pin. "NO MORE INFORMATION NEEDED! You may change back into your gown and hurry along."

"Well, I never," the old gossip hissed, standing with her mouth agape.

"And one more thing you should know," Natalie continued with rising anger. "I never publicly discuss any man's private life, and most certainly not Ben Walters'. He is not my worry."

Natalie viciously stabbed the pin into the pincushion, extracting a visible flinch from Estelle, then reached for the hem of her client's gown to lift it over her head.

"Well, that's a fine-how-do-you-do!" Estelle mumbled under the yards of fabric. "Far be it that you should recognize my concern for your feelings. I know that Ben Walters *is* your worry, and I was merely tipping you off before you ran into the two lovebirds."

Suddenly the gown was off, leaving Estelle looking much like a bony hen with plucked feathers.

Natalie felt hard-pressed to hold back tears. The last thing she wanted was for Estelle to see her cry. She was positive that the whole town would know about it within the hour if a single tear dropped.

Finally, Natalie shuffled her out of the shop, shut the draperies, and placed the "Closed" sign on the door. Her knees felt like they would give out, so she sat in her desk chair and propped her forehead against her closed fists.

"Day is done, Mary. I've decided to close early," Natalie whimpered to her concerned assistant, who had quietly moved into the room.

Mary had overheard Estelle Wilcox's story about the Massachusetts woman and Ben Walters and knew it must have cut Miss Wakefield to the quick. She wished she could say something that would comfort her employer, although she sadly realized that if

Estelle's story was accurate, there was deep trouble brewing for Miss Wakefield's future.

Mary peered over her wire-framed glasses to observe her employer. She knew practically everything about Miss Wakefield's former life and what she dreamed for her future. Most importantly, she had learned that Ben Walters meant more to her employer than any other man on earth and that she had dreamed of someday becoming his wife. After hearing Estelle Wilcox's news, that dream looked like it could die a swift and painful death.

"No need to close, Miss Wakefield. I'll see to the customers today," Mary offered.

Natalie sniffed. "Thank you, Mary. Estelle has me in such a state." She patted her brow with a handkerchief and took a deep fortifying breath. "Would you please wrap those items for Abigail Matthews? I believe I'll run them over to the hotel and save her a trip," Natalie uttered.

Mary frowned. Miss Wakefield *never* made deliveries. Though she certainly understood why she wanted to deliver the goods to the hotel this time. She needed an eyeful of her competition, and Mary didn't blame her.

"Yes, ma'am, I'll get them together straight away."

"I appreciate that," Natalie answered, moving before the tall standing mirror. She smoothed her hair and made a close personal inspection.

"I'm pale," Natalie declared out loud. "And who wouldn't be after a morning with Estelle? You can't imagine what she does to me, Mary." There was a tremor in her voice. "I should change this gown."

"No worries, Miss Wakefield. It looks *wonderful* on you," Mary praised.

Natalie dropped her head. A single tear fell and spotted the front of her gown. Her voice was barely above a whisper. "Not wonderful enough, Mary. Definitely not wonderful enough."

***

Natalie hadn't departed for the Steven Matthews Hotel ten minutes when the bell on the shop door sounded. Mary moved into the shop to lend assistance, finding two unfamiliar ladies by the display table perusing the goods.

"Good day, ladies. May I help you?" The reed-thin pair flashed identical smiles from very similar faces.

"Good day to you. We're new here in Philadelphia and heard pleasing things about this shop. Locals tell us you offer the finest fashion in Philadelphia."

Mary smiled. "Thank you. It is a popular shop for the ladies of this city,"

"Are you Natalie Wakefield, the proprietor?" she asked in a smooth and refined voice.

"No, ma'am. I am Mary Stanton, her assistant. Miss Wakefield has left for the day."

"Oh," the woman exclaimed, turning to the younger woman by her side and then back to Mary. "My daughter and I were hoping to speak with her personally. We need a number of items for future events here in Philadelphia."

"I'd be more than happy to show you fabrics, take measurements or answer whatever questions you have without difficulty. Miss Wakefield will be back on the morrow."

The woman did not answer at first. Instead, she circled the sparkling gown displayed on a form, scrutinizing every detail. Meanwhile, Mary glanced over at the young girl, who stood quietly by a table. The girl smiled when their gaze met.

"Yes, I believe we will do that," the mother answered. "I realize that we are new clients for Miss Wakefield, but rest assured there will be no delay with payment on our behalf. I'd be happy to leave a sizeable deposit for our order if it would help move our requests to the head of the list."

Mary's spine stiffened. This shop had its share of haughty clientele who thought they were entitled to immediate service and any demand simply because they had the wherewithal to buy the very best.

"I'm sorry, we do our work in the order it's received. It would not be fair to our other faithful customers to do otherwise. That being said, there's seldom a delay unless a problem arises with the shipment of fabrics. We pride ourselves on meeting all deadlines. Now, if you will excuse me for a moment, I shall gather some samples and sketches for you to consider."

When Mary left the small fitting area, the daughter whispered to her mother that it didn't look like they would see the shop's proprietor today as hoped. The mother frowned, holding a finger to her lips.

Finally, Mary returned with the promised goods, whereas the selections commenced, followed by an appointment secured with Natalie Wakefield the following Monday morning at ten thirty.

"You've been very helpful, Miss Stanton," the mother commented.

"My pleasure. May I present a complete list of your selections today? Please examine this order, and if everything meets your approval, I will ask you to sign at the bottom."

Mary watched as the woman perused the expensive imported fabrics she had chosen for their extensive order. She pulled the quill from the inkwell and signed her name.

Mary cringed at the careful and beautiful script that spelled **"Olivia Dansbury"** at the bottom of the page.

#

Chapter Three

Ben hung his saw on the wall, tidied the workbench, and swept the sawdust into a neat pile. His workday was done. Generally, he started at the first break of dawn, working well into the afternoon or early evening. But concentration had been too difficult these past hours with the expected arrival of Olivia and her daughter Hope. Ben had invited them to dinner earlier in the week while dining together at the *Steven Matthews Hotel*. From his first morning stir, their anticipated evening arrival had pressed down on him with a heavyweight.

These past days, he had noticed a marked difference in his usual calm comportment. Today his loss of focus had cost him a swollen thumb, which he had hit twice with the hammer, and a cut on his index finger, because of his carelessness with the saw.

Over the past seventeen years, he had thought about how he'd conduct himself if he ever ran into Olivia again. He had convinced himself that he'd tip his hat in greeting and pass by without another thought. But that plan had rapidly dissolved when he learned last week that she had returned to Philadelphia, a widow and was staying at the *Steven Matthews Hotel*. When he found himself before the hotel desk requesting her room number, Ben recognized that he had never let her go.

The years had changed so much. He no longer resided in the small log cabin he had built many years ago but now lived in a splendid two-story brick manse constructed on the same property. Ben had taken painstaking effort with every detail of the structure, crafting cherrywood window seats in the bedrooms, fluted trim surrounding the fireplaces, and spectacular crown moldings at the ceilings. He had filled the home with rich draperies, imported carpets, and handcrafted furniture.

Ben had also constructed a large workshop, barn, and carriage house with the manse. The original workshop had burned to the ground a few years back, and he had since replaced it with a building twice the size of the original. The shop was a large rectangular structure covered in ship-lapped, rough-sawn lumber. The interior walls were paneled with thick vertical pine boards, while the floor boasted sturdy ten-inch-wide planks. Oversize doors had been cut into the end wall for easy entry and removal of materials and finished goods.

The workshop was Ben's haven. No house, no room, no building felt quite like the workshop. Even the manse, with its creature comforts and elegant beauty, could not compare to Ben's peace and contentment in the workshop. Wood walls, wood floors, working with wood, walking through the wood, and the smell of freshly cut wood were heaven to Ben. His single-minded passion and interest in wood-crafting made his custom furniture business a huge success, and his unrivaled talents brought him notoriety and financial gains. Life for Ben was good, rewarding, and, most of all, unruffled.

It had been seventeen years since Olivia had turned her back on the plans they had made together. Ben had never forgotten that ill-fated day when Andrew Dansbury had shown up at Olivia's father's store and swept her away with his charm, education, and money. Ben, twenty at the time, had only begun carving out a living with furniture design and construction. Although he had earned an honest dollar enough to keep a roof over his head and food on his table, he had been no match for Andrew, a William and Mary College graduate and employed in his father's successful law firm. The temptation had been too great for Olivia, and ultimately it had become the bitterest pill Ben had ever swallowed. Now, after seventeen years of emotional indigestion, she was back, and the torment rested in the realization that his need for her was as strong on this day as the day she had left him seventeen years before.

Ben rubbed the back of his neck, then drew his hand across the day's growth on his jaw. "You need a shave, Walters," he mumbled as he exited the woodshop, slamming the door behind him.

***

Max Seigel was Ben's most valued employee, a short, stocky package of energy and boisterous laughter. He ran Ben's home efficiently enough to rival an entire staff of servants and brought to Ben's table an array of mouth-watering dishes fit for a King. His garden boasted plump fruits and vegetables, and he harvested grapes from a small arbor on the property, producing a wine that rivaled the finest from France.

When Max had become Ben's employee five years ago, he had been provided handsome and comfortable quarters inside the manse. Within the first year, the two men had a remarkable fraternal bond. Max had become Ben's sounding board and confidant. Ben was the son Max never had. There was nothing that one would not do for the other, so when Max had shown interest in Ben's original log cabin, which had been vacant for some years, Ben offered it forthwith to this man who had earned his trust and respect. With great enthusiasm, Max transformed it into a welcoming abode, hanging herbs at the kitchen window, a rack of homemade wines in the corner, hand-braided rugs on the wood floors, and comfortable, though well-worn, furnishings throughout the few small rooms.

"I've got a feast cooking downstairs and two hot kettles of water right here for you!" Max chortled as he entered Ben's bedroom with two final buckets of water for his bath. He glanced over and noticed his employer thoughtfully reclined upon the bed. "I made my pumpkin soup, and it's mighty tasty. Sure, hope the ladies are hungry," Max continued merrily while he poured the steaming water into the tub.

Finally, Ben sat up and braced himself at the bed's edge. A frown creased his forehead. He remembered how Olivia had remarked about the dreadfully large servings at the *Steven Matthews Hotel* earlier in the week and how she and Hope could have easily shared a meal. Ben knew that Max would feel hurt if his meal went unappreciated. The manservant took pride in his culinary creations and was used to large gatherings or a table full of hungry business people eating plenty.

"Don't make too much, Max. My guests are very light eaters," Ben suggested as he walked to the window and looked across the lawn bathed in autumn's orange glow. He couldn't define the tightness in his stomach. He felt anxious. An uncommon pressure surrounded him as the evening ahead grew closer.

"When the ladies get a mouthful of my pumpkin soup and roast pork and potatoes, they will eat heartily," Max replied confidently, throwing Ben's jacket over his arm and moving to the door. "Tub's hot! Get in and enjoy. I'll be back after I press your jacket."

Ben lowered himself into the steaming tub, feeling the soothing effects of the warm water on his tired muscles. The bath did little to help his strung-out emotions and unclear mind. Seventeen years had passed, and now she was back. Tonight, she'd visit his grand home and sit in his dining room to enjoy the meals prepared by a hired servant. His wealth had never seemed so glaring before, but maybe that was because money had never been the ticket to his happiness or the most important factor in his life. Actually, before Olivia's return to Philadelphia, Ben had spent little time thinking about his wealth except for how it could help someone in need or perhaps how it could offer the community many evenings of food and festivities. But, since Olivia's return, Ben noticed he had been taking inventory of the material he had gained over the years. He knew Olivia would no longer have reason to criticize his life, home, business, or reputation; deep in his gut, those things troubled him.

***

The manservant stood by the window and watched Ben assist the richly garbed Dansbury women from their coach. It felt odd to see his employer flanked by the unknowns, the older of whom lavished fawning attention on him as they strode toward the threshold of the manse. Max had seen plenty of women attracted to the likes of Ben Walters, but only sometimes had he seen his employer return interest so intensely as he did tonight.

"Such a lovely home, Ben," the richly garbed woman commented as she stepped inside.

"Thank you, Olivia. I can show you and Hope through after dinner if you'd like," Ben returned proudly.

Now closer, Max validated Olivia Danbury's classic beauty. Her pale hair, pulled into a sophisticated chignon accentuated her high cheekbones and graceful neck. Max saw that her life had offered her beautiful clothes and costly jewels and schooled her in the airs of the aristocracy. It showed in her graceful carriage and the controlled calm of her voice.

Max shifted his gaze to the daughter. Except for her soft, brown eyes surrounded by a thick fringe of the lash, she much resembled her mother. He noticed the daughter's brow wrinkle when her mother boldly walked to the sitting room threshold to gaze within.

"This is so unexpected, Ben," Olivia breathed, turning toward him with a smile. "Imagine finding you a bachelor after all these years and without the help of a woman's touch for your lovely home."

Ben moved over to Max, standing in the shadows of the entrance hall, and wrapped his arm around the manservant's shoulder.

"Olivia and Hope, I'd like you to meet my good friend, Max Seigel. He deserves the credit for the condition of things around here. Because of his efforts, things are easy and comfortable for the mind and body.

"Good evening, ladies," Max greeted with his usual warmth.

"Good evening," Olivia delivered with forced courtesy, her ice-blue eyes inspecting him from head to toe.

Hope whispered a hello.

"Max, why don't you pour us a glass of wine before we dine," Ben heartily suggested.

Olivia immediately threw up a protesting hand. "I believe we'll pass, thank you. Hope, and I ate very little today and certainly don't need a headache before dinner."

"I'll try some," Hope cut in softly.

Olivia's head snapped toward her daughter. Her ice-blue eyes sent out a warning. All the while, her voice sounded deceivingly tender. "I think you should wait, dear. Perhaps after dinner."

Hope's shoulders tensed.

"It's a very mild potion, Olivia," Ben insisted. I'm sure Hope could handle it. Bring us a small tray of your sweetened bread also, Max. This will help since the ladies haven't eaten much today."

Max saluted his employer and then turned to fetch the refreshments.

"To the sitting room, ladies?" Ben offered, presenting an arm to Olivia and Hope. Noticing Olivia's pinched expression, Ben leaned close and whispered that she had little to worry about, for their comfort and enjoyment were his utmost assignment for the evening.

The intimacy of the moment sent unexpected warmth through her. The past days spent with Ben proved more exciting than Olivia had anticipated. She saw that the past seventeen years had honed Ben Walters into an extraordinary man. He was no longer the struggling, naïve boy with dreams but rather an accomplished craftsman who had made a name and fortune for himself. This and his tall, impressive physique offered a potent attraction. The most wonderful part was that every indication revealed that his heart still belonged to her.

As they entered the sitting room, Olivia's eyes took careful inventory of his possessions. Pewter candleholders with stout candles rested on deep windowsills. Upholstered high-back chairs and a silk-covered settee were grouped before the fireplace. A thickly woven Persian carpet covered the highly polished wood floors. In the fireplace, a warm fire crackled, and on the mantel, two brass oil lamps burned, illuminating the painting hanging prominently above. Olivia recognized the subject matter of the painting as the small log cabin Ben had built years ago: his first home. She saw Edward Channing's name scrolled on the bottom right corner of the painting, Ben's artist friend from years before.

Olivia's scrutiny continued, spotting the luxurious velvet draperies at each window, and she wondered if Natalie Wakefield had a hand in the making. It ate away at her with agonizing curiosity that she had not yet managed to meet the celebrated couturiere. Olivia desperately needed to know what she was against, even though she felt strongly that Ben was fairly taken with her return.

"What a handsome room, Ben," Olivia praised as she approached the fire.

"Thank you, Olivia," he replied softly, taking her hand.

"How is Edward?" she asked, turning the subject and her gaze back to the painting.

"He's gone. He fell from a ladder at his Lancaster home a few years back."

"I'm sorry, Ben. I know you were very close."

"His daughter, Chrystal, married my nephew, Chase Alexander. Chrystal's like a daughter to me," Ben admitted.

'Have you ever wanted children of your own, Ben?" she asked, smiling at Hope.

He looked directly into her eyes. "Yes, I wanted children, Olivia, but I needed a wife first," he answered frankly.

"And what of that, Ben?" she returned, but the question went unanswered when Max entered bearing refreshments.

Max placed a tray of bread on the small table near Hope and then offered the young girl a goblet of wine. "Take one, young lady, and enjoy." The servant crossed the room to the two at the fireplace. "Mrs. Dansbury? Ben?"

"Ben, I'll take your word this is safe before we dine," Olivia queried.

"Perfectly safe," Ben chuckled as he touched the rim of his glass to hers and Hope's. "To my lovely lady guests. A rare sight in this manly abode."

The meal proved outstanding. Even Olivia, who always limited herself to one small serving and then ate only half of what she took, cleaned her plate and treated herself to Max's delicious apple dessert. Hope ate and drank everything put in front of her, including the refills of wine Max poured when her glass got low.

A lively banter was born between the young girl and the servant while Olivia looked on with disdain. She found it unnerving that Ben allowed Max to take such liberties. The purpose of a hired servant was to see to the guests' needs, not to exchange pleasantries. Olivia figured Ben's humble roots offered little proper protocol and etiquette knowledge. Because of the Dansbury's, she had learned to place humans on their rightful level of importance, their level of worth.

Hope turned to Ben. "Could I be excused, please?" "Max has promised me a surprise after dinner."

Hope's request nearly choked Olivia. Ben, on the other hand, looked well pleased.

"I hope you enjoyed everything, Hope. I'm sure Max has something very special for you," Ben suggested, smiling broadly at the young girl.

Hope purposely avoided eye contact with her mother as Ben helped her from the dining room chair. The young girl knew that fraternizing with hired help was a no-no, and she didn't want to chance a look of disapproval from her mother.

She turned to Ben. "It was delicious, thank you," Hope extended gratefully, then slipped from the room.

Olivia missed the entire exchange between Hope and Ben. Her attention had been taken once again by the dining room draperies. It was unsettling to look at them and think that Natalie Wakefield could have made them for Ben's home. If so, it meant she had spent many hours here among Ben's possessions. The idea of this ate at her, and Olivia found it necessary to discover the depth of their relationship as soon as possible.

"Ben, Hope, and I have found an established couturiere in town. I've asked numerous ladies around the city and feel confident she has a sound reputation. As a businessman, I'm sure you might have heard of her. Her name is Natalie Wakefield."

To hear Natalie's name spill from Olivia's lips was like a solid punch in Ben's stomach. Until now, he hadn't thought about the two women in proximity, let alone Natalie fashioning gowns for Olivia. The intimacy of that whole process made him nauseous. If he hadn't shared that untimely kiss with the feisty redhead, there'd be nothing to worry about. But it had happened, and now the waters were muddied.

"Natalie Wakefield is the finest dressmaker in Philadelphia. You won't be disappointed," he replied.

His words were honestly and sincerely spoken, but his expression showed Olivia a serious issue lie between them. Olivia made a mental note to double up on the ammunition. She definitely needed to be well-armed for this possible opponent.

#

Chapter Four

Life hadn't always afforded the finer comforts Natalie Wakefield now enjoyed. Born fifth in a brood of nine, she, like all her brothers and sisters, had worked hard in her youth to contribute to the feeding and clothing of the family. By the time she had turned eleven, she was taking in mending and alterations. At fifteen, she excelled in fashion design and creating women's apparel. It had not taken long for the ladies in town to circulate news of Natalie's talents for choosing the colors that best suited their complexion or her ability to create the most flattering lines for their body shape. Her list of clients had grown so rapidly that her father had been forced to transform a room in their farmhouse to accommodate her thriving business. He had built a small dressing area in the corner of the room for the privacy of her clientele and framed a large piece of silvered glass so the ladies could admire the perfect fit, color, and flair of the gowns his daughter had so uniquely created.

By sixteen, Natalie had blossomed into a voluptuous young woman. Although short, she boasted a grand bosom that knocked most men from thirteen to sixty off their feet. Forbidden by her parents to wear low-cut necklines, she had cleverly designed the few gowns she'd owned to flatter her upper torso without displaying her bosom. Her gowns had tightly pleated and pinched waists with inserts of darker colors, minimizing her already tiny waistline and increasing her abundant chest. Her attire always enhanced her assets, offering the observer the true meaning of hourglass.

Just before Natalie's seventeenth birthday, Jonathan Wakefield, "Gambler Extraordinaire," caught a glimpse of the feisty young lady's proud profile walking past the tavern window where he was seated. The sight of her abundant beauty commanded his manly parts into proud attention. Jonathan's suave manner, striking good looks, and winning humor had persuaded many females to surrender themselves to his charms. He figured he'd try his magic on this beauty, hoping to add another female to his list of conquests. Without a second's consideration, Jonathan catapulted from his chair at the gaming table and exited the tavern. When he reached her side, he teasingly grabbed an apple from her basket and tossed it in the air, a devilish smirk on his face. Jonathan was accustomed to his antics and suave manner positively affecting the opposite sex, single or married, so he was most unprepared for the reaction he had gotten that day. Instead of falling for his good looks and winning smile, Natalie delivered a forceful kick to his shin, reclaimed her apple from his hand, and swiftly marched away. The gambler had bet on a reaction more in the line of a giggle, coyness, naiveté, or caution, but instead, he was rebuffed by an unexpected bold attack. Surprisingly, for the first time in all his years, love pushed him off balance. Fighting back gained Natalie a position at the front of Jonathan's line. He had liked her spunk so much that he had pursued her until finally winning her hand in marriage six months later.

It had proven Natalie's biggest mistake.

With a fistful of important, established clients on her books, Natalie had strapped herself to a man who had gambled away every hard-earned penny she'd made. Although Jonathan had always been a great listener, had often lifted her spirits with his humor, had made a dashing escort, and had been truly loved by her women clientele, it hadn't been enough. The inability to love her more than his love for gambling had unmercifully snuffed out her desires for him. After seven years of marriage, Natalie had finally reached her limit and wanted out. Jonathan hadn't tried to change her mind either, for as much as he loved her, he knew he loved gambling more and would never be able to offer her the life she deserved. Surprisingly, when the divorce was finally granted, they parted as friends. Neither of them had wanted it any other way.

To start anew, Natalie moved to Philadelphia, set up a business with the few saved coins she kept well hidden from Jonathan, and within a year, found herself back on track with more work than she could handle. Natalie often wondered what her life would have been like without her talent to depend upon. Maybe she would have found a man to love and care for her. But then what of her work? She had sewn for others since she was a child, and those efforts earned a handsome living and a life of independence. Natalie wasn't sure she could have given that up. Though disturbing loneliness had set in in the past few years, convincing her that the right man could persuade her to give up anything.

Shortly after she had relocated to Philadelphia, she was shopping in the busy Market House when her basket was knocked from her hands, tossing the contents everywhere. Natalie swung around to react to the mess and saw an incredibly strong and striking gentleman gathering her goods in his arms. She was transfixed by his handsome appearance and how he handed her the recovered goods with a stretch of his strong forearms and ardent apology. His mannerly and reserved way swept her off her feet. She had been so used to men approaching her with aggression and eyeing her natural bounty with unrestrained desire, while this fellow looked her directly in her eyes and made his apology with no wasted words.

It hadn't taken her long to find out his identity. It seemed everyone knew Ben Walters/Furniture Designer Extraordinary: unmarried, no children, and a faithful Episcopalian. Natalie remembered thinking about how their lives and interests were closely paralleled. Instead of designing and constructing "furniture," she designed and constructed "female fashions." She was also unmarried with no children, and even though she had been raised Presbyterian, Episcopalian sounded fine also. One week after meeting Ben Walters in the Market House, she decided to join Christ Episcopal Church.

Some encounters happened in the following months, but Ben handled them in the same manner as the first; short and rigidly polite. Their relationship had never reached an intimate level. Nothing she did or said had ever enticed him to look at her with more than friendship.

Then two years ago, a band of miscreants had set fire to Ben's workshop, leaving him for dead inside the burning building. Upon hearing of Ben's misfortune, Natalie seized upon the moment and rushed to his side to lend "assistance." Ben had preferred to call it "interference," exploding in her presence with how he didn't need to be mollycoddled, could damn well take care of himself, and whatever he couldn't handle, Max, his right-hand man, could. Heartbroken, Natalie had left his residence with lips aquiver and held back tears.

Though Ben had always been averse to her invasion of his turf, it hadn't taken him long to regret his actions. He soon realized, when left alone, that he missed Natalie's tender loving care. When his strength returned days later, he visited her city residence and apologized for his ungentlemanly disposition, and from that day forward, things between them had greatly improved. Ben soon accepted Natalie's coffee, pie, or dinner invitations, and their friendship flourished.

***

That afternoon Natalie's visit to the *Steven Matthews Hotel* had proved futile. After a long conversation in the lobby with the proprietor's wife, with no opportunity to look at the new arrivals from Massachusetts, she finally gave up. Frustrated, she returned to her shop, drained and filled with anxiety.

Mary approached Natalie, seated at her desk in a dejected pose. The assistant hated giving her employer bad news.

"Excuse me, Miss Wakefield. I know it's been a trying day, but I thought you might want to know as soon as possible that shortly after you left the shop this afternoon, the ladies Estelle Wilcox spoke about earlier visited the shop."

Natalie sat straight up, a look of despair on her face. "Here? Were they merely looking or did they request a fitting?"

"They scheduled a fitting appointment for Monday morning. They desire only *your* attention with their order."

Mary handed Natalie the signed paperwork detailing the fine fabrics and trims chosen by the ladies and the number of items requested.

Natalie glanced at the signature, then blew out a shaky breath.

"I see they have selected fabrics. Have you sized the ladies, Mary?" Natalie asked without lifting her gaze.

"I have not, Ma'am. Mrs. Dansbury was quite adamant that you handle the measurements."

Natalie cursed her untimely departure today. If only she'd stayed in the shop longer, the uncomfortable suspense would be over. Now she'd have to wait until morning and hope for the opportunity in church. A long and dreadful night lay ahead.

***

Natalie took pride in always presenting her best appearance. After all, her wardrobe had been her finest advertisement. On this Sunday morning, she arose an hour earlier, ensuring she had enough time to look her finest.

First and foremost, she selected Ben's favorite pale peach gown. Not that he had ever told her so, but she had guessed by the way he'd always made it a point to have a bit of news "just for her" on the Sundays she wore it. Cinched at the waist and cut to a plunging "V" at the neckline, Natalie never tired of watching Ben struggle to keep his eyes focused on her face.

After her lengthy toilette, she donned the gown, piled her hair atop her head in her usual fashion then artistically applied cosmetics to enhance her eyes and lips. She dabbed fragrance behind each ear for added allure, then placed the stylish new hat she had purchased from Charlotte Becker's Millinery on her bobbing auburn curls. The result was splendid.

Natalie arrived at Christ Church twenty minutes before the service. The mere thought of possibly witnessing Ben Walters with a woman companion unnerved her beyond reason. Yet, the need to lay eyes upon her competitor drove her from the confines of her home, pushing her forward like a condemned woman walking to the gallows. Furthermore, she preferred sitting in her pew with hymnal in hand to pacing the floor at home.

As the minutes ticked by, the church filled with murmurs of children and adults. Unfortunately, Ben Walters' pew sat two rows behind Natalie's on the opposite side of the center aisle. She couldn't see if he had yet arrived without turning around in obvious curiosity. Sheer dint of will kept her faced forward. Then, to her complete displeasure, Estelle Wilcox and her skinny daughter pushed in beside her.

"Good morning, Natalie," the gossip whispered.

Natalie forced a smile as Estelle lowered herself to the kneeling bench. Then with hands steepled at her forehead and her face turned toward Natalie, Estelle murmured a warning. "Whatever you do, Natalie, don't turn around. Ben Walters arrived with the ladies I told you about the other day."

Natalie's hands trembled on the top of her hymnal.

"I followed them in and admitted they are an impressive set."

Natalie ground her teeth. Oh, how she wished the old hen had chosen another pew. Wasn't it enough that she had the pressure of Ben and the Dansburys behind her? Why was she cursed with handling Estelle's abrasive manner too? Natalie dropped her head and prayed for added strength.

The church bells rang out to welcome all, the choir burst forth with hymns of gladness, and the service began. Natalie found it nearly impossible to relax, wondering if Ben had bothered to look in her direction and if he noticed she wore the peach-colored gown he favored. She longed to turn around and get a good look at the two women, for she was dying to know if they were fashionably dressed, accessorized, and attractive. The suspense was almost too much to bear, yet she knew bearing it was a must.

Natalie got her chance at the end of the service when the congregation rose and filed out. She moved from the pew, greeting the familiar folks around her with idle chit-chat while positioning herself for a clear look at the trio across the center aisle.

Her heart stopped when her gaze fell upon the two fair-haired females flanking Ben.

Her heart broke when she saw the happiness that spread across Ben's face. She had never experienced pain quite so sharp.

"It looks like she has plans for that man," Estelle whispered, nudging Natalie's side. "Look at the hold she's got on him."

Natalie's body stiffened. She turned away to greet other people around her to shake off Estelle, but the town gossip stubbornly stuck close, bending her full attention on every exchange Ben and his lady friends made with the surrounding crowd.

"That daughter is a beautiful girl. One thing for certain, she's been well-schooled in the fine art of grace and etiquette. Look how she carries herself, and oh, here they come!" Estelle warned behind four straight fingers.

"Good morning, Natalie."

The rich timbre of Ben's voice penetrated Natalie's senses from over her right shoulder. She turned slightly and saw that he stood close behind her with the two lovely females at his side.

"Hello, Ben," she returned, her eyelashes beginning a nervous dance. She felt tongue-tied and nervous.

He looked at her directly with no apology in his posture or expression. It appeared the opposite as if a surge of pride and euphoria filled him for escorting this pair to church this morning. Natalie felt a sharp pain, thinking the kiss they had shared nights before probably meant little to him, while it painfully meant the world to her.

"Olivia and Hope, allow me to introduce you to a talented friend of mine, Natalie Wakefield," he offered.

Olivia tried hard to hide her shock. Her mind had conjured up a far different vision of Natalie Wakefield these past few days. She had certainly expected a well-dressed individual but hadn't considered the chance that she'd look this dramatic, provocative, and younger than she. From what Olivia remembered of Ben's tastes seventeen years ago, Natalie did not fit the mold. He had always favored more of the helpless, frail female; the female who needed a Protector, a Provider, and it certainly appeared that Natalie Wakefield didn't need support from anyone or protection from anything. Her gaze swept Natalie's form, and Olivia wondered if the businesswoman handled life's obstacles as boldly as she clothed her voluptuous shape. Their gaze clashed, and Olivia reacted with an artificial smile and a barely audible "Hello."

"Hello, ladies," Natalie answered, her gaze drifting from Olivia to the young daughter. "I returned to my shop late yesterday and discovered I have an appointment with you both on Monday morning."

"Hope and I were disappointed you could not assist us yesterday when we stopped. I told your assistant we desire to work directly with you." Olivia arrogantly stated.

Natalie figured this society snob had never worked a hard day in her life and certainly knew nothing about the schedule and responsibilities of a businesswoman. She was tempted to comment, but when she glanced at Ben, she thought it best to hold her tongue. He looked at Olivia with tenderness and pride, a look he had never gifted her. It was a solid warning that this situation would need a careful approach. She swallowed her hurt and answered with professional confidence.

"Mary's efficiency is unsurpassed. I'm sure she can quite satisfy any of your requests. Until Monday, then?"

37

Olivia smiled stiffly, directing her next words to Ben while keeping her attention on Natalie. "Well, Ben, if we are to make it a day?"

Ben turned his attention to Natalie, nodded, and presented a farewell smile. She did not return the same. It was clear, at that moment, how they had crossed over the line of intimacy with a kiss and how that kiss had changed everything between them. Before, they had been friends, but now it was something different. The future was muddied, the timing uncanny, and Natalie felt out of sorts.

"Yes, I guess the day isn't getting any younger. Shall we?" Ben said, offering his forearm to Olivia. Before he turned away, he looked at Natalie, nodded, and delivered his usual gentlemanly farewell.

"Have a nice afternoon, Natalie."

"You, as well, Ben," she returned with a forced smile. Then glancing at Olivia she thought, *And you, Mrs. Dansbury, can stick your head in a bucket of water.*

#

Chapter Five

Indian Summer burst forth, turning the Pennsylvania autumn to unseasonably warm temperatures. As Ben removed his lunch from the sack, he considered the day's beauty and hoped it would hold until the week's end when he'd see Olivia again. He planned to visit the beautiful secluded spot they had frequented years before as young lovers to share a picnic lunch and a few private hours. He felt a growing desire to discuss matters neither had touched on since her return. Thus far, their conversations had been superficial, but time had grown nigh for things to delve deeper into the whys and wherefores of life since they had parted.

Ben's past had been uncomplicated without a wife and children. Olivia's, however, had been quite another matter. She had lived an intimate family life, and he needed to know if that former life had been happy, why there had only been one child, and if Olivia had ever thought about him during the past seventeen years.

Then, without warning, a picture of auburn hair and batting eyelashes flashed into his mind. In the past week, Natalie's image had interrupted his serenity with a frequency that had frustrated him. The smallest memory of something the shapely woman had said or done in the past would suddenly light up his brain, redirect his thoughts and ruin his peace of mind. Like now, when thoughts of her flooded his mind just from biting into one of the delicious molasses cookies, she had baked for him over a week ago.

Damn, she was a good cook.

Ben thought she excelled at almost everything. She never slept past six a.m., was never late for an appointment, never made a bad meal, and always had dessert. Her efficiency impressed him, yet at the same time, overwhelmed him. Her competency convinced Ben that he could do nothing to add to the quality of her life.

He recalled a few years ago when he had stopped unannounced at her home. It had been the only time he had ever seen Natalie without the guise of corsets and cosmetics. She had answered the door at his plea, albeit hesitantly, in her nightgown and robe, with her face scrubbed clean and her hair brushed in silken smooth waves around her shoulders. He had thought her beauty beyond compare. Sometimes in the middle of the afternoon, when working in his shop, on a drive to town in his wagon, or even in the solitude of his bed at night, that picture of her would re-enter his mind and carry him on a reckless path of lust. More recently, his thoughts had centered on the kiss they had just shared. Her shapely form pressed against his, and her nimble fingers massaging his backbone had been a titillating experience.

He strode to the pump, splashed water on his perspiring face, cupped a handful of the cool liquid, and took a hefty swallow. Natalie Wakefield was a beautiful woman and a good friend. Still, Ben knew that after spending thirty-seven years as a bachelor, a self-sufficient, domineering woman like Natalie would never suit as his wife.

The previous night, a windstorm had downed a sizeable tree to the side of Ben's workshop, barely missing the buildings and littering the surrounding yard. The warmth and beauty of the day offered perfect conditions to clean the debris and cut and stack the logs for winter.

Ben rolled up his shirtsleeves and bent to the task with an axe in hand. He diligently labored at the clean-up until the heat finally got so overwhelming that he removed his shirt and tossed it over the tree stump. His broad, muscular, darkly furred chest revealed masculinity in its finest form. Sweat glistened on his back and arms, defining the sinewy strength of his body. The sight would likely cause unsafe heart palpitations to a love-struck and lonely female.

Max rang the dinner bell just as Ben buried the axe blade into the last log. As he reached for his shirt to wipe the sweat from his brow, he caught the tail end of a carriage passing behind his outbuilding at breakneck speed. When the carriage rounded the corner of the barn and drove into clear view, Ben felt an unreasonable irritation and discomfort.

"What in the name of Jesus is she doing here?" he muttered as Natalie approached Hell bent for leather, kicking up a cloud of dust in her wake.

One, who didn't know her manner, might think she had some dire emergency, but Ben, well-seasoned with her antics, refused to panic. When her carriage skidded to a halt before him, he watched through squinted eyes as she brushed a hand across each cheek, aligned her bonnet (a wide-brim affair tied with a length of yellow silk under her chin), and smiled, eyelashes batting fast and furiously. A lock of hair had fallen loose from the bonnet, and her flushed cheeks lent a fetching effect that did not go unnoticed.

When Natalie's gaze fell upon Ben's sparsely clad form, her insides were set atremble. Her hands gripped the reins firmly, stretching her yellow kidskin gloves tightly across her fingers as she tried to keep her hands from visibly shaking. Ben had often appeared reclined naked upon her bed in her dreams, but this vision standing before her was certainly no dream. This was flesh and blood in its finest form.

41

She swooned, watching him wipe the sweat from the back of his neck with his shirt. Her mouth felt dry, and her throat parched. She thought that a tall glass of something very cold would taste mighty good right now as her tongue passed across her lips to wet their surface.

"Natalie," Ben clipped as he slid his arms back into the shirt sleeves and buttoned the front.

"Hello, Ben. It looks like you have been working hard. I imagine the weather has inspired you. Simply delightful, isn't it?" Her eyelashes beat out a rapid rhythm as she rambled on. "I always look forward to a spell of Indian Summer before the cold weather moves in."

Ben wanted her to get to the point. The dinner bell had rung, and he was unwilling to share the event with a guest, especially Natalie. He had spent enough unsolicited hours today with thoughts of her and now desired peace and solitude at day's end.

"Yes, it's been a beautiful day. What brings you to the country?" he asked with as much patience as he could muster.

When she stood up in the carriage, he felt himself losing ground. Once out of the conveyance, Lord only knew how long she would stay, and dammit, he was hungry!

"I need to speak with you about a problem, Ben. I am so glad I caught you at home." Natalie extended her hand.

Ben saw no way out. He lowered the step and reached to assist.

"First of all, I haven't caught you at a bad time, have I?" She had planned her arrival close to the dinner hour, hoping Ben might invite her to join him for the meal. Last-minute incidentals at the shop had delayed her departure, forcing her to lay the leather to her mare's hide to make it out to his place in time. Relief had washed over her when she found him at the workshop with the Dansbury's coach nowhere in sight.

Tired and unwilling to miss out on some of Max's good cooking, Ben got right to the "unavoidable" invitation.

"Max just rang the supper bell. Have you taken your evening meal?"

"Oh, I couldn't, Ben." She checked her timepiece. "Why, I had no idea it was this close to dinner. I get so wrapped up in my work that I overlook the hour of the day. Please, do not let me detain you. I can talk to you another day about the dilemma."

Ben knew damn well she was aware of the time of day and that no gentleman within a thousand miles would turn her back to town now. The conniving female had cornered him, which elevated his blood pressure to the boiling point.

"Blast it, Natalie! You are here, there is plenty to eat, and I'm damned hungry. I don't want to argue, debate, decide what's proper or get down on a bent knee to make you stay. Come the hell up to the house, and we can discuss whatever is on your mind AFTER I get some food inside me."

Natalie tightened the silk under her chin and took a deep breath. "How dare you speak to me like that, Ben Walters? I did not come here to argue, and I certainly don't expect you to get down on your knees for anything where I'm concerned." She jerked her face toward the open yard, her face and posture revealing hurt and anger.

Ben regretted the harshness of his words as soon as they spilled out. Natalie had been so good to him over the past two years, and to

Cyn Garrett

snap at her like that was undeniably unfair. He couldn't explain his behavior and truly regretted his words.

"Look, I'm sorry. I will tie your rig here and send my stable boy down for it later." With the rig secured, Ben offered his arm. "Let's dine. You have treated me to so many meals. It would please me to offer you a place at my table this time."

Natalie wanted to throw a smart comment back but kept her mouth shut. She puffed out a perturbed breath and reached for his proffered arm.

They walked in uncomfortable silence to the front door; after reaching the threshold, Max, who had been watching the couple since Natalie's cloud of dust had settled, opened the portal wide.

"Good evening, Miss Wakefield," Max greeted with a welcoming smile.

"Hello there, Max. It is good to see you again."

"Miss Wakefield will be joining me for dinner this evening, Max. Will you see she has a glass of wine while I clean up?" Ben requested.

"With pleasure," the manservant replied, taking in the couturiere's appearance. "You are looking exceedingly beautiful this evening, Miss Wakefield."

"Max, I have told you no less than a hundred times about calling me Miss Wakefield." She left Ben's side and followed Max to the sitting room. "You must have learned that ridiculous formality from your employer."

Ben's brows drew together at her deliberate stab. He climbed the staircase, listening with growing agitation as she nagged on, closing his chamber door with force.

"I am Natalie, you are Max, we are friends, and there is no need for a stodgy address. Now, Max, my friend, get that wine, and while you are at it, bring yourself a glass too and a little something stronger for my dinner companion. He needs a soothing potion to soften his sharp edge."

Max winked at the feisty gal before he turned to do her bidding. Some moments later, Max returned with the tray of drinks to find Natalie holding the hem of the window drapery in her hand.

"Martha Gingrich made these didn't she, Max?" she asked when their gaze met.

"Yes. You have a good eye, Natalie," Max answered honestly.

"He'd never asked me," dropping the fabric and moving to the chair by the fireplace. "It would mean that I would share an interest in his home. Then he would feel cornered, right?"

"He is very fond of you, Madam," the older man diplomatically replied, offering her a drink tray sample.

Natalie untied the silk beneath her chin, lifted the confection from her head, and placed it on the nearby table. She reached for a goblet of wine and spoke with honesty.

"Yes, Max, he is fond of me, but what he feels for Olivia Dansbury makes me worried. Very, very worried, indeed."

#

Chapter Six

Ben felt completely out of sorts by the time he reached his bedroom. Natalie had a unique talent for undoing him. He wondered what lame excuse she would use this time to elucidate her unannounced trip to his home—horse turds with that nonsense of not realizing the time of day. Ben knew better than anyone that Natalie was always one to remember the dinner hour. Olivia was quite another matter. He would believe it in a heartbeat if she told him she wasn't hungry or she'd forgotten about the dinner hour, but Natalie---NO WAY!

Natalie loved food. She loved shopping at the market and preparing food and absolutely tried and tasted anything set before her. Oddly enough, her fondness for food and everything surrounding it had never negatively affected her hourglass shape. He had often wondered where she had found the time with all her business responsibilities to keep such a well-stocked pantry. She was a woman chock full of energy and efficiency, which he considered why she stayed trim. He had never known anyone quite like her and was convinced that when Natalie Wakefield was made, they had quite ceremoniously thrown away the mold.

Ben removed his shirt splashed water on his face, then grabbed the cake of soap and vented his frustrations on the object. He lathered his neck, across his shoulders, under each arm, across his chest, then rinsed. The water helped lower his body temperature and soothe his angry edge, and he truly hoped that after some of Max's good cooking, he might feel restored to normalcy. He quickly donned a clean shirt, brushed his hair, and then descended the stairs toward the wonderful aromas that beckoned him.

Not until after dessert did Ben request the nature of Natalie's visit. The fortification of food had calmed his edgy disposition, making him far more receptive to hearing her petition.

"So, Natalie, tell me of this emergency and how you need my assistance. I cannot take the suspense much longer."

Natalie had enjoyed the dining interlude so much that she hated ending the pleasantries with business talk. Still, she had to admit that his mellow mood offered an ideal opportunity to make her request. So, without hesitation, she took a bolstering sip of wine from her goblet and then began.

"Ben, I'm in need of your talents. Last week I asked Stanley Musser if he could lend a hand with some needed carpentry at my shop. Unfortunately, he is too busy and can't fit it until spring. Waiting another six months is terribly inconvenient for me, and I had hoped you could sacrifice a little of your time to help my cause. I promise there will be no pressure. I realize your schedule is also full, but perhaps a few hours in the evenings, a Saturday here and there?" She propped her elbows on the table, rested her chin on her fingertips, and looked pleadingly at him.

"I can't, Natalie. I'm sorry." His answer was quick. "My schedule's not flexible right now. I am as busy as Stan. Who knows when I could get to it? I would hate to have things torn up in your shop for any time and inconvenience you." Ben knew he needed to nip this issue in the bud before it could blossom.

Natalie chewed on the inside of her lip. It wasn't hard to figure out why his schedule wasn't flexible. It came down to eight simple letters: D-A-N-S-B-U-R-Y. She pressed on unmercifully.

"This won't be convenient for me in any time frame, Ben, but the total outcome will improve things immensely in my shop. As I---"

"No, Natalie. I'm sorry," Ben broke in. He placed his coffee cup on the saucer, then leaned back in the chair, crossing his arms over his chest in an immutable pose. He knew if she had asked him a week ago, before the Dansbury's arrival, there would have been no problem, but now with Olivia's return . . . impossible. Taking his free time to remodel Natalie's shop would give him less time to rediscover what he had lost years ago with Olivia. What would Olivia think if he were to help Natalie: a beautiful, successful, well-groomed, SINGLE FEMALE?

"I am not expecting immediate results, Ben, whenever you can fit in a few hours. At your leisure." Natalie sat poised on the edge of her chair, tapping her fingertips nervously on the table's edge.

Ben's gaze was drawn to the movement. He studied her fingers and considered the comfort they had provided for him over the past two years: delicious meals, desserts, buttons sewn on shirts and jackets. He saw the hope steal from Natalie's eyes, and with that, guilt began to worm its way under his resistance, pulling apart his defenses and weakening his determination. How could he say no to her? He owed her, and his refusal sounded brutish and damn selfish. Regardless of Natalie's full schedule, Ben recognized that she had always been there to offer help in his time of need. Ben rubbed the back of his neck and rolled his head in a circle to release the tension.

"Natalie, you put me in the damndest position." He closed his eyes and took a deep breath before he continued. "I need this week to finish a few things. Then I could drop by on Saturday to see what you have in mind." Regardless of how much he tried to control his emotions, his voice sounded much like a bear with a thorn in his paw.

"Wonderful! Oh, that is wonderful, Ben," Natalie breathed fervently as she pushed from the table.

Ben came to his feet and stood frozen to the spot as she moved toward him. Something about the look in her eyes, an undulation to her walk, and a vixen's smile on her lips scared him. He was sure trouble was headed in his direction.

"Thank you for a very pleasant evening, Ben," she purred, running the palms of her hands down the skirt of her gown.

"Max!" Ben bellowed out as she drew closer. The servant miraculously appeared just as Natalie reached Ben's side. "Have Ethan saddle my horse and tie it to the back of Miss Wakefield's rig. I'll be taking her home."

Natalie's smile vanished. Then with quick recovery, she straightened her shoulders, lifted her chin, and spoke with a bite in her voice. "Really, Ben, I can drive myself back to town. I wouldn't think of putting you out." Natalie turned to Max. "No need. Simply bring my carriage around, and I will be on my way. Thank you for that delicious meal, Max."

"If you think I will allow you to ride home without an escort, Madam, you have another thing coming. Tell Ethan to saddle my horse, Max," Ben barked.

Max snapped to it. He was in full agreement with Ben. He didn't want Miss Wakefield traveling home alone at this late hour.

When Max disappeared, Ben laid into her with unleashed rage. "You know what? You are the most independent, hardheaded woman

I have ever met. I cannot fathom why you would consider traveling alone after dark. That is one of the most senseless, lame-brained notions you have ever had, and let me tell you, you have had some winners in the past years."

She had no intention of riding home alone. She just wanted to show a little resistance. After all, without resistance, it would appear that she had planned the whole evening. . . which she did! Though how it had turned into this vicious name-calling was certainly something she had not planned on.

"Lame brained! Hard-headed! You have the colossal nerve to call me that, Ben Walters, when you are, in every sense of the word, *King* of Hardheads. I was merely being thoughtful, something you could never understand. I did not come out here to inconvenience you, and I'll be damned if I'm going to knuckle under a bully."

Ben's face turned red with anger. His fists drew tight, turning his knuckles white. "You know what, Natalie? Your mouth needs to be washed out with soap, and if I ever choose to do it, I will lift those petticoats and paddle your backside till it turns red."

Natalie took three quick steps back, one hand held over her heart, the other on her posterior. "You are a devil, Benjamin Walters. I warn you that if you ever try to lift my skirts with anything but in a loving manner, you will find out just how much fight is inside this gal." Natalie's hand flew to her lips as soon as the words were out. Ben's stunned expression showed her that she had gone too far once again.

Silence filled the air. Ben spoke first, a forewarning tone in his voice.

"Before we destroy this enjoyable evening, I will excuse myself to prepare for our journey. Have Max fetch your wrap and prepare yourself for the journey." He turned from her and strode toward the door.

Natalie's reckless reply rang out when Ben reached the threshold. "To preserve my derriere from abuse, I would prefer Max to take me home. He has, without a doubt, better manners than you."

Ben scoured her with a look that would shrivel the bravest of hearts. "Not a chance. I'm returning you personally." He slapped the doorjamb and quit the room.

Natalie crossed her arms under her breast and defiantly turned her back on the door.

***

Olivia and Hope decided to retire early. They had spent the entire day in appointments that ranged from fittings with Natalie Wakefield to researching temporary housing. An attorney friend of Andrew's, who knew much about upscale properties in the Philadelphia area, had shown them a lovely brick home for rent in the nearby neighborhood of Germantown. The present owners offered the handsome, furnished residence for a costly month-to-month rent. He told Olivia while they took their time to scout the area for a wise investment purchase, this property would offer them the comfort they needed. Little did he know that she did not intend to purchase a home. The only investment she cared to entertain in Philadelphia was on a more personal level: marriage to Ben Walters. The house-hunting stint was only her cover-up.

There was one small glitch in her master plan that had to be dealt with immediately. After meeting with the esteemed couturiere in her shop that very same morning, Olivia realized that Natalie Wakefield was quite an adversary and her plan for Ben Walters would not be executed, as she once believed.

When Olivia arrived at the shop for her initial visit with Natalie, the dressmaker displayed an air of confidence, greeting both she and Hope professionally and moving through each step of their fittings with a fastidious thoroughness and expertise. She had performed the work uninterrupted in an area of her shop that had given the utmost privacy. Fabrics had been discussed, and when Natalie felt a better choice of trim or different fabric weight was needed, she did not hesitate to say so. Olivia seethed with jealousy at her smart suggestions and, ultimately, the reason for her success and total confidence in her profession.

She recalled Hope's pleased reaction to Natalie's bold advice for a vibrant, younger style for her gown. It had brought a smile and excitement to Hope that maddened her.

The worst was that Olivia had also realized that Hope had not been the only one influenced by the talented dressmaker, remembering how willingly she had agreed to everything Natalie had suggested.

Of course, decisions had never been Olivia's strong suit. Andrew had always made the choices, leaving Olivia with the benefit of his solid judgment. She would do quite well with a man like Ben Walters, who had never been married and made all of life's decisions without anyone else's interference. Olivia hoped that Natalie's opinionated personality and independent lifestyle would offer little threat to her quest for Ben Walters' attention. Natalie Wakefield had too much to say about every aspect of life, and Olivia knew Ben would never tolerate that.

Then there was the matter of appearance. Although Natalie's talents lent her the ability to create designs that enhanced her body shape and complexion, Olivia believed that Natalie's bold auburn-red hair destroyed any attempt she made at class and refinement. And what a shame to be burdened with such immense breasts, Olivia thought—such a curse when she knew that a man preferred a slim ladylike shape like her own. There were just too many glaring negatives about the couturiere, which bolstered Olivia's confidence in her future with Ben Walters.

"You never said what you thought about Miss Wakefield's suggestions today?" Hope asked, watching her mother from the strategically placed dresser mirror.

"Suggestions? Well, she certainly had plenty of them. But then, we are paying her top dollar, my dear. We want to look our very best, don't we?"

"For Ben?" the daughter questioned.

Olivia reclined on the chaise, draped in a delicate lavender peignoir. "For Ben and all the rich, eligible bachelors in Philadelphia, that might suit your fancy. You know what we have discussed about this journey to Pennsylvania. I do not understand why you ask questions like that. Turn around and look at me, Hope."

Hope turned to meet her mother's gaze and made her statement. "I do not like deceit. Ben Walters is a very nice man, and I am not sure I want to lie to him."

Olivia quickly moved to her daughter's side and grabbed the young woman's chin, giving her head the slightest shake. "Do not even think about backing out! This was decided upon long ago, and we are sticking to the agreement." Olivia's eyes held an implacable determination. She dropped her hand and turned to face the full-length mirror. "You are so sensitive, Hope. Ben Walters loves me? He never *stopped* loving me," Olivia stated, running her hands down the full length of her body. "That's why he's still not married seventeen years after I left this town. This is not painful for him. It is pure unadulterated joy. He will be the happiest man alive when we tell him the news. Furthermore, Hope, if you think so much of him, I would think you'd want to see a little happiness in his life."

Hope hung her head. Her mother had done so much for her over the years that it seemed wrong not to return the favor she had asked of her. The "Plan" had been agreed upon before they visited Philadelphia, and she had convinced herself that it was the right thing to do for Olivia's security. "You are right, Mother. Ben seems very happy with your return. It has been a long day, and I guess I am just a little tired."

"It has been an exhausting day, darling," Olivia tenderly returned, caressing her daughter's cheek. "Soon, all these pressures will be off our shoulders, and we will be able to relax as before. For now, we must gather our energies and proceed. Agreed?"

"Of course, Mother. Agreed."

#

Chapter Seven

A table tucked in the dark corner of the *Plough Tavern* offered a perfect setting for the gambler's suffering. His misjudgment at the gaming table had cost him most of his booty, and now he struggled with what to do and where to turn. He had felt the "slump" a few weeks back yet heeded no warnings. Nothing and nobody could hold him from a game of chance for two reasons: a.) he was helpless to deny himself the exhilaration of a "WIN," and b.) He had never acquired another career talent. Why would he want to anyway? He had been a gambler since his youth, and it offered everything necessary to his comfort in exchange for minimal effort.

He gazed down at the diamond pinky ring, his prized possession. He could not bear the thought that his survival could come down to selling what linked him to the best years of his life. He had also believed the ring had given him the good luck necessary in his business and therefore felt hard-pressed to part with the keepsake.

"Another mug, love?" a husky female voice queried, interrupting his thoughts.

A tavern wench stood before him sharing his admiration of the expensive ring. She was bent low, offering him a generous view of her finer qualities barely harnessed by a low-cut décolletage.

"No, thank you. Nothing," he clipped, leaving a clear message that he desired solitude.

When she sauntered off, he twisted the ring back and forth, as he watched the play of light shoot from the stone. He had not found himself this insolvent in a very long time and agonized over whom he might turn to for help. Then suddenly, a spectacular idea flashed in his mind. His ex-wife! Granted, it had been years since he had last seen her, but they had parted on good terms, and Jonathan had not forgotten how willing she had always been to help others in need. With any luck, she would help him.

Someone had once told him she had set up a business in Philadelphia. He figured the large city of wealthy residents had probably opened multiple opportunities for his resourceful ex-wife. Her work ethic and frugal ways practically guaranteed him that she would have the means to bail him out of this mess. The only concern was that she had not remarried. That scenario would only complicate the hell out of things.

With the decision made, Jonathan slapped the tabletop, pushed from his seat, and left the smoky tavern. He was headed out of York, due east to Philadelphia.

Saturdays were often a whirlwind of activity in Natalie's dress shop. Many customers arrived for their completed orders, while others visited to purchase a comb for their hair, a pair of gloves, or browse her beautiful things.

On this Saturday, the business had slowed by one o'clock, allowing Natalie to retreat to her apartment and warm a bowl of soup for lunch. Just as she was ladling the hot liquid into a bowl, she heard the tinkling of the shop doorbell.

"I'll be with you in a moment," she called out, placing the bowl on the tabletop. She checked her hair in the mirror, straightened her neckline then moved into the shop, noticing a well-dressed gentleman standing by the gown in her front window. The cut of his clothes and his costly pair of leather buckle shoes indicated that he paid close attention to fashion. She was so used to this variety of men who dropped in to purchase a silk scarf, a beaded purse, or, more commonly, a satin dressing robe for their mistress. They usually spared no coin on a purchase in hopes the gift would yield them high rewards.

"Good afternoon. May I help you, sir?" Natalie pleasantly inquired.

The gentleman looked over his shoulder and delivered a familiar smile and a wink that nearly floored her.

"Jonathan!" she gasped.

"Hi, Honey," he returned in a smooth masculine voice.

Natalie could not believe her eyes. Jonathan was the absolute last person she expected to see in her shop. After all, it had been years. What could have brought him here? Uneasiness swelled inside her. She knew his ways and was sure he was not here to wish her well.

He had changed very little. He still had that gorgeous jet-black hair; his trim shape was nattily garbed in an expensive black suit and silver brocade waist vest, and he smelled deliciously of bay rum. He was exactly as she had remembered him. Jonathan looked like a professional, a politician, a man of great importance, oh yes, she remembered with bitterness worming its way through her. . . a GAMBLER.

"How did you find me?" Natalie asked.

Cyn Garrett

Jonathan propped his buttocks against the desk edge, crossed one leg over the other, and folded his arms across his chest. His lips turned up in a lazy smile. "Seems everyone knows where Natalie Wakefield lives in this town. It wasn't difficult at all."

"But, Philadelphia, how did you know that I lived in Philadelphia?"

"Luck, I guess." He reached for a piece of paper lying on the desktop and read the heading out loud. "*Natalie Wakefield, Couturiere of Fine Fashion.*" Glad to see you still carry my name. I can't imagine why, though. I figured by now you'd have a brood of kids in your skirts and a hardworking man by your side. That's what you always wanted, right, Honey?"

"You can't always have what you want, Jonathan," she delivered with a mordant tongue. She was busy at the garment rack, straightening what already hung in perfect order. "Of course, *YOU* never realized that. By the way, have you given up that nasty gambling habit?"

He pushed from the desk edge and moved toward her, causing panic to rise inside her. She recalled his charming manner and how she used to forgive his faults because of his way with words and love.

"I see you're still quick to anger," he teased, stopping only inches before her to touch her hair. "Must be red. It's said that red hair and a fiery temper go hand-in-hand."

"What you know about me is absolutely zero, Mister," she said, slapping his hand away.

He chuckled. "You're forgetting, Honey. I probably know more about you than anybody. All those past years of married bliss haven't slipped your mind, have they?"

58

"Bliss?" I remember them more like a blasted toothache!" She moved over to the display table. She was jolted to another level when Jonathan's hand gripped her shoulders. Natalie yanked away, stepped back then let him have it. "If you want to continue a decent conversation with me, Jonathan, I can accept that, but you will not handle me, nor will I sit quietly and listen to the details of our once-shared life. It has been years. I hardly call us intimate."

She was the Natalie he remembered, and he liked that. She was not married; things looked as if they were going quite well for her in business, and his gut told him that if he watched his step, she'd most likely help him through this little rough spot. He saw it in her eyes.

"I am proud of you, Honey. Of course, I have always known you were destined for success. "The best decision you had ever made was getting rid of me," he admitted, walking toward the shop's back corner.

Just then, the shop bell jingled and halted Natalie mid-word from commenting on Jonathan's remark. Ben was the last person she expected to see and the last person she was prepared for at this emotional moment. He was dressed for a hard day's work in rugged fabrics cut to fit his muscular form.

"Good day, Natalie," he greeted, wiping his feet on the rug inside the shop door.

"Good day to you, Ben," she answered, glancing nervously at Jonathan and then back to Ben. "What do I owe the honor of this visit?"

If she had one wish, she would ask Jonathan to leave quietly without another word spoken and never darken her door again, but, of course, that would not happen. She noticed he was making himself quite comfortable as he lowered himself onto her desk chair.

Then Ben spoke again. "Can I have a word with you about the other evening?"

Nothing sounded better to her. Angry encounters with Ben had never made for a good night's sleep. She wanted to get things back on the right track if it were not for the buffoon relaxing in her desk chair, watching them like a hawk and eavesdropping like it was his God-given right. She wanted a private moment!

Ben noticed the gentleman customer in the corner of the room, so he positioned himself so his back blocked Natalie from the man's view and discreetly lowered his voice to a murmur.

"It wasn't right for me to say those things to you the other evening, and I wanted you to know, well, I just don't know how we get misdirected into those arguments. I want to apologize for that, Natalie."

Ben had moved so close to her that she could think of nothing but the kiss they had shared a fortnight ago. Natalie's heart picked up faster, and Jonathan's presence was suddenly unimportant and forgotten.

"Certainly, Ben. Not to worry," she answered in a breathy whisper.

Ben smiled, running his strong fingers down the outside of her arm. He cupped her elbow and squeezed gently. "Thank you, Natalie. Now, about that project? I had just delivered a cabinet next door and thought I might see what you desire before I head home. Do you have time to show me what you want, or should we do this another day when you do not have a customer?"

Customer! Oh, how could she forget. . .Jonathan. She craned her neck around Ben's side and saw the troublemaker watching them keenly.

"Hey, don't worry about me, Honey," Jonathan commented casually." Take your time and show the man what you want. You and I have all day."

Natalie cast the eavesdropper a dark look. Please leave it to Jonathan to ruin things for her. He had ruined so much of her past, and now he was back to start where he had left off. She wanted him gone!

But when she turned back to Ben, she immediately noticed his wrinkled brow and stiffened posture as he stared down every inch of Jonathan's frame. His reaction was truly surprising, which caused an instant bubble of excitement to swell inside her. Why, Ben looked half-peeved. Downright jealous, to say the least. Who would have thought that Jonathan's presence and attention, after all these years, would have turned out so positive? She readjusted her thinking and thought it might be advantageous to seize the moment. She needed everything possible to reach her goal, and this was not an opportunity to pass up.

"Well, are you sure you don't mind waiting?" she answered Jonathan with extraordinary sweetness.

The suave gambler took her cue. He pushed from the chair and sauntered toward her. "Not at all. I will look through your pretty things while you take the time you need, Honey." He reached for her chin and gave it a tender shake.

Jonathan was taking things to the extreme. But when she turned her attention back to Ben, she noticed his eyebrows were drawn into one straight agitated line across his forehead, and she felt hard-pressed to keep the smile off her face.

Until Olivia's voice cut through the air like a knife, bringing the trio's preoccupation to an abrupt end. The threesome never heard her enter the shop and simultaneously turned toward her with surprise.

"Honestly, Ben, wouldn't the pub hold a livelier atmosphere on a Saturday afternoon than a dressmaker's shop?" Olivia said in a saccharine sweet voice followed by a light giggle.

She stood inside the threshold of the shop, perfectly coiffed, decked in a gown of lemon yellow, and surrounded by an aura of elegance. A stream of light poured in the shop's window and bathed her in a soft glow that offered a youthfulness and beauty rarely seen.

But Ben only saw red when Jonathan moved to her side and bent into a courtly bow.

"A livelier conversation perhaps, yet for a more delightful atmosphere, a man would always choose this establishment," the gambler uttered, reaching for Olivia's hand. "Allow me to introduce myself, Jonathan Wakefield, Natalie's ex-husband," he announced as he drew Olivia's hand to his lips and pressed a kiss upon her slender fingers.

Olivia shot Ben a shocked expression.

Ben, in turn, rolled his eyes heavenward.

And Natalie felt a sense of triumph and grinned from ear to ear.

"Oh, yes, excuse me. I have been terribly rude," Natalie sweetly apologized. "Ben and Olivia, this is my ex-husband, Jonathan Wakefield," she waved gracefully. "And, Jonathan, please meet Olivia Dansbury, a new customer of mine." Then turned to Ben, stretched out both arms with palms facing upward, and said, "And, of course, my *very* good friend, Ben Walters."

Olivia sucked in an indignant breath. Why, of all the humiliating introductions she had ever heard! Customer? And Ben, a *very* good friend of hers? What a slap in the face.

"Very nice to meet you, Olivia and Ben," Jonathan returned smoothly. Then to Natalie, "Don't let me hold you a minute longer, Honey. I can see things are piling up for you. As I said, I will look around at your pretty things, and when you're finished with these folks, we can catch up."

"That sounds divine, Jonathan," the smiling redhead answered, playing along with great fervor. "Now, I have those things you have ordered in the back room, Olivia. Mary wrapped them yesterday. Let me get them for you."

Natalie rushed down the hallway while Ben and Olivia exchanged whispered words. Jonathan covertly watched and listened to the couple's hushed conversation as he strolled around the shop, pretending to scrutinize the lovely accessories displayed on tables. He deciphered from their conversation that Ben would meet the beautiful blonde woman at the hotel after he took lumber measurements for a project he had promised Natalie. Olivia Dansbury's hissed remarks were harder to understand, but Jonathan thought she said something about Ben's poorly placed priorities and how he cared little for her humiliation.

"Here you go, Olivia," Natalie trilled as she reappeared with a package. "I hope you find everything to your satisfaction."

Olivia never acknowledged Natalie as she took the package from the dressmaker's outstretched arms and immediately handed the parcel to Ben. "Are you finished here, Ben?" she clipped.

"No, I am not. I must take measurements for a small project here at Natalie's shop," he stated, handing the package back to the pouting woman. Ben wanted no part in Olivia's redirecting plans. "I will swing by for you at four o'clock, as we decided. Now, I have little time to waste. Natalie, could we be about the details of this project?"

"Gladly, Ben. Follow me. I will see you later this evening, Jonathan," she called over her shoulder.

"Absolutely, Natalie," Jonathan answered while offering his arm to Olivia, who now stood beside him. "Allow me to escort you, Mrs. Dansbury. My rig is out front at your disposal."

Ben stopped in his tracks and stared them down, immediately inspiring Olivia. She turned to Jonathan, accepted his invitation and proffered arm, and never looked back.

As they stepped from the shop, Jonathan called back over his shoulder. "Again, good meeting you, Ben Walters."

#

Chapter Eight

Immediately following Olivia and Jonathan's departure, Natalie requested Ben follow her to the shop's dressing area. "I'd like a platform built for my ladies, Ben. A simple one-step affair in that corner with two mirrors attached to each wall."

He studied the dynamics of her request and figured he could do this favor for her without inconveniencing her or himself overly much. It was the least he could do to repay her for all she had done for him. "I'll take some measurements and make a lumber list," Ben answered.

"Wonderful. Now, if you would please follow me, I have another small favor in my bedroom." She walked deliberately back the hall and into her apartment, leaving Ben no choice but to follow.

With all the visits Ben had made to Natalie's home in the past, he had never once entered her bedroom. He had never even looked inside the room, staying purposely in the dining room and parlor and away from any possible trouble. Now, as he stood at the threshold, feasting his eyes on the intimate details of her personal space, a warm and exciting feeling washed over him. The room exuded the familiar and appealing fragrance that was so much a part of her, and it seemed to wrap around him with exciting promise. It was fresh and clean like the rest of her home and shop. The main difference lay with the personal effects that were scattered throughout. Various bottles filled with creams and a porcelain-handled hairbrush rested on the vanity top. Silk hose hung from a dressing screen in the corner. A small round table with an oil lamp stood beside a chaise with a lace-edged nightgown draped over its seatback. Then finally, his gaze came to rest on the canopy bed piled high with frilly pillows and the precarious tilt of the bed's foundation.

"An underneath strap had torn loose in the middle of the night over a week ago. I had no idea how to fix the thing," Natalie explained, rubbing her neck.

"Where have you been sleeping?" Ben asked as he moved to the bed for a closer examination.

"In the chaise. I feared more supports might give way if I climbed back in the bed."

Ben glanced at the chaise and imagined the discomfort Natalie must have experienced sleeping on the narrow space night after night. With her full schedule, sleep was an essential ingredient to production. Ben checked his timepiece. He had two hours before his date with Olivia and decided that was plenty of time to repair the damage and get things for Natalie.

"Go get those tools I left here while I turn this mattress over." Ben reached for the pillows propped at the headboard. "You don't mind if I put these things on the floor, do you?"

"That is fine, Ben, but---"

As he stretched for the very last one at the far side of the bed, Ben lost his balance and tumbled onto the tilted mattress. The pillows flew like confetti, giving way to yet another leather strap.

"Ben!" Natalie ran to the bedside. She thought he had hit his head and was knocked unconscious, for his eyes were closed, and he lay deathly silent.

Finally, his head rolled toward her with one open, angry eye glaring at her. "What?" he ground out.

"My goodness, I thought you hurt yourself. Here, give me your hand, and I will help you up," she insisted, ignoring his obvious irritation.

Ben shifted to his side for better leverage, completely avoiding her, but the movement on the weakened foundation was enough to tear another strap loose from its stronghold, throwing Ben once again on his back.

"Bennnnnnn! Let me help you." Natalie waved her hand back and forth in front of his face, her fingers wiggling to get his attention.

"It is impossible, Natalie. Move away before you hurt yourself. I will get up myself," he snapped.

"Give me your hands," Natalie pleaded.

Ben groaned with her persistence.

"It is the only safe way up, Ben. My feet are braced, and I have sufficient leverage." She grabbed his hands.

"On the count of three. Ready?" she encouraged.

He grunted an indecipherable sound.

"One. . . Two. . . Three!"

Natalie pulled with all her strength, but Ben's weight pulled her right off the floor and onto the bed. The added weight broke the remainder of the straps, bringing the mattress and its occupants crashing to the floor. It forced a scream from Natalie as she tumbled awkwardly against Ben's form.

There was a moment of silence.

Opening her eyes, she discovered her face was pressed dangerously close to Ben's manly parts. She frantically attempted to pull away, but the heavy weight of her skirts twisted beneath her made it nearly impossible. Somehow, she maneuvered to Ben's chest level and forced herself to consider his angry face. He was lying on his back, hands folded under his head and staring at the ceiling in stony silence.

"I'm sorry, Ben, I was just trying to help you," she whispered with an apology.

Ben wondered just how much a man was supposed to endure. His mission was merely to help with a little carpentry work, and he wondered how, in the name of heaven, it ever came to this twisted-up mess. When her fingers began making circular motions on his shirt front, he grabbed her wrist and pulled her hand away.

"You are a very persistent woman, Natalie. Couldn't you see that there was no way you could have pulled me off this bed?"

She wiggled a little and brought her face closer to his. "I see that now."

Ben groaned with frustration. Natalie purred with contentment when his arm dropped to lie across her waist. But the smooth masculine voice from the doorway suddenly cut off the moment's magic.

"Should I tell Olivia you might be a little late?"

Startled by the intruder, Natalie and Ben jerked around to find Jonathan, arms akimbo, standing in the doorway.

With speed akin to lightning, Ben shot off the bed while Jonathan seized the opportunity to gallantly assist Natalie from her reclined position.

"I was showing Ben my broken bed, hoping he could fix it for me," Natalie hastily explained when she got to her feet.

"You don't owe him an explanation, Natalie," Ben growled, furious that Natalie's annoying ex-husband had caught them in a compromising position. "Get me those tools, Natalie, and I'll fix the damn bed." Turning to Jonathan, Ben snapped out more orders. "And since you don't have anything better to do, give me a hand with this mattress, Wakefield."

"My pleasure. Where it concerns Natalie, there are no limits to what I would do," he answered with a crooked smile.

Except for the sound of shuffling furniture, the room filled with a strained silence.

***

When Olivia returned to her hotel room, she discovered a note from Hope lying on the dresser top. It said that she had taken a coach out to Ben's so that Max could teach her about winemaking. For her life, Olivia could not understand what drew Hope to the older man. And whenever she pressed her over the matter, Hope answered that Max had many interesting stories and a vast knowledge of things she knew little about. She had claimed that she enjoyed being with him. Max was everything Olivia detested.

On this day, however, her daughter's absence happened to suit her quite well. It would give Olivia time alone with Ben for more serious matters. From how Natalie Wakefield played the game, Olivia figured she better start breaking a few rules of propriety. Tonight, she would entice Ben into a more intimate arrangement.

Olivia decided to spoil herself with a lengthy toilette. After a warm bath, she oiled her body with the fragrance Ben had commented on last week, then slipped into a dressing gown and spent the next hour with her hair and nails. At four o'clock, she was a vision of perfection, reclined in the chaise and waiting for Ben's arrival. By four fifteen, he still had not arrived. Olivia began to pace. Late was not Ben's style. The mere thought of him in Natalie Wakefield's company didn't settle well at all, and when four-thirty came, with no sign of him, jealousy surfaced like nothing Olivia had ever felt before. Finally, a knock sounded on her door at ten minutes to five. Olivia jumped up and pulled the portal wide.

"You should be more careful. One never knows what danger lurks on the other side of a closed door." It was Jonathan with both arms propped high on the door frame and a rakish grin covering his face.

"Where's Ben?" Olivia demanded, ignoring his previous comment.

"That is why I am here, Madam. He had an accident earlier today with Natalie's bed and has not yet finished the repairs. It turned out to be a little more than he expected." Jonathan dropped his arms and leaned back on the door frame to watch her building fury.

"We have a dinner engagement," she bit out.

"Ben said you did, and when Natalie heard that, she suggested making the four of us one of her spectacular meals. I offered to escort you over, so Ben could keep working, and Natalie could get the remainder of the meal together."

"Dinner at Natalie's was not our plan. Tell Ben I'll wait until he is finished."

Olivia's voice was so condescending that Jonathan wanted to slap the haughty expression right off her face. "I am not your messenger boy, Mrs. Danbury. Dinner is served at six o'clock sharp. I will be there, and if you expect to see Mr. Walters, you better be there too. Last, I looked at the man; he was not ready for a night on the town. Now, you can come along with me, or if you find that too repulsive, you can hire a town coach when I leave. What will it be, Madam?"

"It will be simple, Mr. Wakefield. Remove your presence and join the gay crowd at Natalie's."

Jonathan pulled his body away from the slamming door in the nick of time.

#

Chapter Nine

By the time Jonathan returned to Natalie's apartment, Ben had finished the bed repair. Ben immediately questioned him on Olivia's whereabouts, but when Jonathan merely rolled his eyes, Ben knew things had not gone well. He hastily gathered his tools, realizing his behavior had been unfair and rude to Olivia. He owed her an explanation for the turn of events.

"My apologies, Natalie, but I must see to Olivia. I promised her the evening and must explain my tardiness," he said to the couturiere without caring for her feelings. Ben grabbed his hat and coat, never noticing the finely set table nor realizing the effort she had made for the meal. He closed the door behind him, leaving Natalie and Jonathan speechless.

A tearful voice answered on the other side when Ben rapped on Olivia's closed portal.

"Who is it?"

"Olivia, it's Ben. May I come in, please?"

He heard the latch turn, and when the door opened, Olivia stood before him with a tear-ravaged face, a handkerchief held to her nose. Ben stepped inside and took her into his arms.

"I'm so sorry," he whispered into her hair.

Olivia remained stiff, unwilling to accept his apology. The pain and embarrassment she had endured these past hours could not be forgotten with one simple *I'm sorry*. He was a cad!

This incident recalled the memory of Andrew's unfailing etiquette. He had never fallen short of gallantry where her welfare was concerned and had always placed her first regardless of the emergency. On the other hand, Ben Walters had embarrassed her at Natalie Wakefield's shop earlier that day by rudely dismissing her. To make matters worse, he then sent her outrageous ex-husband to her hotel room to escort her back to the company she had wanted to avoid. Ben needed a lesson in comportment. If he cared to have a refined woman like herself share his life, he needed to learn the manners he sorely lacked.

"It was the most humiliating thing I have ever faced, Ben. Why did you send that man over here?" She broke free from his arms, turned her back on him, and dabbed at her nose.

"I was in the middle of a repair, Olivia," Ben simply explained. "Wakefield offered to help by escorting you back to Natalie's for dinner."

"Fixing her bed, so I hear. How do you think I felt when I learned you could not keep our date because you had to work on another woman's bed? It worried me sick, Ben." She turned around, and a fresh round of tears poured forth."

He stared at her and thought how *she* had been the one to break their plans many years ago when she had run off to marry another man. Ben wondered if she had ever understood *his* pain. Then he shook the thought and reminded himself that it was best to leave bad memories where they belonged, in the past. Her beautiful face was ravaged with tears over his ill-mannered actions, which troubled him the very most.

"Come here," he coaxed, opening his arms wide to welcome her into his embrace. "I will make this up to you. We can still enjoy a relaxing dinner together in the dining room." He rubbed his hand soothingly up and down her backbone. "Would you like that?"

She nodded against his chest.

"Good. There is a changing room down the hall. I will clean up, then go to the dining room and reserve a table while you get together. I will be back in fifteen minutes."

A disturbing thought invaded his mind when Ben closed the door behind him. In the course of one afternoon, he held two very different women in his arms: one of slender, incomparable beauty and refined manners and the other, a saucy redhead with an unleashed tongue and a body that could tempt a saint.

Ben salvaged the evening by treating Olivia to an enjoyable meal in the hotel dining room. Ben had always said good night at her door, but she invited him to share a nightcap tonight.

"Do you remember that afternoon eighteen years ago when we made love by the pond?" Olivia whispered as she moved inches before him with desire burning in her eyes. "I remember it as if it were yesterday, Ben."

Ben drew her up against him. "I've often wondered how your husband reacted when he realized you were not a virgin on your wedding night."

Olivia stiffened. "Why must you bring Andrew between us?" Ben was spoiling the mood she had worked hard to create throughout the evening.

"I guess because it's where he's always been."

Olivia pushed away and walked to the bed's edge. "I was young and very foolish, Ben. It took less than a month of marriage to discover that I had made a terrible mistake." She wrapped her arms around the bedpost and looked at him with regret.

Ben didn't move a muscle. He hoped that Olivia had lived in hell with Andrew Dansbury, a rightful punishment for causing him so much pain. He had never understood how she could have given up all they had shared.

"It was too much for me to understand then, Ben. Andrew was older, worldly, and persuasive if you will. He promised me a life without wants or struggles. And I foolishly thought it would be wonderful to spend my life never wanting again. Most of all, I saw an opportunity for our children to gain everything I had never had: clothes, a beautiful home, and a fine education. It had not taken long to realize my foolishness. Weeks after our wedding, Andrew told me he was sterile. It nearly destroyed me, Ben. I became cold and detached because of his deceit and moved from our bedroom. Soon I realized I was pregnant with your child, a bittersweet revelation. Although I carried your child, I had lost you. Hope has been my only happiness all these years.

"Andrew was only too happy to claim another man's child," she continued. "He loved her as if she were his blood. Andrew threatened that if I ever allowed the secret of Hope's lineage to escape, he would take Hope from me, and I would never see her again. I prayed for the day when I could tell you the truth. When Andrew died, I finally saw my chance. My deepest desire was to return to Philadelphia and make up for all the hurt I had caused you. I wanted you to know your beautiful daughter."

Ben moved next to her. His voice was low, his eyes deep and probing. "Hope is my daughter?"

Olivia nodded, a tender smile on her lips.

"Does she know?"

"Yes," Olivia simply stated.

"Why didn't you tell me sooner?"

She sniffed for effect. "I was afraid. I needed to make sure your life had not been complicated with a wife and children, and perhaps I needed time to settle in and get reacquainted. Believe me, Ben, if you had found happiness with another woman and had made a life together, I never would have revealed these particulars about Hope." Olivia wrapped her arms around his waist and tilted her face to look into his eyes. "I never would have caused you any more pain than I already have."

Ben was filled with a bizarre combination of feelings: overwhelming joy mixed with an undercurrent of resentment and slight distrust.

Then the door latch rattled, and Hope entered, her arms full of packages.

"Oh, excuse me," the young lass uttered with discomfort, realizing she had just interrupted a private moment.

"Hope," Ben said with tenderness.

The look in Ben's eyes and the tender tone in which he greeted her spoke volumes. When she glanced at her mother and saw the look of satisfaction covering her face, Hope knew the deed had been done. After spending an enjoyable day with Max and learning the wonderful, honest ways of Ben Walters, Hope felt a sudden sharp discomfort with her part in this trap her mother had concocted.

"Did you have a nice evening?" Hope queried, working hard to maintain a level voice.

"Yes. I guess you might say it turned out quite well," Ben answered, studying her closely.

He searched her features for something that resembled him. She did not have the Walters' trademark sapphire blue eyes, but warm brown eyes fringed in dark curling lashes. There was no part of the squared Walter's jawline either. Her heart-shaped face was as delicate as a flower, and, for the most part, Ben concluded that she looked like Olivia with her slender shape, pale hair, and facial similarities. He wanted to believe she was his daughter, for a child of his own had always been his strongest desire. He only wished he could see one thing about her that marked her as HIS. She was smiling at him, and his heart opened to her. He wanted nothing more than a daughter as beautiful, sweet, and gentle as this young woman and felt a surge of pride swell inside him to call her his daughter. He was helpless to stop his reaction.

"Your Mother gave me the most wonderful news this evening, and I want you to know, Hope, that whatever joys have come my way in the past, none can compare to the joy I feel tonight. Although I have heard it from others, tonight, I can tell you firsthand that there is no greater joy than becoming a father." Ben kissed the top of Hope's hair.

Hope glanced at her mother, who was smiling like a Cheshire cat. Hope had been repeatedly reminded about what she owed Olivia, so she bucked up, smiled lovingly into Ben's kind face, and stated the words she knew her mother wanted to hear. "Father, it is wonderful to be here with you at last."

***

Jonathan relaxed at Natalie's table with a post-dinner brandy. He listened to the satisfying, long-forgotten sounds of domesticity as his ex-wife finished the dinner clean-up. He reflected that she certainly had not lost her touch in the culinary department. Her splendid meal, coupled with the intimacy of her company, had given Jonathan one of the best evenings he had had since they parted. A pang of regret shot through him for his inability to hang on to her love. She was a fine catch for a man.

"It is funny to see you at my dining table, Jonathan. I thought when we had said goodbye, it had been forever."

"Forever is a long time, Honey."

She laid her coffee cup on the table and removed her apron. "Yes, I guess you are right. Whew! What a day! I am exhausted."

"You're a hard-working woman. It does not appear that you've slowed down over these years. Everything is so clean and comfortable around here."

"Yes, and do not get any ideas about comfortable, Jonathan. We have said our goodbyes, and that is how I want it to stay, apart, as friends."

Jonathan swirled the amber liquid around his glass as he carefully studied her. "We *are* friends, aren't we, Natalie?"

"Heaven only knows why. After all the agony you put me through, I shouldn't allow you within fifty miles of my front door."

Jonathan detected softness in her voice and knew she had long forgiven him for the pain he had once put her through. By darn, he honestly wanted to make it up to her, and, for the first time since he had known her, he wished he did not have to ask for a favor.

"How many men stand at your front door?" he teased.

"I would rather not get on that subject. Most especially with you, Jonathan. We both have our own lives now."

He leaned forward with his forearms braced on his knees. "I see that you let Ben Walters further than your doorstep."

Natalie's expression turned dreamy at the mention of Ben's name, and that look caused a ripple of jealousy within Jonathan. She had once looked at him with that excitement and passion, but now those loving looks and heartfelt desires were only for Ben Walters, the lucky bastard. He was the man who had captured her whole heart and occupied her entire mind.

"I have been thinking about a plan to better your chances with your lover boy. Though, I must warn you the plan includes my _personal_ talents," Jonathan touted.

"Ben Walters is _not_ my lover boy," Natalie snapped.

He chuckled. "Wait a minute, Honey; you forget whom you're talking to. Nobody knows better than me about the looks you give that man. You are in love with him, and Olivia Dansbury stands in your way."

Natalie's head dropped while her fingers moved worriedly back and forth on her lap. She could not hide that Ben Walters was the man she wanted with all her heart. Olivia Dansbury's arrival had caused her to lose ground with Ben more rapidly than anything else had in the past two years. She knew if she had any intentions of making him a permanent part of her life, a plan of strategy was essential, even if it was at the cost of involvement with her ex-husband. Time was running out. She needed help.

"All right, I'll listen to you, Jonathan."

"Terrific. Now here is the plan. I suggest we spark Ben's jealousy by pretending reunited love."

"What?" she screeched.

"Hear me out. Have you seen those unfavorable looks he shoots me whenever I get close to you? Except for the fact that I was once your husband, I have given him no reason to act that way. I know what he is worried about, Natalie. He is worried that you and I will rekindle our relationship, which does not sit well with him," Jonathan stated firmly. "I would love to give him a little competition and watch him squirm. Word has it; Ben Walters has little competition where you are concerned. Well, let me tell you I am here to court you in high fashion and give him whatever it takes to shake his tree. What do you think?"

Natalie was slightly insulted by how he put it but decided to let it slide. Quite frankly, he was right with his assumption, and since she had no other plan, perhaps she would try Jonathan's idea. What could she lose?

"O.K., Jonathan, say I go along with this plan. What do you want out of it?"

"I need a small loan, but I will pay you back, and I mean every word I say. I *will* pay you back."

She should have known. Deals with Jonathan always involved money, though Natalie figured it might be money very well spent this time.

\#

Chapter Ten

As planned, Jonathan arrived at Natalie's apartment Sunday morning bright and early. He climbed the back-porch steps and then paused to check his appearance in the window before he knocked. The sun glinted off his diamond pinky ring, creating a shiny light over his reflection in the window. He adjusted his red silk cravat, winked approvingly at his image, then tapped lightly on the door to announce his arrival. A moment later, he heard the clatter of Natalie's heels. Natalie's lovely face appeared when the curtain parted, and the portal swung wide.

"Good morning, Jonathan. Come in and help yourself to coffee. It is on the stove," talking over her shoulder as she retreated. "I am not quite ready. I only need a minute."

Jonathan was so happy to be back in her company. Her loveliness had not faded since they parted many years ago. These past days together, she reminded him of her ingenuity and how she had always designed the cut and color of every gown she wore to hide her drawbacks and enhance her finer points. He knew better than anyone that Natalie possessed many "finer points," As much as it did not seem possible, he saw she had gained a handful more since their marriage. Jonathan felt positive that the weeks ahead in Natalie's company would prove very pleasurable, indeed. At last, she stepped into the hall and moved toward him, a wool cloak draped over her arm.

"Your beauty is a feast for my eyes, madam. I believe my first day of employment will require much self-control." Jonathan moved close to inhale her alluring scent.

"Do not push it, Jonathan. You know the rules," she sharply reminded him, handing him the cloak.

"Push it? I'm only playing the loving ex-husband, as we agreed. You want my loving attention to appear sincere, don't you?" he chuckled.

"Sure, go on and laugh. I am sure it's very funny to you. The more I thought about it in bed last night, the less I believed in our silly plan."

"Come on, Honey, don't feel defeated this early in the game. We haven't even given it a try," Jonathan encouraged, tucking her arm in his and giving her hand a consoling pat. "Relax! All good things take time."

"I have been after this 'good thing' for too long! I think I have run out of time, Jonathan," Natalie sulked.

"Trust me; you have not run out of time. Stick close, do what I say, and keep the faith. Patience, patience," he cajoled as he closed the apartment door behind them.

***

After learning that Hope was his flesh and blood daughter, Ben had barely slept a wink. A mixture of bitter sadness for having missed out on Hope's childhood, and resentment, because Olivia had turned her back on him years ago kept him tossing and turning throughout the night. It was torturous trying to rationalize why he felt willing to accept Olivia back into his life after all that had happened in the past. He had allowed her to waltz out of his life seventeen years ago, then waltz right back in with little to no accountability for her actions. She had a grip on him in ways he could not define, especially now with the newfound knowledge that Hope was his daughter.

To add to his confusion, visions of Natalie Wakefield kept popping into his mind at ridiculous moments, causing disorder and questions about the plans he attempted to make for his future. He knew he had to stop thinking about the redhead, cease his concern for her well-being, and focus more on the details between Olivia and him.

Yet the longer Natalie's pew remained empty, the more his stomach rolled with unrest. Ben could not remember a Sunday morning Natalie had missed church or been late for services, and he worried that something serious had come about. He knew he had done a solid repair on her bed, though he would not put it past Natalie's big oaf ex-husband to have dived on the bed next to her or foolishly performed some other act of buffoonery to make her laugh, breaking the bed again and some bones in the process. The thought made him sick.

Jonathan Wakefield was becoming a virtual pain in Ben's backside. He was perpetually joking and smiling with that big toothy grin, always saying things to Natalie that held a slant with every meaning, an ulterior motive to every idea he suggested. Quite frankly, it made Ben mad as hell. He had never thought much of men like Jonathan: pretty boys who never broke a sweat. The gambler's callous-free hands and jewelry-adorned finger showed that he had never worked a hard day in his life. It mystified Ben that Natalie, who had always practiced a strong work ethic, would allow her good-for-nothing-lazy- gambling-ex-husband back into her life to take hold of everything she had worked so hard for all these years. These thoughts repulsed him, and a sudden wave of disgust washed over him, making him want to bolt from his pew and find out exactly what had detained her.

"Are you all right, Father?" Hope whispered, gently squeezing his hand.

"I'm fine," he lied, glancing down into Hope's concerned expression. He returned her squeeze for reassurance.

Then from his peripheral vision, he saw movement on the other side of the aisle. Natalie and her incorrigible escort arrived just as the steeple bell rang. It truly bothered Ben that Natalie tolerated this scoundrel encumbering her orderly life.

Ben's gaze dropped to Jonathan's possessive hand on Natalie's waist as he ushered her into the pew. The intimate touch suggested last night might have been far cozier for the two than Ben cared to consider. He prayed Natalie was not getting in over her head. With all she had told him about her ex-husband's gambling habits and the trouble it had caused in their former marriage, Ben certainly hoped she would not be foolish enough to make the same mistake twice.

Ben was in for his second-morning upset when the processional hymn began. Who would have thought the no-good freeloader would possess a baritone voice so full of tone and control that folks around him would stop and listen in awe at his God-given talent? In Ben's opinion, it was one more superficial attribute that said nothing about the man.

The Vicar stepped before the altar, spread his arms in welcome, and invited his congregation to open their prayer books to page three hundred and eight.

Ben breathed relief; finally, the buffoon's moment was over. However, seven minutes later, the pain returned when another hymn began, and then painfully twice more before the service finally ended. Ben could not wait to escape the confines of the church. Jonathan's voice reverberated against the church walls during the hymns with such a disturbing presence that Ben could not find the peace God always provided here on Sunday mornings.

He felt exhausted.

He wanted out!

Many folks moved forward to greet Natalie's escort, narrowing the center aisle and path that led to the door. Meanwhile, Ben suggested to Olivia and Hope that they hurry along to make the most of the day. Fortunately, both ladies offered no resistance, filing from their pew and quietly passing the interested throng of friends around Natalie and Jonathan. Ben heard Estelle Wilcox's voice loud and clear from the group's center when they passed.

"You must be Natalie's husband . . . ahem, excuse me, I mean ex-husband. We have heard so much about you, and now we finally meet. Let me introduce myself, Estelle Wilcox, one of Natalie's faithful customers."

A crease formed on Ben's forehead. When they reached the churchyard, he never noticed the brilliant sun in the sky or the mild temperatures. Instead, a blinding confusion filled his mind, robbing him of whatever good surrounded him. He assisted Olivia and Hope aboard, then rounded the back of the rig and foolishly allowed himself a parting glance at the church. The Vicar stood with a small group at the door; Natalie and Jonathan were in the center. He was shaking Jonathan's right hand while his left hand fondly gripped Jonathan's shoulder. Natalie stood to the side smiling brightly. It was a common Sunday morning sight following services: peaceful, happy faces exchanging good wishes for the day and week ahead.

Ben kicked the dirt and shook his head in disgust. He climbed aboard his rig, slapped the reins on the horse's hide, and never looked back.

\#

Chapter Eleven

In Jonathan's typical wily manner, he managed to secure a room at the *Steven Mathews Hotel* next to the room Olivia and Hope occupied. This convenient proximity enabled him to eavesdrop on their conversation by resting his ear on a drinking glass and then placing it against the wall separating their rooms. Tonight, Olivia and Hope's conversation was quite interesting; Olivia's attitude was lofty.

"I want Ben to review the property before we decide, Hope. I know nothing about the neighborhood and would not feel comfortable until Ben approves."

"Mother, Germantown has the finest homes in the area. Furthermore, I cannot imagine Russell offering it to us if it were less desirable. He is an old family friend and aware of your standard of living. He knows what you expect."

"Only the very best, I'm sure," Jonathan whispered under his breath from the other side of the wall.

"You ask too much of Ben," Hope bit out as she moved to the armoire for fresh undergarments.

"He is happy to accommodate me, Hope. He has been a man without a purpose for so many years, and now he finally has us to dote over. Can't you see his joy?"

Jonathan wished he could see Hope's expression. She did not answer her mother's question, and he wondered if she agreed with her opinion.

"Now, you *will* join us Wednesday morning," Olivia demanded.

"Where, Mother?"

"To visit the property for rent. We will go as a family. I am sure your father will want you present."

"No, I am sorry, but I can't do that. I promised Max I would help him with the party preparation."

"What party?" Olivia snapped.

"Ben is having a costume party. I am sure he plans to tell you about it this evening. I hope you will wear a costume, Mother."

A noticeable silence fell in the Dansbury's room. Jonathan pressed his ear firmly against the glass and waited.

"Mother, did you hear me?"

"I heard you, Hope. Now you hear me. Do not start with your free-willed ways. This is our future, and it is nothing to take lightly. I want you to tell me immediately if you know anything important to our plan. I do not know when you learned about this ridiculous costume party, but I see you did not feel it important enough to inform me. I am your mother, Hope. Have you no respect?"

Another silence prevailed.

"If Ben is having an affair at home, I should have known first. And in answer to your question about the costume, I will *not* be wearing a costume."

Jonathan screwed up his face. He should have figured she would resist wearing a costume. He, on the other hand, could not wait. A costume party sounded like great fun and offered a marvelous opportunity to annoy Ben again. Jonathan's face broke into a devilish smile as he considered the great costume idea that came to mind. He would run it by Natalie tonight at dinner.

***

When Estelle Wilcox looked across the aisles in the Market House and caught sight of Natalie at a vegetable stand, she quickly doled out the coin for her sack of potatoes and hustled over next to her.

"Have you heard?" Estelle whispered when she drew close.

"Heard what?" Natalie answered with disinterest. She adjusted the parcels in her arms, then continued down the aisle, never looking at her aggravator.

Estelle followed. "I heard this after you left church on Sunday. By the way, Natalie, that man of yours has the most divine voice I have ever heard. I could listen to him sing all day long. Simply heavenly voice! I caught the tail end of Clayton Brenner's conversation when I passed him in the churchyard."

Natalie kept moving. Today her schedule was chock-full. There was no time for Estelle's mindless chatter. She stopped before a stand of cabbages and picked up a head to feel for firmness.

Estelle moved close and dropped her voice to a whisper. "Natalie, brace yourself. You will not believe this, but Clayton said he heard that Hope Dansbury is Ben's flesh and blood daughter. I was stunned, to say the least, and the worst is that Ben Walters is flaunting it around town like there is nothing sinful about a bastard child!"

Natalie's fingernails dug into the surface of the cabbage. Her world tilted. A sharp stab of pain seized her heart. Hot tears filled her eyes. Although Estelle kept rambling on, Natalie lost concentration and heard nothing more. All she wanted was the sanctuary of her home where she could gather her wits and convince herself that this was just more of crazy Estelle's unsubstantiated gossip.

"As I see it, Ben Walters better make this whole thing right in the eyes of God and marry that woman! Imagine!" Estelle continued, knocking on the skins of pumpkins piled up in a wooden crate. When things drew silent, she finally looked up and saw that Natalie was no longer beside her but rather exiting the side door of the Market House. "Natalie? Natalie!" she called out. "Huh, she needs to slow down. She is always in to hurry," she blathered to the girl behind the stand. "By the way, did you hear about Ben Walters? It is simply scandalous!"

***

All was silent when Jonathan rapped on Natalie's apartment door. He rapped again, and still nothing. He tried the door latch and was surprised to find the door unlocked. He had learned these past days that if Natalie was home, she answered her door. If she was not home, her door was ALWAYS locked. Simply put, something was definitely wrong.

"Natalie!" he called out as he stepped into the kitchen.

Jonathan checked the room. There were no pots on the stove, no delicious aromas in the air, and worse yet; there was a definite chill in the air. He opened the stove door and saw she had let the fire burn out.

"What the devil is going on here?" Jonathan mumbled.

He moved up the hallway toward Natalie's bedroom, and when he reached the threshold of her room, he peered in and found her huddled in her bed with her back toward him and the covers pulled up over her head. Jonathan moved to the bed's edge and touched her shoulder.

"Honey? What's wrong?"

Her head whipped around, revealing a tear-streaked face and startled expression. She had been so involved with her misery that she had never heard him enter the house.

"Oh, Jonathan. I didn't hear you. Sorry." She blew her nose into the saturated handkerchief that she held tightly in her hand.

"You should lock your door, Honey. It could have been anybody that let themselves in." His hand stayed on her shoulder and soothingly rubbed back and forth.

"I forgot," she admitted in a pathetic voice, offering no more explanation.

Jonathan had never seen Natalie in this state in all the years of knowing her. He was at a complete loss for what to do.

"Are you ill?" he finally asked.

No answer.

"Would you like me to make you something to eat?"

She shook her head.

"Want to tell me about it?" Jonathan took a seat beside her on the mattress.

She blew her nose again and shrugged her shoulders. Then the hall clock chimed six times. Natalie groaned."I am sorry that supper is not ready, Jonathan. It has been a bad day."

His eyebrow lifted. "Very bad, I would say. I cannot say I've ever seen you in this state."

"Can't say I've ever felt like this b-be-fore either." There was a catch in her voice, and then she lost control and broke into tears. She covered her face with her hands.

"There now," Jonathan said with tenderness. He took her into his arms. "Your old friend's here with plenty of time on his hands. Why don't you tell me what this is all about?"

He held her in his arms, rubbing her back to help ease her pain while she cried.

"It's useless, Jonathan," she began. "I have lost him forever."

"Who? Ben?"

She nodded her head.

Jonathan continued rubbing her back. "Why do you think you've lost him forever?"

"It is not only Olivia I need to fight. Estelle Wilcox overheard Clayton Brenner telling people in church on Sunday that Hope is Ben's flesh and blood daughter." A fresh round of tears burst as soon as Natalie made the proclamation.

Whoa, this *was* bad news, Jonathan thought. Nevertheless, he did not want to jump to any conclusions. After all, just because Estelle Wilcox said she overheard it did not mean it was true.

"I'd never take Estelle Wilcox's word for anything, Natalie. She is nothing but gossip. I would not give it any credence until you hear this from the man himself." Jonathan took her by the shoulders and looked into her eyes. "Where is that feisty gal I have always known?

Where is your fight? You are the only person I have ever known that has never given up on a dream. Why would you give up on this? And remember, we are in this together. You have got me on your side, Honey. We can work this out."

She sniffed, then eked out a limp smile. "Thanks for your support, Jonathan. You are very sweet. Right now, I do not know what I'd do without you. I hope you have some ideas."

"Some of the best ideas I have ever had, and I mean to share them with you. Let's get going."

Jonathan looked at her sad tear-streaked face and remembered all the times he had let her down. One thing he knew for sure, whatever the outcome, he would stand beside her until the end. Just once, he wanted to be there for her when the going got tough.

***

When Ben came in from the workshop that evening, he discovered his lovely daughter had already left without bidding him goodbye.

"She was in a hurry, Ben. I think she must have made arrangements with somebody this evening," Max offered as he continued stirring the sauce on the stove.

"Arrangements? I hope to hell it is with a male companion. I worry about that girl."

"Do not worry about Hope. She knows what she wants from life," the manservant pointed out.

"Yeah, what's that?"

"Peace, friendship, opportunity to make her own decisions. She has had precious little of that."

Ben suddenly realized that Max knew more about his daughter than he did, and that fact humbled him. It made him realize that most of his time had been focused on satisfying Olivia's whims and little on learning about his daughter's past or desires for her future.

"She told you so?" Ben asked with wonder.

"Not straight out. You know I lend an ear and learn more about Hope whenever I am with her. Like the party next Saturday night. Did you know that she has never dressed in costume? And I will tell you why. Her mother thought it was too frightening when Hope was a child and childish now that she is an adult."

"There must have been more solid reasons why Olivia discouraged costuming. I will speak with her about it tomorrow," Ben answered in defense.

"Olivia and Andrew made most of Hope's decisions over the years." Max continued, unimpressed with Ben's support of Olivia. "Your daughter has a thirst for friendship too. Her mother and father selected her friends, none of which would have been her choice, so she tells me. She claims I am the best friend she has ever had and the first one someone else has not chosen for her. Poor little gal says that making apple cider and costumes are the finest things she has ever done. Sadly, she must experience these wonderful joys for the first time with an old man like me."

Ben looked perturbed. "What about a love interest?"

Max shook his head. None. That's not what's important to her. Friendship is what she is after. More importantly, friendship with people of her choice."

That night, when Ben retired to his room, he retrieved the small gold ring from its resting place. It had been in the velvet box, in the same corner of his drawer, for seventeen years. He suddenly realized the mistake he was about to make by offering the ring and a lifetime of promises to a woman he was not sure he even knew. Time changed people. His enthusiasm over having Olivia back in his life again and the newfound knowledge that Hope was his daughter overrode his common sense. He needed time. He wanted to learn more about his daughter and the kind of woman Olivia had become. More so, he thought he might listen to that little voice that told him to make Olivia wait! After all, he had waited seventeen years, and now it was her turn.

Ben placed the ring back in the velvet box and tucked it away in his drawer. Next Saturday would be the first test. He wanted to see how well Olivia did with *his* party at *his* home and, most of all, with *his* friends.

***

At the dinner table, Jonathan listened to Natalie talk about Ben's savvy business sense and sharp intelligence every night. Jonathan was baffled that Natalie, whom he always considered to have an above-average intellect, graded Ben so high. If he was so smart, why didn't he see through Olivia Dansbury's selfishness? It took Jonathan only a few encounters with her to realize that she was a spoiled brat with no one's good in mind but her own. Jonathan deducted that where women were concerned, Ben Walters was as dumb as a board. After all, no one with even a modicum of intelligence could enjoy the company of an empty, shallow, conniving woman like Olivia Dansbury. Jonathan knew her exterior beauty could never compensate for the ugliness of her inner soul. Even though Jonathan had made his share of mistakes in his life, he had learned one very important lesson after living with Natalie Wakefield for seven years: the simple fact that true beauty lies within. Jonathan knew even a dunce could see that Natalie was the finer catch and concluded that Natalie's estimation of Ben's intelligence was way off the mark.

#

Chapter Twelve

After escorting Olivia to her room on Wednesday evening, Ben trod a path directly to the hotel dining room. He needed a strong and numbing libation. A tremendous workload awaited him in his workshop, along with remaining preparation for the party at his place on Saturday. To have spent an entire day looking for the perfect property for Olivia, with no solid results, put him in the foulest of moods. He hoped the alcohol might help soothe his anxiety caused by the precious lost hours.

"Good evening, Mr. Walters," the server greeted as he approached his table.

"Good evening. Bourbon, please," he requested.

"Anything else, sir?"

Ben shook his head. "Just the bourbon."

His day had involved a trip with Olivia to the northwest neighborhood of Germantown. This area boasted mansions such as *Cliveden* and the *Deshler-Morris House,* once inhabited by George Washington. Olivia had learned of a property for rent in this neighborhood through an old family friend and wanted Ben's opinion before she decided. Upon Ben's inspection, he found the condition of the residence superior. He assured Olivia she would be hard-pressed to find a finer accommodation anywhere, but Olivia would not decide until she adequately secured a butler, chambermaid, and cook. She had shown him, in one afternoon, all that she expected from life. Truly, Andrew Dansbury had pampered her. He had gifted her with a lifestyle far different from the one she had lived seventeen years ago, and this disturbed Ben to realize that domesticity had played no part in her marriage. On the other hand, he had found Hope excited and inquisitive about chores around the home. Work interested her, and Ben thought, in this respect, she was much like him.

The server arrived with Ben's drink, quietly placed it on the tabletop, and retreated without a word. He wasted no time taking a fortifying swallow of the amber liquid in hopes the drink would relax him after the painful events of the day. The tension was getting out of control, causing restless nights and, worse yet, forcing mistakes and delays in business. Inadequacy was not Ben's style. He had missed a promised deadline for a customer's trestle table and made two miss-cuts in a wide piece of mahogany which he was finally forced to throw on the burn pile.

Though Ben hated to admit it, he knew that part of his preoccupation stemmed from Jonathan Wakefield's sudden arrival in Philadelphia. The Card Sharp's, slick, sugar-coated ways put a sour taste in Ben's mouth. He believed Jonathan Wakefield untrustworthy and worried that Natalie would be lured back into his arms only to lose what she had worked so hard for.

Ben was shaken from his thoughts when a spirited group of people filed past the dining room entrance. Their lively banter frustrated him even further, for he realized that the people around him were having the time of their lives while his world was filling up with trouble. A familiar laughter from the passing throng grabbed his attention even more. He leaned back in his chair to study the group closer, only to find that the laughter belonged to Jonathan Wakefield, walking arm in arm with an attractive woman toward the gaming salon.

This was too much. To catch the bastard escorting another female around the hotel and playing Natalie for a fool was unspeakable. Ben had remained quiet on many things, but alas came a subject he could not ignore. Natalie was the most generous, loving woman he had ever known, and this scoundrel would not take her for another ride, at least not if he could help it.

Ben checked his pocket watch: nine fifteen. A little late, but with his schedule this week, he had no idea when he would have another chance to warn his friend of the mistake she could be making again in her life. He needed to see her right away.

***

Natalie stepped out of the warm bath. Her skin glowed and smelled sweetly of roses from the recent scrubbing. She was uncommonly fatigued from worrying about her unsuccessful attempts to gain Ben's favor. For so long, she had been in love with him and prayed that someday he would return that same affection to her, but with the newfound knowledge that Hope Dansbury was his daughter, she worried that she very well could lose the battle for his love.

Wrapped in a warm velvet dressing gown, Natalie sat at her vanity and removed the combs that secured her upswept coiffure. As was each night's ritual, she ran the brush through her thick mane while fantasizing about the man of her dreams. An apparition of Ben, lying in her bed against a mound of pillows, always appeared in her vanity mirror. Ever since the week she had arrived unannounced at his workshop and caught him shirtless, his vision now appeared naked from the waist up. That recent experience had unmercifully whetted her appetite, and she longed to see more of the man.

A firm knock on her apartment door shook her from the pleasurable thoughts. Natalie assumed it was Jonathan. He was the only person who dared to drop in on her after nine o'clock at night.

"Just a moment," she called out, hustling into the kitchen. Before she unlatched the door, she tightened the belt around her waist and pulled the collar of her dressing gown high about her neck. "Who's there?"

"It's Ben. May I come in for a moment, Natalie?"

Natalie's hand froze on the latch. There was no one she cared to see more than Ben, but in her present state, with her face scrubbed clean, hair down, and nothing on but her dressing gown, she could not let him in. She always wanted to look her very best for Ben, especially now that Olivia was in the picture.

"Oh, Ben, I just stepped out of the tub, and I'm not presentable."

"Go put something on, and I'll wait," Ben impatiently answered.

"I am not unclothed, for pity's sake, Ben. I have my dressing gown on. It is just that I'm not presentable for male company."

"I have seen the robe before, Natalie. Open up!" Ben barked, jiggling the latch. "Please, Natalie, open up."

He sounded distressed. Natalie yanked the door open with one hand while holding onto both sides of her collar with the other.

Ben pushed past her and moved to the warm stove. "I'm sorry if I seemed abrupt, but I didn't relish the idea of your entire neighborhood catching me at your door at this hour," he said by way of an apology.

"Huh, wouldn't want to soil your reputation, Mr. Walters?" She secured the lock on the kitchen door and then turned her offended look on him.

Kiss Me Once

My reputation is not necessarily the one at stake here, Natalie. The reason for my visit tonight is because I am concerned about *your* reputation and *your* future."

Natalie's eyebrows lifted though she returned no comment.

With arms firmly crossed over his chest, Ben continued. "We've been friends for years, and dammit, I simply cannot allow your jackass ex-husband's undisciplined behavior to go without comment."

"Those are harsh words for a man you barely know, Ben," she simply stated as she glided past him, a length of leg peeking through the opening of her robe with each step.

Ben's attention was drawn to the flashes of the flesh offered by the parting fabric. It redirected his thought process. "Do you wear this ensemble when that good-for-nothing-gambler comes over?"

Her head dropped to view the front of her robe. "This?" she innocently asked.

Ben's eyes rolled heavenward. "My God, woman! Don't you remember what this man did to you? How can you let him back in your life?" He spread his arms in supplication as he walked in a complete circle.

Ben did not realize how much Natalie meant to him until he said it. He possessed blood-boiling jealousy for all the fun-filled moments Jonathan Wakefield had spent in her company, all the private conversations they had shared, and even the simple pleasure of holding her hand. Ben tried not to think of intimacies more than this, for the thought of her sharing her love with that no-good gambler cut Ben to the quick. The cruelest part was that it had taken a complicated set of events to make him realize exactly what he wanted in life, and now it was too late. He had a moral responsibility to Olivia.

101

"What I do with my life is none of your business, Ben Walters. Furthermore, people change. Just because Jonathan had a few nasty habits years ago does not mean he has not mended his ways."

"Don't be a fool. The man has not stopped gambling, and take it from me, Natalie; he has picked up a few other failings."

"What do you mean?" She propped her hands on her hips and took a confrontational step toward him. "Explain yourself," she demanded.

Ben made the mistake of glancing down at her neckline. The neckline of her dressing gown was now spread wide, showing the upper swell of her breasts. Damn, he wished she would move back a step.

"I'd rather not go into details," he muttered.

"You have no right baiting me with things. Either you tell it all or keep your concerns to yourself."

"He's a rake!" Ben nearly shouted in response. "I saw him with my own eyes, and I cringe to think how he will use his charms on you and every other woman in town to get his way."

Natalie's gaze leisurely swept down over him. Then her finger reached out and flipped the end of his cravat. "Better watch out; he might use those charms on Olivia, and then where would you be, Ben?" She smiled sweetly, fluttering her eyelashes.

Ben grasped her by her upper arms and pulled her close. "You go too far, madam. I should have known better than to attempt to warn you off. Your senses have been knocked askew by a handsome face."

"You don't ------"

Ben cut her off before she could say another word. "I have always admired you, Natalie. You have a good head for business and an independent nature that shows the strength of character, but I am greatly disappointed when you are willing to put all that aside just because a man gives you a little attention."

"Maybe we are two of a kind. A pair of fools, waiting for our long lost lovers to return and save us from eternal loneliness," she snapped back. "And I do not know about you, Ben, but I am thrilled that Jonathan has returned in such fine shape after all these years. It makes for a most inspirational affair." Natalie turned away to face the wall, squeezing her eyes shut with regret for how she lied.

A long silence prevailed before Ben moved up behind her. He breathed in her clean scent. His gaze drifted over her thick, lush tresses and down her magnificent body, remembering how good it felt against him many nights ago. She had pushed him past the point of friendship and goaded him into an intimate exchange, and from that moment on, Ben had not been able to think of her as he once had. Their kiss had changed everything inside of him, and, as much as he did not want to admit it, it had confused his thinking about Olivia.

"I am sorry. I did not come here to insult you or offend you in any way."

Natalie turned around, all anger gone from her face. She rested her hands on his lapels. "I appreciate your concern, Ben, but I can handle myself just fine."

He pulled her close. She looked too tempting, with the relaxed neckline of her dressing gown displaying the fullness of her breasts. He drank in her beauty, noticing a rapid pulse beating on her creamy throat and an unbridled hunger burning in her eyes.

"So, you say, but I still worry about you," Ben whispered before his lips claimed hers.

He kissed her hard, recklessly desiring the return of that same tremble, that same sensation he had felt when he kissed her weeks ago. Once again, her soft, pliable lips surrendered to his touch as the passion from nights before returned with force strong enough to set him on fire. Instinctively, Ben placed his hand at the base of her spine and pressed her firmly against his full length. He wanted her to feel the effect her kiss had on his body. His trip here was to warn her of Jonathan's actions, but in the back of his mind, it also had something to do with what was happening right now. Confusing as it was, he realized that her embrace was the potion he needed to soothe his frayed nerves, and he found himself trapped in a complicated mess.

Then, without warning, the thought of Olivia and Hope interrupted his focus. It seized his mind with a vengeance born of guilt and tore him from the pleasure. Ben broke from their embrace and walked over to the stove.

"Ben?" Natalie questioned in a trembling voice.

He could not face her. He ran a hand through his hair, then picked up the coffeepot, swirling the remaining liquid inside.

"I can make a new pot, Ben," she offered.

"No. No, thank you." Ben gathered his resolve. "Sit down, please. I need to tell you something."

Natalie lowered herself into a kitchen chair, tightening the collar of her robe around her neck. She felt a sudden chill with the tone of his words.

"I had made an irresponsible mistake years ago that has only recently come to light. I . . . respect you, Natalie, and feel I owe you, and only you, an explanation. Olivia and I were lovers many years ago, and I have recently learned that Hope is our child conceived from that affair. I wanted you to know from me before you heard it from others."

Too late, Ben. Estelle beat you to it! Her eyes opened wide to hold back the tears. It was hard taking this news from Estelle but twice as hard hearing it from Ben.

"You are. . . important to me. . .and we have shared. . . a lot. I am so sorry, Natalie."

He moved closer to her, but she instantly took a step back. Her tears spilled forth.

Ben's eyes squeezed shut in pain. There was nothing more to say, no gesture appropriate enough to offer for the pain he inflicted, so he turned on his heels and quietly walked out her door without another word between them.

Natalie remained seated until she could no longer hear his footsteps. The cards were stacking up against her. She knew his sense of integrity too well. No matter what Ben felt for her, she doubted he would walk away from the Danbury's. She stood up and walked back to her room, laying across her bed and struggling to hold on to her dream. It was getting harder and harder to believe in Jonathan's plan.

#

Chapter Thirteen

With each passing day, Hope Dansbury grew deeper in love with her new life and friends in Philadelphia. For all the years she had lived in her luxurious Massachusetts mansion, there were never moments like the ones she now spent at Ben's home. Each day was an inspiration, sharing and learning life's simple joys: cooking, winemaking, gardening, and, most importantly, enjoying an interesting conversation. Ben called her his favorite guest. They talked of everything from how he began his furniture design and construction trade to female things such as women's fashions, dance, and sometimes the opposite sex. Ben willingly offered his opinion and sensible suggestions with whatever she asked, and, in turn, Hope held Ben in the highest regard. More significantly, Ben had shown her more love in a few weeks than Olivia had in seventeen years.

As Ben's party drew near, Hope's anxiety increased. With all that Ben and Max had shared with her over the past weeks, they both had refused to assist her with a costume for the event. Their answers to her request were firm.

"I'm sorry, young lady, but you're on your own," Max had answered. "The fun of a costume party lies in who's behind what disguise. If I help you, then *MY* surprise is gone."

Ben did not even look at her when he answered. "Can't help you. You will come up with something. I know you will find a way."

Hope was desperate. She could not complete her costume and knew only one person skilled enough to assist her with the problem: Natalie Wakefield. Although her mother had repeatedly warned her that friendship with the couturiere was out of the question, Hope reasoned that friendship needn't be objective. She merely needed Natalie, on a professional level, a capable seamstress, to rectify the gross errors she had made with her costume, and in fact, today offered the perfect opportunity. Her mother was in Clarksboro visiting an old friend and was not expected back until the following afternoon. Meanwhile, Hope figured she might engage the help of the dressmaker with her costume before her mother's return. Hurriedly she stuffed the costume in a satchel and set out toward Natalie's shop with an anxious heart.

Sitting at a table in the hotel dining room, Jonathan Wakefield took special notice of Hope's brisk steps as she crossed the lobby that morning. She wore a determined expression and carried a large bag under her arm. He could tell she was on a mission of urgency, and it roused his curiosity. Jonathan pushed from his seat and set out to follow her, for quite simply, there was nothing better to do with his time on this autumn day. Jonathan recognized that the young girl was heading toward his ex-wife's shop two blocks from the Steven Matthews Hotel. There was something mysterious in that satchel, and he aimed to find out what. Jonathan picked up his pace and closed the gap between them.

"Good day, Miss Dansbury," he greeted. Jonathan pulled on each shirt cuff, then straightened the silk cravat around his neck.

"Oh! Mr. Wakefield," she answered with a start.

"Quite a spectacular day, isn't it, young lady?" he said, gazing at the sky above.

"Yes, it is," she returned. Hope shifted the sack in her arms and then picked up her pace. His long strides assured her that her efforts to outpace him were futile.

"Looks like you are headed my way. Are you going to my wife's shop with that?" Jonathan pointed to the satchel.

Hope glanced down at the mentioned sack and then back to him. She was amazed at his acumen. Did he have a sixth sense? A fine sweat broke out on her upper lip. Not only was she on her way to ask for Natalie Wakefield's help, but now the ex-husband was escorting her there. Hope could only think of the pickle she would be in if her mother found out. She felt sure it would look like a double dose of disrespect.

"Don't you mean your *ex-wife*, Mr. Wakefield?"

"You are quite right, Miss Dansbury. Due to my foolishness, Natalie is my ex-wife. I have made my share of mistakes, but none have topped the error I made the day I let Natalie walk out the door." he answered with regret.

Hope glanced over at his dejected expression and felt like a heel for using such harsh tones. She liked Jonathan Wakefield regardless of what her mother said about him. His suave, debonair manner made her feel truly womanly; his high spirits and the friendly smile never failed to put her in a good mood.

"I don't have an appointment," she said by way of an explanation. "Perhaps I will intrude. I should not assume Miss Wakefield is free this morning."

"She is a generous lady; I'm sure she will make time for you. Do you have a large request?"

Oddly enough, Hope felt safe divulging her dilemma with this gentleman. Something told her he would keep the secret. "I have a problem with my costume for the Saturday evening party and need assistance. Where sewing is concerned, I find myself at wit's end."

"I see. Well, you are asking the right person for help, then. Natalie is brilliant with a needle and thread. I am on my way there, also. I have my final fitting today."

Hope giggled.

"Funny, you think?" Jonathan asked with arms spread wide.

"It is the way you put it. A fitting? I do not believe many men frequent her shop for fittings."

Jonathan chuckled. "I guess you are right, but I'm the exception to that rule. The fitting is for my costume."

"Aha! Well, I am positive she has created a magnificent one for you. Alas, we have arrived," Hope announced when they reached the shop's steps.

The tinkling of the shop's bell brought Mary to the front. "Good day, Miss Dansbury, and to you too, Mr. Wakefield."

"Good morning to *you*, Mary," Jonathan replied with high spirits. "Is Natalie about? I only need a moment of her time, and then she can see to my friend here."

Hope tried not to flinch when he called her his friend.

"Yes, certainly, she just walked back to her apartment. Follow me, sir." Mary ordered.

"Thank you," Jonathan answered.

"Please take a seat, Miss Dansbury. Miss Wakefield will be right with you," Mary offered the young girl.

"Thank you, ma'am."

The longer Hope waited alone at the front of the shop, the more it occurred to her that this mission was the worst idea she had ever had in her seventeen years on earth. It was a decision born of desperation. She had felt so terrified over creating an inadequate costume for Ben's party that she had gone to the extreme peril of crossing enemy lines for aid. She realized how ludicrous this was and knew she had to escape before Natalie appeared. What would her mother think, and what grief would she have to endure because of her decision to involve the enemy? She moved toward the shop door for a quick escape, but Natalie's voice called out just as her hand reached for the handle.

"Hello, dear."

Hope froze. Her pulse quickened. Slowly she turned around and saw Miss Wakefield standing in a stream of sunlight by the dressing room door. Her hair was beautifully coifed, and she always wore a radiant smile.

"Oh . . . hello, Miss Wakefield."

"Jonathan tells me you need assistance with your costume for Saturday's party. You have not changed your mind, have you?"

"I am not sure what to think, ma'am. I need help, yet it suddenly dawned on me that you are far too busy with your important clients to assist me with this project," she answered.

Natalie stepped close to Hope and pulled the sack from her arms.

"I think I should be the one to determine who is an IMPORTANT client, dear. Let's see what you have."

Hope was speechless. There was no turning back now; if she were honest with herself, she did not want to turn back either. She needed help in the worst way, so she put herself before Olivia for the first time in her life and followed her plan.

"Thank you very much, Miss Wakefield. I appreciate this," she softly replied.

Jonathan then re-entered the shop. "Tell you what, Honey, I'll come back later, and you can take your time with this pretty young gal."

"Good idea, Jonathan," Natalie answered. "We'll finish yours later."

Hope watched wide-eyed as he moved close and kissed Natalie full. Hope blushed from her head down to her toes, for she had never witnessed such a passionate exchange between a man and woman before. And, in broad daylight! And, in a public establishment! She had seen little affection between Olivia and Andrew, much less an unabashed kiss like this one. Hope knew she should have turned away but was helplessly mesmerized by the scene before her.

"Goodbye, Hope. I will leave you in competent hands," Jonathan offered after he pulled from Natalie's lips. He squeezed Natalie's waist in farewell.

Upon Jonathan's departure, Natalie invited Hope into her private quarters.

"We will have more peace back here, away from the shop's traffic," Natalie explained.

Hope felt truly honored by the gesture. She had never seen Miss Wakefield's quarters. She noticed it was quite different from what she had been used to. The great halls of the Dansbury's manse rang out in hollowness, giving forth a cold and uninviting air. In sharp contrast, the dressmaker's apartment was compact, beautifully accessorized, and smelled of lavender. Hope felt surrounded by warmth.

"Your home is lovely, Miss Wakefield," Hope commented as they traveled down the hall into the kitchen. "And thank you for taking time from your schedule to help me with this costume catastrophe."

"It is my pleasure, dear. Let's see what you have?"

Hope pulled the drab, brown-gray fabric from the bag, a length of rope, and a pair of soft ankle-length boots. "This is it," she said in a flat voice.

"This is what, my dear?" Natalie asked, holding the fabric at arm's length.

"My costume. It is a monk's garb," Hope muttered.

Natalie's eyebrows drew together. Her concern had nothing to do with Hope's inability to sew. She wondered why she had chosen this hideous idea when the costume party offered the opportunity to create and wear something magnificent.

"I told you I couldn't sew," Hope added, feeling Natalie's dismay. "Am I asking too much of you, Miss Wakefield?"

Natalie dropped the fabric on the table, took Hope by the shoulders, and looked straight into her eyes.

"We will start over. I want nothing to do with this or any other idea that hides your beauty. A monk's garb? Was that your mother's idea?"

Hope felt immediate tension with the negative slur. "It was my idea," she admitted.

"Well, it's a poor choice, child. We will create something that will be a joy to wear." Natalie stated, smoothing Hope's cheek tenderly with the back of her hand. "Sit down while I put the tea kettle on. We need to relax and decide upon a truly appealing costume."

Hope filled with giddy happiness.

***

Ben loaded his tools into the back of his wagon, climbed aboard, and set out for Natalie's shop. Olivia's early morning departure to Clarksboro allowed him to start the promised project in Natalie's shop with no interference from Olivia. He certainly did not need a repeat of her hurt feelings like the day he had fixed Natalie's bed, so he wanted to get this done and his schedule clear before Olivia could complain. Ben slapped the reins on the steed's back, and the wagon lurched ahead.

Yep, he thought, *that is exactly what I want to do, start that damn platform and get it done before Olivia returns.*

No, it's not! Whom are you trying to fool, Walters? The platform is an excuse. What you want to do is smooth things over with Natalie.

Ben's shoulders slumped. His brow wrinkled. "Like hell," he burst out.

He knew the last thing he needed was time alone with Natalie Wakefield, though nothing could stop the pleasant memory of her lips on his, and that alone erased his scowl expression and left in its stead a smile. He sat forward and rested his forearms on his knees while the reins hung loose in his grip. She had a body that aroused his ardor to dangerous heights and hands that touched him with a promise of mortal pleasure that one man could even dream of feeling.

Then the wagon wheel rolled over a large rock and jolted Ben from his daydream.

"By damn, Natalie Wakefield. Get out of my mind!" he shouted, startling the mare into a few quick steps. "Giddy up, you old bag of bones! I want this job started and finished as soon as possible."

#

Chapter Fourteen

Ben pulled his wagon to the rear entrance of Natalie Wakefield's establishment. The back door offered the shortest distance to carry his materials, plus access through this entrance had presented the least interruption for Natalie and her clientele in the front showroom. He grabbed his toolbox from the back of the wagon, slipped the wide leather strap across his shoulder, and strode to the door. He tapped firmly against the glass to announce his arrival.

"Excuse me, dear, while I get that. Please help yourself to more tea," Natalie offered as she hustled down the hall to answer the caller at her kitchen door.

When she reached the door and pushed the curtain aside, she was surprised to see Ben standing there with his toolbox slung over his shoulder. A spark of hope ignited inside her. Butterflies fluttered in her stomach, and her heart raced with anxious anticipation. Everything had sounded so final between them when he had last left her home, and now, to her sheer delight, he stood at her door, ready to work again. Natalie's eyelashes started a rapid dance.

"Ben!"

"Good morning," he said in a straightforward tone. "With any luck, I'll be out of here today."

Natalie swung the door wide. "That's wonderful, but I didn't expect, well, I mean, I wasn't sure you would find the time for me, Ben."

Ben pushed past and lowered the heavy toolbox to the floor without comment.

"Would you like some help with your materials, Ben," she offered.

"I can handle it myself. Thanks just the same."

He kept his answers short, discouraging lengthy conversations between them. He wanted to do the job and be gone when Olivia returned from Clarksboro.

When Ben returned to his wagon for the lumber, shades of doubt washed over him. He knew Natalie would hover over him like a mother hen while he built her platform, and Olivia would return from Clarksboro angry and hurt, wanting explanations for his actions.

It was not like him to set deliberate hurdles in life. It would have been so easy to say "NO" to Natalie, which would have steered him clear of a bad encounter with Olivia, but instead, he chose the hard road.

He delivered the last materials to the fitting room and laid out the boards when Natalie and Hope entered.

"Oh, Father! What a surprise!"

Ben was surprised as well. He spread his arms wide in welcome. "Good morning, young lady. I thought you had gone along with your mother today."

"My costume was far more important. Thank goodness Miss Wakefield was willing to assist me."

116

Natalie wrapped her arm around Hope's shoulder and gave her a bolstering squeeze. "Your daughter intended to wear a most wretched disguise to the party on Saturday evening, but I reassured her that we will create something breathtaking, a costume that will make her father proud."

Ben was once again reminded of Natalie's graciousness and helpfulness to others. Even after the news he was forced to deliver the other evening, Natalie had still offered her precious time and talent to help his daughter. His reason for being here today was truly reinforced. If Natalie could help Hope, he could certainly help Natalie.

"I imagine Miss Wakefield has something lovely in mind for you," Ben stated, gazing at his daughter.

We have discussed many ideas, all far better than what I had, Father."

"What *was* your idea?" he asked.

Hope looked at Natalie and then back at Ben. "You don't want to know."

"Do not worry. We are going with something entirely different, aren't we, dear?" the couturiere offered. She held a silencing finger to her lips.

The last thirty seconds of conversation never penetrated Ben's brain, for his attention had been taken hostage by the well-dressed dandy who had entered the room and stood behind Natalie. Ben was further incensed when Jonathan put his manicured hand on Natalie's shoulder and lightly squeezed. His diamond ring caught the sunlight and shot a sparkle of color into the room.

"Jonathan!" Natalie turned and was greeted with surprise.

"Hi, ladies, I'm back," the gambler announced.

"Back from what? The pub?" Ben bit out.

"Good morning to you too, Ben, but as a matter of record, I am returning from church. The vicar has requested my assistance with the children's choir over the holiday season."

"Plan on hanging around that long?" Ben spat.

"Longer than that if I have anything to do with it." Jonathan quipped, turning a look of tenderness on Natalie. He rubbed his index finger over the tip of her nose. "What fantastic idea have you imagined for Hope's costume?"

That question was like a punch in Ben's gut. How did the ass know anything about his daughter's costume? It was only eight-thirty in the morning, and *he* had only found out about it fifteen minutes ago.

"We thought of a beautiful costume, Jonathan, but it's a secret until the party," Natalie answered. "We must get to work or run the chance of not finishing on time. Ben, we will leave you to the platform, and Jonathan, you must run along."

Ben was incensed. He only wanted to take a slab of lumber and rap the man alongside his head. Courtesy for Natalie was the only thing that held him back from knocking the gambler's perfect white teeth down his songbird throat.

"Quite understandable," Jonathan answered. "I merely stopped for that sample of red velvet for the vicar. I forgot about it yesterday. If you tell me where it is, I will grab it and get out of your way," Jonathan promised.

"Ask Mary; she knows," Natalie answered.

"Thanks a lot, Honey. Good day, Hope." Jonathan glanced over his shoulder and took a stab at Ben's pride. "Now, watch your fingers, Ben. There have been many slips with the hammer by men far more proficient than you."

Natalie's eyes rolled.

Hope flushed vivid red with embarrassment.

Ben's color matched Hope's, although his sprouted from boiling anger, unlike hers.

Jonathan was out the door, down the steps, and up the street before Ben could muster a comeback.

An uncomfortable silence prevailed.

"Well. . . let's get to work, Hope," Natalie hastily suggested, leading the young woman down the hall.

Ben never noticed their departure. Jonathan Wakefield's audacity so maddened him that he could not move a muscle. He wondered what Natalie saw in this unskilled half-wit who had never worked a day in his life. Didn't she realize the mistake she was making for the second time in her life? He picked up his hammer angrily, thankful for the project ahead, to pound out his frustrations.

By mid-afternoon, Ben had most of the platform constructed. Much to his surprise, Natalie had neither fussed over him nor interfered. Except for giggles, muted voices, and an occasional rattle of the teapot, Ben was virtually undisturbed. In fact, Natalie had not even asked if he wanted anything to eat or drink, which was most unlike her. At last, his curiosity got the better of him. He laid down his tools, walked to the closed bedroom door, and listened to the women exchange a moment before he knocked.

"Because, my dear, you must bait them. Dangle the worm before their very eyes. That is what this costume will do. I guarantee you will have the finest catch of the evening."

"But, Miss Wakefield, do you think this is too revealing? Look at this, for example. Perhaps we might sew it a bit higher so that I don't show so much flesh,"

Ben wondered what was going on behind the closed door. Knowing Natalie and her knack for plunging necklines, Ben figured an unacceptable creation was underway for his young daughter. He had to speak with her . . . alone. He wanted her to curb her enthusiasm for the "delectable" and focus more on the "creative" for *his* sake. After all, he was new at this "father" thing and did not need Natalie to create a costume for his daughter that would draw men from every end of the room.

Ben rapped on their door without further hesitation before calling out his request. "Excuse me, ladies. Could I have a word with you, Natalie?"

"Enter, Ben. We are all decent in here."

Ben opened the door at Natalie's invitation to find Hope dressed in Natalie's creation. The sight left him speechless.

#

Chapter Fifteen

When his gaze fell upon his lovely daughter, Ben was speechless and transfixed with awe. Instead of the distasteful garb he expected, she was swathed in resplendency. Her fit bodice of apple green silk and skirt constructed of layers and layers of uneven green organdy complimented her lithe form and pale beauty. Tiny pink satin flowers encircled her waistline and dotted the flowing skirt. A crown of the same pink blossoms wreathed her head, allowing her thick golden hair to flow freely down her back.

Standing before his lovely daughter, Ben felt ashamed of his boorish intrusion. Natalie was the most trustworthy person he had ever known, yet ironically, he had not trusted her with this task. As he studied all the creativity she had put into Hope's costume and the obvious joy it had offered his daughter, he felt truly humbled for thinking Natalie would create anything less than outstanding.

"Miss Wakefield deserves all the credit. Isn't it beautiful?" Hope exclaimed, pirouetting before him.

"You're quite beautiful, my dear. I see that you ladies have worked very hard."

Ben turned to Natalie and saw pride and happiness on her face. He wished he could show her how much this gift of time and togetherness she had given his daughter meant to him, but he could not; he would not. It would only give Natalie false hope, and he did not desire to hurt her more than he had already.

"I'm so excited about your party," Hope commented, wrapping her arms around Ben's waist.

"It will be a fun evening, I'm sure," Natalie added, lifting Hope's heavy tresses off her shoulder and smoothing them down her back. She then turned to Ben. "Are you finished for the day?"

"Yes. Can I have a moment of your time in the fitting room? It will not hold you long, and then I'll be on my way."

"Yes, I would love to see what you have done thus far. Continue with the flowers, Hope, and I will be back in a moment."

Ben led the way to the fitting room. Natalie followed, chattering in her usual style.

"I can't wait to see your progress. Did you get much done today? Sorry, I didn't check on you, but we've been so busy."

When she entered the fitting room, she fell silent. She was stunned by the elaborate two-step dressing platform he had constructed. It stretched across the entire corner of the room.

"I must frame the mirrors, and then I'll return next week and hang them. I hope this is what you expected."

"Honestly, Ben, it is nothing as I expected. You have done a far grander job, yet I should have known your work would exceed my expectations."

Natalie stepped on the platform, walked from edge to edge, and turned around in a complete circle. "It is truly marvelous. Perfect! What do I owe you, Ben?"

"I think we are even, madam. Thank you for Hope's costume." He started to gather his tools, a satisfied grin covering his lips.

"She is your daughter, Ben. I loved helping her."

"Even so, I know you have a lot of scheduled deadlines, and I'm sure the time you gave Hope will pressure your workload." He reached around her to grab the hammer that rested on the windowsill. "You are a very generous woman, Natalie."

"No more generous than you, Ben. With your workload and everything you and Max must prepare for the festivities, I certainly did not expect you to build the platform so soon. I wish Jonathan were a little handier. Then I would not have had to bother you."

Suddenly, he stopped what he was doing and turned toward her. Ben stared at the smooth column of her throat and noticed the rapid beat of her pulse. At that moment, he felt the urge to pull her close so he could feel her heartbeat and share her warmth, but he denied himself the smallest step closer. Instead, he stood frozen in time until the words that he had no right to say tumbled from his lips with painful honesty.

"What are you doing with him, Natalie? He is no good for you."

There was a moment of silence before Natalie's mouth opened to answer, but before she could utter a word Hope entered the room, forbidding Natalie's reply.

"Miss Wakefield?"

Natalie squeezed her eyes shut in frustration before reluctantly turning toward Hope to answer. "Yes, Hope."

"I don't know what I've done wrong, but I'm having trouble with this flower."

Natalie reached for the flower and examined her work.

"You have a knot in your thread."

"Oh," Hope answered, moving closer to watch the couturiere correct the error. She glanced at her father, who stood with legs braced apart, staring sternly at the floor.

"Are you all right, Father?" she asked.

Ben turned toward the young girl, forcing a smile, then hefted the strap of his toolbox over his shoulder. "Yes," was his simple reply before he quit the room.

When the outside door slammed shut, Hope looked at Natalie with surprise. Natalie did not comment. She returned the fabric to her without comment and turned down the hall.

***

"Heat my bath water, Max, and bring it to a boil. I have the urge to scald myself tonight!" Ben called out as he climbed the stairs to his bedroom.

Twenty minutes later, Max entered the Master suite with two large buckets of hot water. Ben was wrapped in his thick robe, perched on the edge of his bed, waiting in brooding silence. After Max returned with the second round of hot water, Ben ambled to the tub and submerged his body in the soothing water. Max was about to close the door and return to his kitchen work when Ben's voice reached out.

"It's a dog's life, Max."

It was not like Ben Walters to talk like that. He was a man of positivity, high energy, and love for life, though Max had noticed some unsettling changes in his employer since the Danbury's arrival in Philadelphia. Perhaps it was time to hear him out, and with any luck, he would have the opportunity to voice his opinion about the course Ben's life was taking.

"Hope asked Natalie for assistance with her costume. They spent the entire day together at Natalie's shop while I built the platform. I knew I should have said yes when Hope had asked for help. Instead, she went to Natalie for help and made a mess of this situation. By damn, that reckless redhead made my daughter a costume that would test the saints. What is it about her, Max? Why does she have to do things in such a provocative way?"

Max knew Ben's annoyance was not with the costume but something much deeper. "Natalie knows what she's doing. I am sure the costume is very tasteful," Max answered confidently as he stared into the fire.

"She sets upon me at every opportunity. Doesn't she know I am nearly betrothed?" Ben brought both hands down and slapped the water.

Max looked at the younger man, holding the tub's sides in a white-knuckled grip. A bead of water was about to drop from the end of his nose. The picture made Max smile.

"She does not give up easily, but most people in love *never* give up," the manservant honestly replied.

"She must lay off. Tomorrow, when Olivia returns, there will be hell to pay for that damn platform, to say nothing of the costume Natalie has created for Hope."

Now we are on to something, Max mused.

"There is no crime in any of that. Don't forget the wonderful things Natalie has done for you. She is your good friend, Ben, and there is no reason to end an innocent friendship because of Olivia Dansbury."

Max had no idea that an "innocent friendship" no longer existed between them. Their passionate exchange weeks before changed the whole dynamic of their relationship.

"I don't think Olivia would understand that," Ben muttered, returning the back of his head to the tub's edge.

Max offered no consolation. Instead, he turned the subject in another direction. "So, Hope has a new costume, eh? The party should be fun."

"I see the event as tortuous," Ben groaned. "Olivia doesn't want to dress in costume; I will have to keep a sharp eye on my daughter so that the wolves don't eat her alive, Natalie will probably come in something the slick gambler can't resist, and worst of all, I will have to stand there like the perfect host and accept it all!"

"You're right," Max quipped.

"Max, this is not a light subject. I need your help. You are experienced with the ways of women. Helda taught you much about their motives and clever schemes. Help me! What should I do?"

The older gent walked to the bedroom door. "You need help only because you have not committed. Olivia or Natalie, Ben. Whom will it be? You need to make a choice. Finish your bath, fill your belly, then take the evening and give it some serious thought."

"Natalie Wakefield is not under consideration for marriage. She never was! The woman does not need a husband; more importantly, I don't need an iron-fisted woman in my life."

"Natalie never struck me as iron-fisted. Her free-loading ex-husband forced her into survival. That does not mean she wouldn't welcome opinion and a warm body in bed. I think the problem stands with you, sir. Perhaps she is too much female for you."

With that, Max quit the room, leaving Ben feeling like a hornet in a corked jug.

***

Just as he had promised Natalie, Jonathan left the shop and delivered the velvet to Christ Church. He hadn't explained his afternoon gambling plans at Duffy's Tavern. He wondered why he still felt he had to hide his gambling from Natalie. She knew what he did with his time. That was the whole essence of their agreement: she would loan him the gambling money in exchange for his undivided male attention. So, what was this peculiar feeling he always got when she asked him about his day? It had been years since he felt guilt for being a gambler, but now back in Natalie's company, guilt had been re-born.

When Jonathan entered Duffy's Tavern, a rowdy group of tars from a corner table called for him to join them. It was the same seedy group of sailors he had lost a few unlucky hands to a few nights before, and he figured their affability toward him was because they hoped to do it again.

"He's back!" one called out as Jonathan drew close. "We saved ya a seat, Mister Dandy."

"That's mighty generous of you, gentlemen," he answered with an amiable smile.

Jonathan slid into the chair and studied the glazed eyes of each man who sat around the table. It was obvious the tars were well into their cups. He felt sure he could dupe these slackers with his sleight of hand, and that, coupled with a little luck, was sure to turn a profitable result today.

The tavern wench carrying a sudsy brew sidled close and rested her arm on his shoulder. "Will ya 'ave a mug, my love?"

The ale served at these dockside taverns was not his drink of choice, but he realized the men watched him closely, expecting him to accept and drink hardy. Jonathan smiled at the used-up, unclean lass and nodded.

"Yes, my dear, and another round for my friends, if you will."

As Jonathan placed the gold coins in the serving wench's apron, he studied her hardened appearance and realized how lucky he had had Natalie's attention these few short weeks. He had had his share of tavern wenches for so long that he had forgotten the delight of sharing the company of an extraordinary woman like Natalie. Natalie had been a beautiful girl when he had married her, but nothing compared to the lush, womanly temptation she had become over these past years of absence. Simply put, playing the loving suitor proved an easy task.

Oddly enough, he began to wish that Ben Walters would not have so damn much going for him. Jonathan knew he posed no competition for Ben in any way, and he guessed that was why he enjoyed inflicting pain on him whenever the opportunity presented itself. After all, why wouldn't he when Ben's strengths only highlighted Jonathan's shortcomings? He loved watching Ben's painful reaction whenever he called Natalie honey, kissed her, or caressed her arm or waist. It was as if he'd thrust a knife into Ben's belly, and Jonathan had to admit he truly enjoyed doing that. Yes, with sizeable regret, Jonathan had finally realized that what he had carelessly discarded years ago was possibly the best hand he had ever held.

#

Chapter Sixteen

Ben and Max were down to the final details with their costumes.

"You should have grown your own then this wouldn't have been necessary," Max complained while fashioning a beard from remnants of hair he had clipped from Ben's head earlier in the day.

"Olivia would not have approved of my untidy appearance while I grew the thing. I do not need a beard anyway. Why do you insist on this?"

"Robin Hood wore a Van Dyke beard. It is as simple as that."

"You're a stickler for details, Max."

"Perhaps, but authenticity is what costuming is all about."

"If authenticity is what you're after, then you better figure out a way to get fire from that dragonhead of yours."

A tap sounded on the kitchen door.

"I'll get it," Max offered, chuckling at Ben's costume advice. "Good *early* morning, young lady; come in," the servant welcomed.

Hope waved her hired coach on, then stepped into the warm, homey kitchen.

"Why do you knock on my door? You are not a stranger. You are my daughter, and welcome to come and go as you please," Ben stated as he helped her with her wrap.

Hope winced at Ben's reference to her parentage and directed the conversation to a lighter subject.

"I hope I am not too early, but I can't wait any longer. I am so excited."

"It is good to have a woman here to help us. Has your mother returned from Clarksboro?"

Her voice immediately lost its luster with Ben's question. "Yes, she'll be here later. She has a fitting with Natalie Wakefield this morning, Father. I told her I had asked Miss Wakefield for help with my costume, and she was very displeased. She said I waited until she was gone and did it behind her back. I shudder to think what Mother will say to Miss Wakefield when she sees the platform you built."

Ben frowned. "Am I not permitted to do a service for an old friend?"

"Mother feels it isn't proper, just like when you repaired Miss Wakefield's bed. She finds things like that disgraceful and ---" Hope couldn't finish the rest of what Olivia had said.

"Disgraceful and what, Hope?" Ben walked over to the stove and poured himself another cup of coffee. When she did not answer, he turned to face her directly. "Disgraceful and what?"

"Crude and ill-bred," she finally answered.

Ben took a sip of the dark brew and stared silently at the wall with thoughtful intensity. Olivia's snobbery was beginning to grate on him. He noticed the differences and the changes her former life had made on her more and more. She had gone from a shopkeeper's daughter to a wealthy attorney's wife at an impressionable age and had, like this, become intolerant of things beneath her social standing. He was not going to lash out at Hope with an angry rebuttal. She was innocent in all of this. Olivia was another matter. It was time she learned that life with Ben Walters would not be as it was with Andrew Dansbury.

"Well, young lady, I'll settle this later with your mother. For now, we have much to do in the way of preparation, and I think it is time we get started," Ben answered, tapping the tip of her nose with his finger.

Hope smiled. "Lead me to the chores," she answered, stepping on tiptoes to kiss his cheek.

***

Olivia arrived at Natalie's shop by ten o'clock, determined to set a few things straight. There had been enough flirting and flaunting with Ben, and she meant to end it. Upon her prompt arrival, she found Natalie at her desk with a quill. Olivia waited for her to acknowledge her presence.

"You're right on time, Olivia. Follow me, and we will begin." Natalie instructed as she placed the quill back into the inkwell and then moved from her desk.

Olivia silently followed, but when they reached the fitting room, and her gaze fell upon the new platform, her silence came to a swift end. She was filled with incredible rage, realizing that Ben had purposely waited until she was in Clarksboro to do this personal favor for Natalie. It elevated Olivia's blood temperature to the boiling point. She was furious, humiliated, and, worst of all, out-smarted.

"I'll take your cape, Olivia. Please step behind the screen. I will help you out of your gown when I return."

But before the couturiere could leave, Olivia started an interrogation. "So, when did *this* new addition take place?"

"My new platform?" Natalie spread her arms wide and stared at it with adoration. "Isn't it marvelous? Ben built it when you were out of town. I guess your little foray offered him some free time, so he could work through the evening hours and finish it in record time." Natalie's last sentence was delivered as she walked out of the room with her client's cloak over her arm.

Olivia's rage consumed her. She punched downward with both fists and stomped her foot in complete exasperation. It was high time she clarified a few things with this bold redhead, and she wouldn't wait another day to do it. She stuck her head out into the empty hall and shouted her demand.

"Natalie, I need you in here immediately!"

A few moments later, Mary appeared at the fitting room door. "Excuse me, ma'am. Miss Wakefield had an emergency. She asked that I take over."

Olivia turned her outrage on the woman. "What do you mean an emergency? I have never heard of anything so unprofessional in my entire life."

"Emergencies arise in all our lives, Mrs. Dansbury. I am perfectly capable of handling this final fitting, so if you desire your items completed when promised, I suggest we begin."

Olivia blew out an appalled breath of air. "Oooooooh! I never!"

Mary ignored her outburst. "Let me help you into your gown. If you could step on the platform, please, I will begin."

A jolt of unmitigated hatred shot through Olivia's body when her slippered foot touched the surface of the platform. It was very clear that her plan for her future needed revision. Natalie Wakefield wanted to play tough, so that is exactly what she'd give her.

***

Jonathan arrived at Natalie's doorstep that evening by six o'clock sharp. His spirits were high, his pockets full, and his stomach empty. Boy, he could not wait to see what she had prepared for dinner tonight. Long days at the card table had offered little nourishment, and he looked forward to the nightly interludes at Natalie's dinner table. It had been years since he felt domestic stability, and he wondered why he had once felt marriage confining. Now older, this tranquil setting somewhat appealed to him.

He reached Natalie's back door and tapped on the windowpane. Her lovely face appeared between the parted curtains before the door swung wide.

"Jonathan, come in. You must look at the wonderful job Ben did for me." She pulled him down the hall toward the fitting room. "His talent never fails to amaze me. I am so thrilled with the results. What do you think?"

A stab of jealousy pierced the gambler. He had felt so high from his day of winnings, and the last thing he wanted to talk about was that pain in the backside, Ben Walters. He wanted to enjoy her wonderful cooking and gaze upon her lovely features. He was searching for comfort, Natalie's hospitality, delicious food, and undivided attention. Instead, he got blasted with a shower of accolades for Ben Walters. Look what Ben did! Guess what Ben said? What do you think Ben thinks? It was downright sickening.

"Well, isn't it marvelous?" She stepped on the platform and turned a dainty pirouette.

"Looks like an easy enough project to me, honey. Certainly, nothing out of the ordinary," the gambler replied.

"Sure, Jonathan. I guess you would have no problem building the same," Natalie sarcastically remarked.

"It has been my observation that you hold the brute in far too high esteem," he growled, turning from the room. "What's for dinner?" he asked. When he reached the kitchen, he moved to the stove and lifted the lid to the pot. "Mmmm-mm! Corned beef and cabbage. That is one of my favorites."

Natalie stood at the threshold and stared at Jonathan with irritation. He was holding the pot lid while inhaling the delicious aroma of the meal. She suddenly realized that perhaps this game was wearing over much on his ego.

"Getting tired of the act, Jonathan?" she clipped.

He looked over his shoulder. "Now, why would you say a thing like that?" He turned around and moved closer. "It's great being with you again," he stated in a low tone. He took hold of her upper arms.

Natalie saw the strange light in his eyes and lifted her shoulders to shrug him off. "Jonathan, you are the wiliest fox I have ever had the misfortune of knowing. If you cannot hold up to your end of the bargain, let me know now! As I told you initially, our relationship ended years ago."

Jonathan saw she meant every word. Resolute determination appeared on her face, that same look she had given him years ago when she had said goodbye.

"Whoever said anything about trying again?" he said with a forced laugh. "I know the rules. I know the promises."

She watched him with a wary expression and saw he was determined to act casual and unaffected. He moved about the kitchen, touching things and running his fingers along the tabletop.

"Did you have a good day?" he asked to regain her cheerful mood.

"Delightful. And you?"

"Yes, I dropped the material off at the rectory and gave considerable thought to the song selections for the children's Christmas choir," he answered, removing a brandy bottle from the corner hutch. He did not feel comfortable telling her anymore about his day, so he maneuvered the conversation elsewhere. "I am anxious to know how you made out with Hope Dansbury. Were you able to fix her costume?" He poured two small glasses of the amber liquid, extended one to Natalie then sat at the kitchen table.

Natalie immediately placed hers on the sideboard and then moved to the stove. "We started from scratch and created a wonderful costume." She emptied the contents of the pot into a pewter tureen. "After talking with Hope, I have a lot of speculation about the Dansbury clan. Jonathan, I want you to help me find out a few things." She placed the tureen in the middle of the table and reached for Jonathan's plate.

"Your wish is my command, Honey. Anything you need," he offered, lifting the stemmed glass to his lips.

"I want you to find out all you can about Olivia Dansbury. Your flirtatious ways with women will surely make extracting the details I need simple." She placed the delicious dinner in front of him and then reached for another plate, only to ladle out an extremely small serving for herself.

Jonathan stared at her minuscule portion. "Don't you feel well?"

"I need to eat less," she admitted, spreading the linen on her lap.

"Why?"

Natalie stared at the plate in front of her. "Because I think I could better my chances. I worked with Hope today and realized her mother's shape is as slender as hers. You know, Jonathan, Ben has not paid this much attention to any woman since I've known him.

"Natalie, look at me. I am sure Ben's attention toward Olivia Dansbury has little to do with her shape. It has more to do with a memory that Ben never let go of. Granted, he is happy that Olivia is well preserved, but up against you, there is no comparison. She's a bag of bones!"

"Well, that bag of bones has gotten the attention of Ben, the man I love. I am on a diet!"

Geez! What's wrong with you? Your figure is fabulous! Let me tell you something. When I arrived a few weeks back, I expected to find a twenty-seven-year-old, plump, married woman with a brood of kids at her skirts."

Natalie's spine straightened.

"Instead, I found that you had not changed much over the years. The changes that did take place made you more beautiful than I remembered. I would put money on it that Ben Walters thinks your body is perfect. In fact, I know not only what Ben Walters and every other man think when they look at you."

Natalie's expression turned indignant. "Since I have been in the flower of my youth, I have had to put up with men and their lecherous minds. Is a woman's upper endowment the only important thing to a man?"

"It certainly is a point of consideration, love. The mere thought of those soft mounds resting in a man's hands or anywhere else against a man's body can certainly shake a soul."

"Oooooooo!" She pushed herself from the table and walked to the stove.

Jonathan scanned her back and took in her hourglass figure. He simply could not understand her. Why would she ever want to look like Olivia Dansbury? His hands ached to touch her and have her return those caresses with the same fervor she did years before. What a temptation!

Natalie turned to face him; arms crossed over her bosom as if to hide the topic of conversation. "I think you are wrong, Jonathan. Not wrong about men, just wrong about Ben. If I were a little thinner, I might catch his eye, and at this point, I will do anything possible to win a better edge."

"There is no talking a woman out of something once she's got her mind set. Do whatever you want to make yourself miserable, Honey. Please don't take any of my opinions seriously. After all, what do I know?" Jonathan downed the brandy and poured another.

She saw that she had hurt his feelings this time. He was trying to help her through this whole mess, and she was being ungrateful. Natalie moved to his side and placed her hand on his shoulder.

"I appreciate all you have done for me, Jonathan. You have been a good friend, and I have tried hard to keep my spirits up. Why don't we just forget about this now and finish your costume?"

Jonathan shot to his feet and pulled her close. He looked hopeful. "Does that mean tonight you'll sew on my tail?"

Natalie put her hands against his chest. Her tone changed from congenial to the firm. "The finishing touches go on tonight, Jonathan, but don't get any ideas."

"When can you start? I am certainly ready if you are." His eyebrows wiggled above a wicked smile.

#

Chapter Seventeen

Little daylight remained when Olivia's coach pulled up before Ben's home. She had expected a much earlier arrival, but numerous personal obligations had delayed her. Ben had assured her earlier that week that the details of the party were adequately covered. Still, she doubted that completely and wanted to ensure no mistakes or forgotten particulars with the event. After all, she felt certain the community considered her the soon-to-be Mrs. Benjamin Walters. She wanted to reassure everyone that the gatherings at the Walters' residence would now be handled with complete finesse and elaborate detailing.

When Ben failed to appear at the front door, Olivia grudgingly accepted the driver's assistance to escort her into the safety of the manse. A crackling fire and the smell of freshly baked bread and assorted other foods assailed her senses. Her curiosity was peaked, and this drew her deeper into the dwelling.

She was stunned when she saw the tasteful party decorations that adorned the rooms. Somehow, she had expected a plain setting with none of the flare displayed before her. She was surprised by the creative approach taken with every detail as she moved from room to room. Groups of stout candles mingled with pine boughs and gourds of every size sat atop tables and windowsills. Fruit-filled cornucopias rested at the sides of fireplaces, and pine and nut garlands draped the mantels. She was astounded at the transformation of the drawing room, where chairs and other furnishings had been removed for dancing, and a festoon of ribbons had been gathered about the chandelier to form a canopy of color. Then in the dining room, a ten-foot lace bedecked table displayed two magnificent brass candelabrums flanked by low-lying floral arrangements. In the corner of the room, wine bottles stood inside brass tubs held up by wooden tripods, and between the containers, a table displayed rows of sparkling wine goblets. It was a sight to behold and held no second to any gathering she had ever held at her Massachusetts estate.

Then a sickening thought shot through her. Could Natalie Wakefield have assisted with the detailing and special attention given to the rooms? After all, the couturiere had made a hasty exit during her fitting that morning for a so-called "emergency," Who knew that the "emergency" was not Ben's party production? She would not put it past her either. Natalie Wakefield was a woman who could not be trusted.

Olivia heard faint laughter from some distant location in the house. It sparked unmitigated anger because Ben ignored her arrival, and Natalie possibly duped her. As she rushed toward the voices, she was more convinced that if Ben Walters wanted any part of her and Hope's life, his friendship with Natalie Wakefield would have to end this minute. With no warning to those on the other side of the kitchen door, she swung it wide, expecting to confront the interfering female immediately. But when the collective crowd assembled around the fireplace turned and faced her, Olivia was surprised Natalie was not among them. Olivia stepped inside and suspiciously looked to each corner of the kitchen in search of her, but she was nowhere to be found.

"Olivia!" Ben exclaimed, shooting from his seat. "Welcome."

Hope, alive with excitement, moved next to Ben. "Oh, Mother, this will be a wonderful party. Wait until you see the house we decorated and the delicious food Max has prepared."

"I have already seen the house, dear. You have been quite busy," she answered Hope while looking at Ben with a forced smile.

"I had outstanding helpers," Ben commented, wrapping his arm around Hope.

"So glad you had Hope to see you through. She has been my right arm at most of my social events, and I am sure her ideas and knowledge came in quite handy."

"No, Mother," Hope interrupted. "It was quite the contrary. Max and Ben have taught *ME* much about entertaining."

Olivia moved to Ben's other side, wrapped her arms around his waist then laid her face on his chest. She shot her daughter daggers as she complimented Ben in a saccharine sweet voice.

"I am impressed, darling. You are a very competent man."

Olivia was unaware that Max had witnessed the entire exchange from his vantage point. Quite simply, she had ignored his presence until he moved from his position by the fire and spoke.

"Excuse me, if you will. I must test the brew for tomorrow evening and wonder if you would like to join me, Hope?"

"Yes," the young girl answered with fervor.

The combination of the old man's rude interruption and the objectionable nature of his request unnerved Olivia.

"Brew?" she snapped in a high-pitched voice.

"Tis only apple cider, Mother. I shall bring some back for you, and I promise you will love it," Hope suggested, ignoring her mother's attitude as she rushed toward Max's retreating form.

Ben waited for the door to close behind them before questioning her. "What's wrong, Olivia? You seem displeased."

Olivia's disapproval was palpable when she entered the kitchen, and Ben felt incensed.

"I don't understand why our daughter insists on spending so much time with a man who is old enough to be her grandfather," Olivia returned with disgust.

"What do you have against Max?"

"I understand your relationship with the man, darling, but it is improper for Hope to spend so much time with him. After all, he is a servant! Certainly not the same class of person- well, she should have friends on her same social plane. Hope is a very well-schooled young woman. She should associate with friends of her same caliber."

Olivia's words truly struck a dangerous nerve with Ben. It was not the first time she had voiced her disapproval of Max, and though Ben had ignored it before, Max meant too much to him to permit Olivia's continued insolence. He had pined over losing her for seventeen years, torturing himself with thoughts of her intimacy shared with another man. Now she was back in his life, professing her love for him, and quite frankly, he was not sure what he felt for her. These past weeks had shown him the person she had become: a woman full of self-importance and arrogance. She was nothing as he had remembered from years ago, and he was beginning to wonder if Hope was the only thing they had in common.

"The Danbury's have taught you much about social etiquette, Olivia," Ben stated. He saw her lips turn up into a pleased smile. "Had you been here with us to enjoy the day, you would have also added a special touch to the party." Her smile grew wider. "But then you would have had to tolerate Max, and I'm sure that would have caused you great discomfort."

Olivia flinched, and Ben noticed, but she recovered quickly as she gazed into his eyes.

"Oh, darling, I have hurt your feelings. I am sorry," she whispered, giving him a soft squeeze.

Ben never moved a muscle when he ground out his next words.

"Our worlds are far apart, Olivia. Hope has had seventeen years of your world, and now I am going to show her a little of mine,"

Olivia pulled back and took his hands in hers. "Our worlds are the same, darling. You have a fine standing in your community and a large circle of affluent friends. Most of all, we share a beautiful daughter."

Ben did not respond.

"I apologize for what I said about Max. My only concern is that Hope could founder," Olivia stated.

Those words added additional fuel to Ben's burning anger. "Our daughter will not founder, Olivia. You do not give her enough credit."

"And you do not know her well enough to make that judgment. Hope needs direction," she replied with unrelenting fervor.

Ben may have only known his daughter for a few short weeks, but he realized it was long enough to learn that Hope was a sensible and caring young woman void of airs and attitudes like her mother. In fact, Ben was puzzled about where Hope had acquired her loving ways, for it was certainly not from Olivia. He could not find many similarities between the two women at this juncture.

***

Olivia could have spit! She realized too late the error she had made by voicing her negativities about Max Seigel. Because of it, she found them aboard Ben's coach and bound for the city after only a few hours together. As they drove through the night, Hope's fatigue and Ben's silent mood presented Olivia little to keep her mind off thoughts of Natalie Wakefield and the stumbling block that existed.

She had learned from Vonnie Miller, her friend who lived in Clarksboro, that Natalie Wakefield was a force to be reckoned with. Vonnie had been a client of Natalie's for the past two years and, in turn, knew everything about her business reputation, her personal circle of friends, and her economic position in the community, and, most of all, her relationship with Benjamin Walters.

Short of a muzzle, there was nothing Olivia could have done to shut her up that day. Vonnie had rambled incessantly about Ben Walters' and Natalie Wakefield's finer points until Olivia felt dreadfully nauseous and envious. It had convinced her that all the couturiere's silly little games with Ben Walters must cease. After all, Natalie had made it all these years alone just fine. Natalie did not need Ben Walters as she needed him. With Andrew gone, Olivia needed a man to accompany her and give her a strong position in the community as Andrew had done. That man would be Ben Walters if it took every womanly wile she had.

When the coach stopped in front of the *Steven Matthews Hotel,* Ben jumped to assist the ladies. The trio ambled up the staircase toward the Dansbury's rented quarters in complete silence. Finally, when they reached the threshold of their room, Ben spoke.

"I will send my coach for you tomorrow morning. Get a good night's rest."

"Thank you, Father," Hope answered, then kissed his cheek. "I cannot wait for the party. It will be wonderful."

"I agree with Hope," Olivia added after her daughter entered their room. "It will definitely be a fine evening."

Ben studied her expression to extract the depth of her sentiments, but she was impossible to read. Olivia had often offered loving words, though she had never shown love and excitement and never acted with spontaneity. He realized now how he needed that in a woman.

Olivia leaned close, and their lips met, a perfunctory move that ended the evening.

"Until tomorrow, then," Ben said.

"Yes, darling. Good night." Olivia slipped inside her room without another word.

A crease marred Ben's brow as he moved down the hall. Damn, her kisses left him cold. It was as if each kiss was an obligatory act, and the worst part was that he had not yet touched her the way a man in love touches a woman. They were adults playing like children, and he felt bottled up with frustration.

He immediately knew what he needed when his boot hit the coach's step. He was headed to Natalie's. He could not explain his feelings nor his boldness in arriving unannounced at her doorstep at nightfall. However, when he drew to a stop before Natalie's shop, Ben alighted from the conveyance with aggression and unexplained excitement. He was happy that a lamp still burned at her kitchen window and hustled toward the welcoming light. His euphoria faded when he reached the door and distinguished two silhouetted figures through the curtains. He had never considered the possibility of

Natalie entertaining company this late, and when the company's voice held a masculine tone, it raised his hackles no small amount.

"Ooooooo! Make sure you put that thing in the right place, Honey. It needs to feel right, you know?"

Every nerve in Ben's body stood at attention when he realized the masculine voice belonged to the good-for-nothing-gambler.

"How does that? Feel good?" Natalie asked.

"Could you move your hand, please?" Jonathan instructed, then after a moment of silence came his purred reply. "Yeah, that feels terrific."

Ben knew he had to get out of there. His presence was bordering on voyeurism, plus listening to more of this bold chatter could quite possibly turn hazardous for any number of individuals right now. He had gotten into enough trouble the other day when he had walked in on Natalie and Hope. He did not need more trouble, for sure. Yet the thought of something indecent behind the door kept him glued and curious.

When Natalie burst into a fit of giggles, Ben leaned close to peek between the break in the curtain, and that is when a big, black tomcat rubbed against his leg, scaring the hell out of him. His forehead accidentally hit the glass, and the conversation ceased inside. Ben did not waste a minute. He lit out for the street like a bat out of hell.

"Get me the gun," Jonathan whispered. It mattered little to Jonathan that he was dressed in his costume: red horns pointing upward, pitchfork tail sewn in place and swinging freely. He yanked open the kitchen door and, with wide-braced feet, pointed the gun into the inky night. His satanic backlit shape filled the doorway. No soul was in sight except the stray cat rubbing against the door frame.

Jonathan took a bold step outside and heard the scuffle of feet scrambling toward the street. Then the figure passed under the burning street lamp, giving him a full view of the intruder.

"Walters," Jonathan hissed.

"Who was it, Jonathan?" Natalie fearfully whispered when he turned back into the house.

He locked the door behind him. "It was nothing, Honey. Just a cat."

"That scared me, Jonathan. I thought someone was out there."

"Nope, everything's all right, not to worry." He did not want her to know anything about this, not yet. "I'll tell you what, it's getting late, so I'm going to slip out of this costume and head back to the hotel," he announced as he walked down the hall. Instead of turning into the fitting room, he continued through the shop, parted the curtains at the front window, and peered outside to discover Walter's coach near the end of the block. He smiled at how well his plan had fallen into place. Yes, sir, all the attention he had bestowed upon Natalie was bothering Ben Walters, making Jonathan smile with pure satisfaction. He grabbed his tail, pulled it high, and whispered with glee.

"You better gather your strength, Ben Walters, because all Hell will break loose tomorrow night!"

Jonathan told Natalie before he departed that he was tired and needed his bed at the *Steven Matthews*. She knew better. Oh, he was going to the *Steven Matthews* all right, but not for sleep. Natalie was positive he had plans to enjoy the hours in the gaming salon. Once a gambler, always a gambler, she mused. Not that it mattered to her anymore. After all, she was not his keeper. All she wanted from him was his end of the agreement, though lately, she wondered if Jonathan's participation had even helped.

Olivia Dansbury was tougher competition than Natalie had ever dreamed possible. Her lithe form and pale beauty gave Natalie dreadful feelings of insecurity.

Standing before her oval mirror, she untied her robe and let it float to the floor. Natalie studied her naked reflection and admitted that *lithe* she was not. Lithe females were tall: long-legged, graceful, and slender-armed with swan-like necks, just like Olivia! She realized her height alone squelched any chance of being lithe. Though she did consider that even though her legs were shorter than her competitor's, they fit her proportion well. She stuck her pointed foot out, rotated her ankle, examined her calf, and concluded they were good legs with slender thighs, shapely calves, and thin ankles.

She then moved onto her waist. So, what if it wasn't eighteen inches anymore? Who cared? She wasn't eighteen years old anymore, either. She propped her hands on each side of her waist and sucked in as much air as possible. To her dismay, it only proved to make her breasts appear larger.

"I do not have a snowball's chance in Hell. I will never be lithe." She stood on tiptoes. "If I were just a little taller." She turned to view her profile in the mirror. Her auburn hair fell to touch the bottom curve of her buttocks. She patted her derriere. "Not too bad," she smartly quipped until her self-examination reached the landscape of two perky nipples resting on the tip of her sizeable breasts. Her shoulders slumped in defeat. Her insecurity returned.

"OOOOoooooooo, Natalie, you had better stay on this diet, or you're done," she warned her reflection.

Then suddenly, a rush of tears poured forth so forceful it drove her to her bed. She buried her face in the mound of pillows, crying out the pain of losing Ben to another woman. She knew it was more than Olivia's lithe shape that tipped the scales in her favor. Ben's daughter Hope is what gave Olivia Dansbury the winning edge. Natalie saw the pride in Ben's eyes every time he gazed upon his beautiful young daughter. She noticed how he had interacted with children at every social or church event they had attended over the past years. Young people were important to him; she always thought he would make a wonderful father. And now, after all these years, Olivia Dansbury was back with her lithe shape and a young daughter.

If she was honest with herself, she had little to no ammunition compared to Olivia Dansbury. Still, something kept her chained to the plan Jonathan set forth, and determinedly she persevered. Only a few tricks remained, and she would use them at the party tomorrow: a provocative costume and an ex-husband full of devilish antics.

#

Chapter Eighteen

Jonathan awoke to Olivia and Hope's heated discussion in the adjoining room on the morning of Ben's party. He again grabbed the drinking glass and pressed it against the wall to catch all the details. The topic of their discussion was highly confidential and very shocking.

"After everything Andrew and I have given you, how could you think of doing this, Hope? We have sent you to the finest schools, bought you the best clothing, and introduced you to society's finest families. You owe me, young lady!"

"Not like this, I don't. It is wrong! They are two separate subjects, Mother. Yes, you took me as your child when my mother died and gave me all that you claim, but I was your sister's child! Ben Walters has no part in this, and I can't allow him to believe otherwise?" Hope yanked fresh undergarments from the armoire drawer.

Olivia cast daggers at her daughter's back. "It is too late, Hope. If you tell Ben the truth, he will hate you," she threatened.

"I would sooner him know the truth now than after you've cleverly trapped him into marriage. I know what it feels like to be lied to by people you love."

"Andrew and I did it for your good. We were protecting you, Hope."

"Protecting me? I do not think so, Mother. I believe it was more about you," Hope said with clear contempt.

Hope had never forgotten that night long ago. She was twelve years old and had slipped out of bed for a sweet snack. She had made her way through the silent manse almost to the kitchen door when a loud clank sounded from her father's study. When she rushed into the room, she found Andrew slumped in a large leather chair with his arm hung limply over the armrest. A few feet away, an empty liquor bottle rested on the floor. The scene frightened her for many reasons, the strongest being that her mother would find him in this condition and unload her wrath on him.

"Father?" she had implored. She remembered his eyes that night and the regret that stole from their painful depths.

"Hope, I'm sorry," he had responded slurredly.

"Sssshhhhh. It is all right, Father. Let me help you to your room. Do not let Mother find you like this."

"We should have told you so long ago. Keeping the secret was selfish and wrong, but I did it for her. She was all I ever wanted, and I did it because I thought I'd lose her."

"Father, please. I will help you to your bed." she insisted, pulling on his arm.

"No, listen to me!" he had shouted.

His tone had frightened her, for in her twelve years, she had never remembered her father raising his voice to her.

Kiss Me Once

That night, in Andrew Dansbury's drunken stupor, he had confessed the whole, unbelievable, heartbreaking truth to Hope. He had blubbered and slurred his way through how Leah, Olivia's older sister, had given birth to a baby girl six months after Olivia, and Andrew had married. In the hours following the difficult birth, Leah had died of complications, and to amplify the moment's misery, her husband, Stanford, overcome with grief, had taken his life.

"I tricked Olivia, Hope," the drunken father continued. "When I had first laid eyes on her, I knew I wanted her for my bride. I had not told her I could not produce offspring until after we were wed. She hates me for that, Hope. She desired children of her own, and I shattered her hopes. Then Leah and Stanford died and left you behind. It was Olivia's chance for a baby, and she took it with great relish, insisting that we speak nothing of your natural parents. You were Olivia's child; that was how the world would know it. It was so important to her. It was so damn important to her. I went along with it, thinking I could win back her love, but I was wrong. She is a cold woman, Hope. Olivia's a cold, heartless woman."

Hope had never forgotten how she struggled to get her father to his bedroom with a minimal sound that night. When she had completed the mission, she had silently returned to her room, climbed into her bed, and spent the remaining long night in tearful misery. She had cried for her mother, who had died in childbirth, a mother she had never known. She had cried for Andrew, a man so in love with Olivia that he thought life would be nothing without her. And at last, she cried for herself and the complicated feelings she now felt for Andrew and Olivia Dansbury. The following morning confused her further when Andrew acted as if the incident the evening before had never occurred. Olivia was right about all they had given her, but Hope had also never forgotten the pain their lies had caused her. She had vowed never to hurt any human being like Olivia and Andrew Dansbury had hurt her.

153

"I don't think a decent human being like Ben Walters deserves this, Mother," Hope bit out.

"Ben has never had a family. He is thrilled to know he has a daughter after all these years. Why can't you let this alone and go along with my plan? Why must you make this so difficult for me? Ben very well could be my only chance at gaining what I have lost since Andrew's death," she finished in a strained voice.

"Father left you with enough money. You do not need Ben." Hope removed her nightgown and stepped into the tub of hot water.

"You are so naïve. Money is not the only thing a woman needs," Olivia snapped.

"Excuse my ignorance, Mother, but since I can't remember when you slept in the same bed with Andrew, what else do you need?"

Olivia stepped over to the tub's edge and slapped Hope's face. "Where have you picked up this vulgarity? Never mind, do not answer that. I am sure your servant friend Mr. Seigel has taught you much about the gutter."

Hope touched her stinging cheek and glared at Olivia.

"I have had enough of your insolence, Hope. You keep this secret until I marry Ben, and after that, I will give you enough money to return to Massachusetts. That way, you do not have to force yourself to live around the lie!"

Hope turned her face away from her mother's angry expression, knowing now that her new friends were the ones that deserved her loyalty far more than her mother.

Jonathan Wakefield lowered the glass from the wall on the other side of the adjoining wall. He was absolutely stunned by what he had just learned.

"Soooooo, Hope's not Ben's daughter after all," he drawled, moving toward the window. He pulled the drapery away, lifted his face to the inviting rays of morning light, and smiled.

"Good morning, Mr. Sun. I believe it is going to be a beautiful day after all."

***

When Ben entered the kitchen the morning of his party, he came face-to-face with an open-mouthed, fang-toothed, green-faced dragon head sitting in the middle of the table. The paper mache creation made him chuckle. Max never failed to entertain him with his humor and wealth of talents.

Ben stirred the coals in the fireplace, laid some logs atop, and then placed the coffeepot on the grate above the stoked flames. He took a seat.

"Damn," he complained, rubbing his sore neck. Last night had been the lousiest night of discomfort he could remember. It was completely void of any significant rest and filled with bad dreams that kept him tossing and turning until dawn. In one dream, Natalie and Jonathan had been chasing one another in and out of her bedroom and through her apartment, wearing next to nothing and laughing with complete abandonment. It sickened Ben. At one point in the middle of the night, he shot straight up in bed after his dreams produced a scene where Jonathan had tackled Natalie's nearly naked form on the bed, spilling her auburn hair across the pillows.

Over the past weeks, he had tried to forget Natalie and concentrate on Olivia, but to his self-disgust, it had not worked, and seventeen years had changed so much. Olivia was definitely not the girl he had remembered, and he had to admit that the years had also changed him. In fact, other than Hope, Ben realized they shared no common ground. The worst part was that he felt a stronger connection with the daughter he had just met than with the woman he once shared the ultimate intimacy with. He did not like what Olivia had become: a cold, self-seeking individual with little depth. And the most puzzling part was how Hope had turned out to be such a wonderful, lovely young woman. Ben wondered if perhaps Andrew Dansbury deserved more credit than he had given him.

Ben sat forward, propped his arms on his upper legs, and clutched his coffee mug between his knees with two strong hands. His belly roiled with uncertainty. Not only did these harsh facts about Olivia disturb him, but he was tormented by the building desire he continued to feel for Natalie. The kisses they had shared over these past weeks had stirred his libido to mammoth portions. In fact, this very minute, he felt his loins harden just thinking about the auburn-haired temptress. He needed her, dammit. He needed her warm embrace, her moist lips on his, kissing away the fatigue of his day and leaving a promise of pleasurable moments together. Now the whole damn thing was complicated because of her ridiculous, troublemaking ex-husband, Jonathan-good-for-nothing-Wakefield.

The kitchen door swung wide and brought him out of his reverie.

"I thought I saw the light on over here."

It was Max. He hung his heavy outer coat on a peg and then moved to examine the dragon's head. "Hey, look at him! Kinda handsome, eh?" Max exclaimed. He walked around the kitchen table, taking in every angle of the open-mouthed, fang-toothed creation, and occasionally glanced at Ben, who stared glumly into the fire.

"What got you awake so early?" Ben grumbled.

"Excitement, I guess."

"Excited for what? To watch my daughter attract the attention of every man in the room or to watch Olivia make a fool out of herself for attending without a costume?"

Max did not comment. He reached for a mug on the shelf, poured himself a cup of the black brew, and sat near Ben. "You can expect Trout Snyder and his little brothers around six o'clock. Trout told me they worked up new tunes to keep the folks on the dance floor all night."

"My daughter is what will keep the men on the dance floor tonight! I shouldn't let her wear that costume."

"I thought you had changed your mind, Ben. You agreed that her costume is lovely."

An angry crease formed on Ben's brow as he sipped from his mug.

"I think this is not about Hope but something more. Why don't you spit out what is bothering you?" Max dared.

Ben shot to his feet and threw the remaining contents of his mug into the burning flames. "It's about my world being turned upside down, Max! It's about throwing a party with the possibility of all hell breaking loose! And most of all, it's about women!"

Max could not decipher much more of what Ben mumbled as he stormed out of the room and down the hall.

**

As much as Jonathan hated leaving his seat at the card table, he knew there would be hell to pay if he did not make it to Natalie's place by five o'clock. He promised her a prompt arrival so she wouldn't suffer unnecessary anxiety. He kept that promise by reaching her property on the hour. Jonathan lifted his hand to tap on the door, but before his knuckles connected with the wood, Natalie yanked open the portal and welcomed him inside.

"Come in, Jonathan. Thank God you are here. Are you hungry?"

Jonathan could not answer. Before him stood such beauty that it left him breathless. Natalie was draped in a form-fitting shimmering gold fabric that showed every perfect curve of her body. Her hair was tucked beneath a smooth black wig that fell straight to her shoulders. On the crown of her head rested a headpiece fashioned of stiff iridescent material fanned from ear to ear, which made a dramatic backdrop for the open-mouthed cobra head placed on a band across her brow. She had artistically applied a colorful array of cosmetics, adding to her mysterious and seductive charm. Her silken limbs hung bare except for numerous gold bracelets on her wrists and a gold serpent wrapped around her upper arm. Jonathan felt his breeches grow tight, imagining exactly what Mark Anthony felt in Cleopatra's company.

He moved close.

Natalie took a step back.

"I see you've spent the afternoon in the tavern," she suggested, waving her fingers before her nose.

"Fool that I am. It seems there were far better sights here. You look absolutely delectable, honey," he answered, his lecherous gaze running down the entire length of her body, absorbing every detail. He noticed the subtle affects her diet had made on her shape. He had once thought there was nothing she could do to better her appearance, but now realized her diet had changed her from beautiful to breathtaking! The tempting scent of her perfume drew him closer. He had to touch.

"Stop it this minute, Jonathan!" Natalie picked up a wooden spoon for defense. "Your costume is in the fitting room. Get dressed while I ladle some soup."

"How about a little nibble of you," he asked, moving closer.

Natalie raised the spoon and slapped it smartly across his cheek without warning.

"Ooow! "Why'd ya do that," he asked in a hurtful tone.

"I have made the right costume for you, Jonathan. You are a devil if there ever was one. Now, get dressed before I decide to forget this whole plan."

"You are a hard-hearted woman, Natalie. I merely complimented you, and you slapped me for no reason." Jonathan grumbled his complaints down the hall until he disappeared into the fitting room.

Natalie looked at the spoon in her hand and smiled. Jonathan's persistent flirtation was an absolute challenge, yet her ego had been bolstered over these weeks by the constant attention and compliments he had showered on her. His reaction to her this evening was especially welcomed. She had worked hard with her diet and designing her costume, and she prayed it would have the same effect on Ben this evening that it had on Jonathan.

Fifteen minutes later, Jonathan emerged from the fitting room in six feet three inches of form-fitting red, complete with a pitchfork tail. His hood fit tightly over his head with two stuffed horns jutting from the crown. The only thing uncovered was his face. Natalie burst into uncontrolled laughter at Jonathan's personal addition to the costume. He had fashioned a thin horse-hair mustache and pasted it to his upper lip. The effective addition was exaggerated in length, stretching well beyond his cheeks, and waxed into a curl that reached eye level. She had never seen anything so humorous and thought, for all the hard work she had put into Jonathan's costume, the mustache brought personality to the guise.

"So maybe I can lure you into something devilish with this?" His eyebrows moved up and down while he twisted the end of his mustache between two fingers.

Natalie's laughter died. "I have heated some soup. Come and eat so we can be on our way. It is getting late."

Jonathan took a seat at the table across from her. "I hope you are a bit warmer to me tonight at Walters' party. Remember, honey, we are supposed to be reunited, lovebirds." Jonathan tasted the soup. "You're a great cook," he commented. He noticed she had not served herself a thing. "You're not eating?"

"I'll have a little something at the party."

"I told you before you needn't worry about your weight. You're a beautiful woman."

Silence hung between them. Jonathan saw her staring at her empty soup bowl when he looked up.

He added, "Walters thinks so too---"

Her head snapped up. "What?" she asked with surprise.

Jonathan took a few more spoonfuls of soup, wiped his mouth, and then pushed from the table to walk over to her side. "I said. . ." He placed his finger under her chin and tilted her head back so their eyes could meet. "You're a beautiful woman."

"No, not that! I want to know how *YOU* know what Ben thinks. Jonathan, we have been playing this part for weeks, and I don't see it working."

"You are blind! The man is seething with jealousy. He cannot stand me, Natalie, and you know why? Because he sees me kiss you, he sees my hands on you and your loving reaction to all of it." Jonathan lowered before her to one knee. "Give me credit for at least knowing a man's mind. I have been only cordial to the brute, and he can barely speak civilly to me. Why? I will tell you why. Because I am the man in Natalie Wakefield's life, and he never had to deal with sharing you before I came to town."

"He almost kissed me the other day," she softly admitted.

"When?" Jonathan was forced to taste a little jealousy himself with her admission.

"The day he built the platform, but Hope walked in, and he broke away."

"See, what did I tell you? He is confused. If he loves Olivia, he certainly would not be kissing you, honey. Now, I've been doing a little research. I want you to trust me tonight. I discovered something in your favor that might turn everything around."

"What do you know?" she asked with eagerness.

"Just play your part, honey, and do what I tell you. You will find out soon enough."

#

Cyn Garrett

Chapter Nineteen

Ben had shown Olivia and Hope upstairs to the guest quarters two hours before the party so the ladies could rest and refresh before the evening event. At six o'clock, when they had not yet emerged from their adjoining rooms, Ben climbed the stairs and knocked on Olivia's door to check if all was well. Olivia opened the door a crack to deliver her apology for their delay, promising they would be down directly. Ben questioned nothing more and returned to the lower level to greet the excited, incoming crowd.

Trout Snyder and his brothers were assembled in the corner of the drawing-room, warming up their instruments for their impending performance. Ben lifted his arm in greeting, chuckling when he noticed Trout's attempt at a costume. Locals gave him the nickname "Trout" years ago because he was always seen with fishing hooks attached to either his hat or his coat lapel. Tonight, his costume consisted of his usual fishhook-covered straw hat, but he had also added a wicker fishing creel attached to a leather strap that crossed over his chest. Ben chuckled at his minimal effort, which was more than he expected from Olivia tonight.

Ben felt a surge of satisfaction as he scanned the festive rooms alive with a party atmosphere. Once again, Max and the staff had seen every detail. The lighted lamps and candles cast a beautiful glow on the decorated rooms. The punch bowl and wine glasses sparkled, and the tables overflowed with baskets of fruits and nuts and platters of smoked meats and cheeses.

Gazing down the long hall, he noticed Max standing at the front door dressed in his green dragon costume. He was greeting early arrivals: a goblin, a sorceress and a swashbuckling pirate. The pirate took Max by surprise, pressed his wooden sword against his dragon throat and pretended to pull a fang from his paper mâché head. With quick reflex, Max grabbed the pirate's eyepatch and pulled it away from his face, forcing him to plead for mercy and release his hold. The surrounding spirited crowd cheered for the little dragon's victory.

Ben's interest was taken by the sorceress standing by Max's side. Her hair was tucked into a tall coned-shaped hat draped with sheer fabric that concealed her face. Her height and body shape resembled Natalie Wakefield, and the costume was beautifully constructed, much like something the dressmaker would create. Anticipation mounted as he moved closer, but when she spoke, he realized it was not whom he hoped, but rather Rebecca Shay, a flirtatious young woman who never failed to be the Belle of every Ball.

"You certainly make a handsome Robin Hood with that beard, Ben," Rebecca called out at Ben's approach.

"The beard is Max's addition. He's my detail man." Ben answered, stroking the object with a smile. "Might I say, you've definitely outdone yourself with *YOUR* costume, Rebecca. From a distance, I must admit, I took you for another guest. Quite a beautiful disguise."

As the next half hour passed, many costumed high-spirited guests poured in, filling the manse with laughter and excitement. Ben moved through the crowd, inviting each guest to partake of the food and drink and enjoy the music Trout and his trio provided. He was extremely rewarded with the enthusiastic costume participation of the crowd. It reinforced his choice of party themes and the imminent success of the evening, despite Olivia's disapproval. Olivia had considered the party a silly event, and her decision not to dress in costume had fired off the anger that manifested a sore spot inside Ben. Would she see that this party was no "silly event" but an evening of excitement and camaraderie? In these past weeks, he realized their interests were far different and their choice of friendships and acquaintances quite the opposite of what he remembered as a twenty-year-old man. The past seventeen years had brought him a bucketful of challenges, yet none felt as life-altering as the one he now faced with Olivia.

He again checked the staircase, though this time surprised to see Olivia and Hope finally descending, *both* dressed in costume. He was taken aback that Olivia had produced a costume for the evening after bemoaning the silliness of his party idea. And more surprisingly, the costume was in no way a simple, thoughtless creation but rather a high-neck, body-hugging gown of flesh-colored fabric covered in sparkling beads. The eye-catching and provocative gown was accessorized with an elaborate feathered mask attached to a beribboned stick she held in front of her face. Her blonde hair was swept high in an elegant coiffure to finish the look and secured with a jeweled and plumed comb.

Then Ben turned his gaze on Hope and swelled with pride. She was, simply put, an extraordinary vision of beauty. Thoughts of Natalie and the hard work and love she had put into his daughter's costume filled his mind. He felt ashamed that he actually questioned Natalie's intent that afternoon at her shop. He had known for years that her fashions changed women from ordinary to extraordinary, and he wondered why he had believed she would do anything less for Hope. He felt indebted to the couturiere for her generosity, talent, and enduring friendship. She always gave to others, making special moments in their lives, as she most definitely accomplished for his daughter on this night.

Kiss Me Once

Anxious for her arrival, he glanced at the front portal when it again opened to welcome guests. To his disappointment, it was not Natalie. He knew her costume would be one of the most outstanding of the evening and was most anxious to see it. She was a pro at creation and an enthusiastic guest no matter what the event. He thirsted for her presence and figured her delay had everything to do with her reckless ex-husband's reluctance to leave the card table. Ben was suddenly snapped out of his musings when he felt a jab in his side.

"Uh," he barked out at the surprise attack. "Watch where you put the tip of that thing," Ben warned when he turned toward the assailant.

It was the Pirate, sheathing his wooden sword while staring at the two lovely visions descending the upper level. "And who, may I ask, are your lady guests? I have been out of the city since late summer, and there appear to be some big changes while I was gone."

"You've much to catch up on, you galivanting cad," Ben stated, swiping the pirate's chin with a closed fist. "Life has changed for many of us in the past months. This beautiful garden nymph approaching is my daughter."

"Your daughter?" the younger man uttered in disbelief.

"I will explain at a more convenient time. I warn you; I will watch *your* every move this evening. She is innocent and certainly not for the likes of a joker such as yourself."

"Sorry for our delay, Father. It took us far longer than we expected," Hope whispered when she reached Ben's side.

"No apologies. I can see it was worth the wait," Ben answered with pride, pulling her close.

"Good evening, darling," Olivia softly greeted.

165

Ben turned his attention to her and inspected her full length. He was confused but had to admit she had pulled off a dazzling costume. "You've reconsidered?"

"Anything for you." She reached for his hand and entwined her fingers in his.

Meanwhile, the pirate soaked up the exchange with consuming interest. Ben had been a close friend of his for years and knew he was not one to make rash decisions or make many mistakes. So, how did Ben embroil himself so suddenly with these two women, one of them a DAUGHTER?

Kirk wrapped his arm around Ben's shoulder in great camaraderie and smiled broadly at the ladies. "Reward me with an introduction, Ben."

"Ladies, may I introduce Kirk Matthews, a close friend of mine." Ben then turned to offer Kirk the introduction he desired. "Mrs. Olivia Dansbury and my daughter, Hope."

Olivia offered her hand, coupled with a most beguiling smile. "A pleasure, Mr. Matthews."

"Kirk, please," he returned, pressing a kiss on her fingertips, then turned his attention to the younger female. "Miss Hope," he greeted, reaching for her hand.

The young girl smiled and dipped into a shallow curtsy while Olivia, whose interest was greatly stirred by this young man, pushed on.

"My daughter and I are guests of the renowned Steven Matthews Hotel. Is this your establishment?" she asked with hopeful curiosity.

"My parents own the hotel. I trust you've been comfortable?"

"Extremely so, it's a first-class accommodation, and the staff has efficiently handled our requests. We won't be staying much longer, though. Hope and I are considering other options," Olivia continued.

"So, you're relocating?" Kirk queried.

"Yes, I'm originally a Philadelphian and would love to make Philadelphia our home again. We want to be close to those we love," Olivia answered, smiling at Ben.

Kirk glanced at Hope and detected discomfort in her posture, but she forced a smile when their gaze met. It didn't take a genius to see there was more to this story than what the moment allowed, but there was no rush for Kirk. An evening of good food and fun lay ahead, and after months away, he was geared up to enjoy every minute. Not to mention, there was a beautiful new girl in town named Hope, and he was going to treat himself to her company.

Max approached the small gathering, twisting his hips so the large tail of his dragon costume swished back and forth on the floor. The group stepped back to give him room and applauded at his comical show, except Olivia, who crinkled her nose at his buffoonery.

Hope was in awe of his costume. "Max! I love this!" Hope trilled as she ran her hand along the paper mache head, feeling the pointy fangs and the long fabric tongue.

"Thank you, young lady. Personally, I'm finding the get-up a bit cumbersome, yet I must admit I'm enjoying the comments. I wanted to say hello before all the young men swept you away this evening. I see that our friend Natalie has worked her magic again. Your costume is outstanding, young lady."

Olivia was incensed by Max's acknowledgment of Natalie Wakefield's handiwork. She didn't need to hear the undeserving praise of that arrogant, interfering dressmaker anymore, yet she was helpless to stop the accolades from the surrounding group.

"Yes, she did a beautiful job. She's a lovely lady," Hope answered, avoiding eye contact with her mother.

"I fully agree", Kirk interjected. "In fact, I believe her handiwork should be shown off on the dance floor. Would you care to dance, Miss Dansbury? Afterward, I could introduce you to my band of mischievous acquaintances, a fun-loving group always anxious to welcome a new addition to the evening."

Ben cut in just then. "I beg you to stay close by my side tonight, Hope. There are those who cannot be trusted, and I worry that you could be led astray," Ben's tone was teasing, but he cast Kirk a warning glance.

"I promise to stay within eye-sight for safety's sake, Father." Hope lightly bantered.

Kirk clasped his hands behind his back and straightened his shoulders. "Not to worry, Ben. I assure you my comportment will be nothing less than a gentleman."

Hope looked at Ben for approval.

"He *HAS* been known to handle himself as a gentleman, but I shall be watching. Enjoy the evening, my dear."

Kirk led Hope to the dance floor, and Max moved on, leaving Ben and Olivia at the room's edge.

"There is a young man worthy of our beautiful daughter, darling," Olivia remarked as she watched Kirk waltz Hope around the dance floor.

Ben's brow wrinkled. After sharing only a few minutes of conversation, he was angered at her rapid assessment of a man she considered worthy of her daughter's attention. "If you own a hotel, is that enough to qualify a man's worth?"

Olivia jerked her head toward Ben. "Ben! What a crude thing to say. Of course not. It is merely clear that the boy has had a proper upbringing. He's very dashing. Very gentlemanly."

Very undisciplined. Very much a Ladies' Man. You know nothing about the boy, Olivia. Ben's gaze took a slow journey down her bedazzled form. The vision confused him. "What persuaded you to dress in costume?"

A significant moment passed before Olivia answered. "I realized how much this party meant to you. I didn't want to ruin your evening by not participating. Please be patient with me, darling. I feel certain we can smooth out our rough edges. We've been apart for so long and have lived very different lives."

Yes, he thought, their lives were vastly different. So different, he wondered if they could find any common ground.

"So, where did you get the costume?"

"The gown is old. Hope helped me with the mask and my hair." She stepped on tiptoes to kiss his lips, but before their lips met, the crowd pushed by, knocked her off balance, and she missed her mark.

The mob moved to the front door, spouting oohs and ahs for the couple who had just arrived. It tweaked Ben's curiosity no small amount.

"Our new guests are causing quite a stir," Ben commented, stretching his neck for a better view.

He took Olivia's hand and moved toward the assembled crowd.

When they drew close, Ben saw that the newly arrived guests were something to rave about. The woman dressed as Cleopatra wore a provocative gown of shimmering gold and an iridescent snake headpiece over a smoothly coiffed ink-black wig. Her partner was dressed as a red devil with a long, curled, pencil-thin mustache that he twisted between his thumb and forefinger. Ben chuckled at the humorous detailing of the devil costume when he first approached until their eyes met, where his laughter shut down like a cellar door in a windstorm.

"Wakefield," Ben muttered under his breath.

To witness the damn red devil stroke the Queen of the Nile's bare arm with a self-assured smile spread across his mustachioed face made him sick to his stomach. Ben's gaze traveled the full length of Natalie's body. Her costume was alluring in design and style, hugging her voluptuous shape to display every curvy detail. She looked different and mysterious with the heavy application of cosmetics and her straight, black wig covering her auburn tresses. When their gaze met, a flame ignited inside him. He felt a desire rise, making his already tight breeches extremely uncomfortable. Ben never noticed that Olivia had been watching every expression on his face and saw the admiration in his eyes.

"Perhaps we should enjoy the spread of food, darling? I am ravenous," Olivia suggested to drag him away from Natalie.

"After I welcome the newest arrivals," Ben firmly countered. He placed Olivia's arm into the crook of his and pushed closer to stand next to the new arrivals.

Ben fixed his gaze on Natalie's face, then slowly let it travel from her headdress, down her shimmering golden body, to the tip of her dainty feet. Her costume ignited a heat inside of him that he could barely control. The silken fabric clung to every curve of her shape, displaying an alluring and sensual result.

"Good evening." Ben's voice was low and directed only at her. "You have certainly outdone yourself, Madam. Your costume is a work of art."

"She's the work of art, fellow," Jonathan interjected, his hand gliding up and down the length of Natalie's arm.

Ben glared at the caress and then shot Jonathan a look that could kill. He raked Jonathan's form with disdain. "Guess you feel mighty comfortable in that devil costume, eh Wakefield?"

"Yep, sure do. My honey made it for me. Though sadly, I won't have any more fittings." Jonathan said with exaggerated sadness as he tweaked Natalie's nose. "You know what, Ben? That was the best part. Especially the night she sewed my tail in place," Jonathan quipped, then further harassed him by pulling his tail around and wiggling the pitchfork end in front of Ben's nose.

Ben batted the tail down to submission.

Natalie quickly responded to end the silly skirmish between the men. She was not sure how much needling Ben was willing to take from Jonathan, but one thing she didn't want was Ben's meaty fist making contact with Jonathan's handsome face.

"You have also done a good job, Ben. Did Max help you?" Natalie interjected in an attempt to divert the dangerous course of things.

"Max made the whole costume down to the beard. I am no good at this kind of thing," he answered, running his hands down the front of his tunic.

Natalie turned to Olivia, who wore a saccharine sweet smile and held the feathered mask to her chest. "Did Max help you also, Olivia?"

"Hope helped me. She is a very clever girl."

Then with clear intention and perfect timing, Olivia dropped the mask and revealed her figure-hugging gown beneath.

Natalie was immobilized when she got the full view of her gown. She realized more than ever the tremendous threat this woman made to her happiness. If this gown didn't get Ben's attention and every other man in the room, nothing would. The fabric clung so faithfully to her body that it appeared like the glass beads were pasted directly on her flesh. Her experience in dressmaking assured her that only a shape like Olivia's could wear something this form-fitting. Sadly, Natalie was forced to admit that Olivia looked stunning.

"I believe a more descriptive term for your daughter is delightful. She's an innocent young woman who never uses calculating measures to achieve her goals. *Clever*, Mrs. Dansbury, is what you are!" Natalie slipped her arm through Jonathan's and smiled. "Well, Ben, I believe it is time to enjoy the fruits of your labor. Shall we, Mr. Lucifer?"

"I'm looking forward to it," Jonathan answered with a devilish wink.

And together, they moved toward the lively music, leaving Ben to stare brazenly at Natalie's retreating form and Olivia insulted and enraged.

#

Chapter Twenty

"I might as well forget it, Jonathan. I cannot compete with her," Natalie uttered dismally.

"Whatever you do, Honey, do not hang your head. Straighten up! I would wager they're standing back there watching our every move." Jonathan wrapped his arm around Natalie's shoulder and lifted her chin so their eyes could meet. "Everything is going to work out. Trust me." He pressed a warm kiss on her smiling lips.

Olivia missed the exchange while speaking with surrounding guests, but Ben caught every ugly detail. He called out to the little green dragon distributing a tray of drinks throughout the crowd.

"Max!"

"Yes, sir, what may I do for you? A glass of wine?"

"Bourbon. Straight up. Fill the glass."

Max asked no questions. He headed directly for the decanter. Ben's tone and liquor request answered everything. Trouble was brewing.

"You promised you would have something to eat tonight. Here, take this," Jonathan said, handing Natalie a plate from the buffet table.

"Actually, Jonathan, I'm not hungry."

"You are taking this too far, Honey. You do not need to lose another pound."

"Did you see her? She has the body of Venus."

"And a heart as cold as stone."

"Ben doesn't know that," Natalie snapped.

"I think he does," Jonathan answered with cool composure as he picked a canapé off the tray and gently pushed it into her mouth. "I want you to eat something, and then we will dance after that. It has been years since we've waltzed together, and I, for one, can't wait. Of course, your costume might be a bit restricting," he chuckled, looking down at her tapered skirt. "

Ben had retreated to a dark corner of the room to nurse his drink, keeping a watchful eye on the bothersome couple who stood at the buffet table.

"What the Hell," he hissed when Jonathan placed the canapé in Natalie's mouth.

Their intimate exchange felt like someone had plunged a knife into his heart. He was not used to another man paying this much attention to Natalie; more so, he wasn't prepared for the painful attack on his emotional state. Ben lifted his bourbon glass and took a hefty swallow, welcoming its fiery path down his throat.

For the past two years, Ben had felt his desire for Natalie grow, yet he had done absolutely nothing to develop a more intimate relationship with her. He suddenly realized that he had left it ALL up to her, even the first kiss, and now admitted that things had not been the same for him since that moment. The passionate memory of their intimate exchange stood between every move he made and every move he couldn't make: his relationship with Olivia and his responsibility to Hope, the innocent one in the whole mess.

Then there was Jonathan. Ben agonized over the gambler's intentions. Did Wakefield intend to rekindle the fire he once shared with Natalie? Was the man sincere, or was he merely taking her for all he could get? Worst of all, Ben was maddened that it had taken Jonathan's re-entry into Natalie's life to make him realize how much _he_ wanted her.

"Darling? What are you doing here in the corner?"

Olivia's voice was barely above a whisper when she approached, yet Ben, whose mind was deeply rooted in painfully private considerations, thought it sounded more like a shout from the mountaintop for all to hear. He pushed away from the wall and bit out an answer.

"It has been a hectic week, a busy day. I thought I would take a moment for myself."

"The host has responsibilities, darling. Do not be rude," Olivia scolded, placing a well-manicured hand on his sleeve.

Ben swirled the amber liquid in his glass, never looking at or commenting on her reprimand. He had thrown so many successful parties over the years that her words were ineffectual.

"Would you like something to eat?" she asked.

"I'm drinking. No, thank you."

Olivia's nose wrinkled in disgust. "So, I noticed. Don't you think it is a bit much this early in the evening?"

Ben simply shrugged his shoulders and then defiantly took another sip.

She ignored his gesture and turned her attention toward the dining room. "The food smells delicious. Shall we sample the fare?"

Ben remained silent, took her elbow, and obligingly moved toward the food-laden table where Natalie and her escort lingered. As they selected plates from the far end of the table, Olivia played the perfect hostess and exchanged pleasantries with a costumed couple. Meanwhile, Ben continued down the table, pretending to survey the food, when all he cared to do was move closer toward the Queen of the Nile.

Jonathan noticed Ben's approach and excused himself to offer Natalie the opportunity. "I will be back shortly, honey. Nature calls. Could you keep an eye on this for me?" He laid his plate on a nearby table.

"Sure," Natalie answered.

When she turned back to the buffet table, Ben stood directly across from her, drinking in her exotic beauty.

"Hello, again," Ben muttered.

"Oh, Ben! Wonderful party. But then you always throw successful gatherings."

Natalie bit into a marinated vegetable while she studied every detail of the man before her. She loved how his costume fit snugly down his muscular legs and how the beard enhanced his rugged good looks. She wondered for a split second how it might feel to be kissed by him with the soft facial hair. Olivia knew! She had miserably witnessed Ben and Olivia's passionate exchange when she arrived at the party. It further distressed her to imagine that Olivia may have felt far more than his mustache these past weeks. What magic did Olivia possess to lure him, she painfully pondered. Was it her beauty and charm? Was it the intimate memories of their past together? Or maybe the daughter they shared?

"Aren't you hungry? You will insult Max if you don't eat," Ben commented, noting a tiny drop of vegetable juice on her plate.

"I'm not eating much these days," she honestly replied.

Ben walked around the end of the table, moving close beside her. He noticed she had lost weight and wondered if she had been ill and, if so, why she had not told him. Then he remembered there was no reason for her to inform him of anything like that anymore. He felt miserable that their relationship had changed from good to bad in such a small space of time. The small intimacies they had once shared were gone. Now Natalie's good-for-nothing ex-husband was taking advantage of everything she had, and Olivia had an ever-living ring in his nose. He honestly did not care who witnessed his next move. He could not take another minute of this mayhem. Ben gently grasped Natalie's upper arm and drew her close.

"I need to speak with you, Natalie."

"Certainly, Ben, go right ahead," she answered, turning to him with a warm smile on her lips.

"No, I mean alone."

"Well. . . we *are* alone, Ben."

He let out a short breath and tightened his grip on her arm. "We are _not_ alone, Natalie. Any minute now, your jackass ex-husband will be back."

"So? What difference does that make?" she asked with a trace of irritation creeping into her voice. "Jonathan is welcome to hear whatever you have to say. We hold no secrets from one another."

Ben tilted his face toward the ceiling and closed his eyes. "Natalie, listen to me. This is _about_ him, and it's for your own good. You are making a big mistake, and I am concerned."

Natalie's eyebrows drew together. "Well, concern yourself no longer, Mr. Walters. My life and what I do with it is none of your business. Furthermore, your worry for my well-being is extremely inappropriate. Remember, you are nearly betrothed." Natalie looked over his shoulder, spied Hope and Kirk Matthews approaching, and thought it best to release a warning. "And I suggest you get a smile on your face because your daughter is moving this way."

Ben turned his head and saw the young couple approach. "Meet me in the study at ten o'clock. Be there," he snapped.

"I will n---" Natalie was unable to finish her rebuttal.

"Miss Wakefield, your costume is magnificent," Hope called out as she approached. "I didn't know it was you until Kirk told me."

Natalie shot Ben one last angry look and then turned her attention to the young couple. She took Hope's hand and squeezed it gently. "Thank you, dear. You look beautiful. Now, Mr. Matthews, how did you know it was me?"

"No one is as clever as you, madam. You are always the best dressed at any affair."

"Very flattering, but I'd guess you probably heard someone call my name."

"You can blame the leak on our host. I could see it in his eyes. The look was a dead giveaway," Kirk teased, wiggling his eyebrows and elbowing Ben.

Ben angrily lifted the glass to his lips and drained it in one swallow. "Excuse me, please. I must see to some matters," he grumbled, then stomped off.

Natalie watched Ben retreat through narrowed eyes, shrugged her shoulders, and turned her attention back to the young couple. One thing was for sure; Ben Walters would not tell her what to do. She had to admit that meeting him in the study put an anxious tickle in her tummy. She most definitely looked forward to the time alone together.

A rage brewed within Ben. The belligerence Natalie had shown him when he asked her to meet him later was more than he could take tonight. Once again, she proved true to form. She was the most mule-headed, independent woman he had ever had the displeasure of knowing.

The mantel clock chimed eight, which, in turn, forced an audible groan from Ben. Why had he told Natalie at ten o'clock? This meant two hours of agonizing wait without guaranteeing she would even show. He knew he'd be driven mad by his apprehensions and anxieties if he didn't calm down and relax. It was tantamount to his well-being that he endure the next hours with a cordial demeanor for the sake of himself and his houseful of guests.

Ben moved to the drawing room doorway and let the melodious strings of Trout's violin soothe his inflamed senses. He watched the pairs of costumed guests glide around the room in time with the music, the rhythmic sway of their bodies lulling him into a calmer state.

A short while later, Ben caught sight of a shimmering gold gown wrapped in the arms of a red devil moving across the dance floor. A sharp pain pierced his heart when he noticed that due to the constraint of her narrow skirts, their dance was made up of small steps and undulating hip movements. Watching them was tortuous, so for survival's sake, he grabbed his coat and marched from the manse to join the gay crowd by the bonfire. Ben figured a bite of cold air would offer more appeal than the smarting atmosphere of the room.

*****

Hope could not recall a time in her life that had proved more exciting than this evening. She credited her good fortune to Natalie Wakefield, for without the dressmaker's talented costume creation, she felt certain she would never have attracted this wealth of attention. So many men had asked her to dance that it was impossible to keep all the names straight, apart from one very persistent partner, of course, and that was Kirk Matthews. She did not mind his diligence, though, for his lively conversation and handsome good looks afforded her the most enjoyable moments of the evening.

"At least five songs have played since I last danced with you," Kirk complained as he swept Hope around the dance floor.

Hope smiled and shrugged her shoulders in answer.

"I'm claiming the next *two* dances if anyone asks," Kirk tightened his grip around her waist. "Then, after the dances, I thought we might enjoy a drink and a bite to eat, and what's so funny?"

"You are very bossy," Hope teased.

"Assertive. I prefer to be called assertive. Bossy implies arrogance. Assertive is simply a sensible step to resolve the difficulty. I prefer assertive."

"I see," she answered with a delightful giggle.

"Follow me; I want to show you something," he said, pulling her from the dance floor.

"Where are we going?"

Kirk drew her through the manse and down a hallway into the narrow service area that linked the kitchen to the dining room. A lantern hung on the wall, casting a mellow light over the two built-in hutches flanking each side of the walls. The room was empty.

"In here," Kirk whispered, pushing her against the hutch.

Hope laid her hands on his chest. "In here? You certainly know Ben's house very well. What's in here?" she asked, with a flushed excitement covering her face.

"You and me," Kirk returned, pulling the black eye patch from his face.

"So... that's what you look like." Hope joked to cover up her nervousness.

When Kirk moved his face closer and kissed her lips, he felt her innocence and wanted no part of scaring her off with his practiced charm and well-seasoned ways. She was a girl worth learning to know, an enticing package of beauty and brains. One would not want to forget whose daughter she was either. Kirk surmised that Ben Walters would break him in two if he slipped up in any fashion with this fresh and charming young sprite.

Then to the couple's surprise, the kitchen door swung open, and Ben's voice filled the room.

"By damn! I cannot find peace anywhere!"

Kirk held a finger to his lips. They listened to Ben pace back and forth across the wooden kitchen floor and stopped to poke around in the fireplace.

"Arrrrrgggggghhhhh! Anything to kill the pain! Annnnnn-yyyyy-thiiiing!" Ben growled.

Kirk figured they had better high-tail it out of there before Ben discovered them. He was not interested in getting tangled up in his fury, for Kirk knew his friend well and realized that would be a most problematic scene.

#

Chapter Twenty-One

Natalie was escorted from the dance floor by her devilish ex-husband into a small assemblage of spirited young folks. Kirk Matthews was at the center of this group, telling tales of his recent travels, which had them laughing heartily. Hope was among this crowd, enjoying Kirk with much enthusiasm.

"You certainly look like you're having a grand time," Natalie said as she approached the beautiful garden nymph.

"Someone told me that my father throws the most successful gatherings in Philadelphia, and now I am truly convinced that he does."

"He does have the best parties, dear, and this ranks up there with one of the cleverest."

It was from the opposing side of the room that Olivia watched the group with scrutiny. It was exciting to see her daughter had thus far kept the avid attention of the young Matthews boy, yet on the other hand, Hope's interaction with Natalie and Jonathan Wakefield put a bitter spin on the scene, especially when Jonathan and Kirk asked for the hand of their opposite partner then escorted them to the dance floor. Kirk and Natalie's coupling was insignificant, but her daughter wrapped in the arms of the red devil was something far different. It made her nauseous.

Hope could not have looked more entertained, with her head thrown back in laughter, as Jonathan's ridiculous tail swung around in wild abandon, slapping the legs of nearby dancers. He was making an absolute spectacle of himself, and Olivia thought that if it weren't for his coordinated dance ability, the moment would have produced enormous embarrassment for Hope. But just like his exceptional vocal talents, his gift for dance and the lovely woman in his arms had captured everyone's attention. It nearly caused steam to emerge from Olivia's ears and nostrils.

She studied every detail of the man dancing with her daughter, from the sparkling diamond pinky ring down his red-clad frame. The costume's material clung faithfully to his body, which allowed a defined picture of the lean frame beneath. Olivia admitted that his good looks would make any woman swoon, yet she had learned long ago that good looks were good for nothing if a man did not have a nickel to his name.

"You're a wonderful dancer, Miss Dansbury," Jonathan commented, taking Hope into a sweeping turn.

"Thank you, sir, but a woman can only be as good as her lead. Perhaps it is you who deserves the compliment."

Jonathan flashed Hope a big toothy grin, which died a swift death when he spotted Olivia along the dance floor's perimeter, staring him down with a very unfavorable expression.

"Your mother doesn't look as if she's enjoying herself."

Hope searched the room for Olivia's whereabouts until she finally found her on the edge of the dance floor, staring at them with disapproval. Hope shrugged her shoulders. "Do not worry about Mother. I am not sure anything makes her happy."

Jonathan's eyebrows shot high. "Well, your father must certainly make her happy. According to my ex-wife, Ben Walters is one of the kindest and most generous individuals Natalie has ever met. She sings songs of praise about him every day. In fact, sometimes it is a little hard to take. But when I think about all he has done for Natalie over the years, I guess I can't expect any less from her. I mean, they were virtually a couple. Ah, that was, of course, before you and your mother arrived."

"Yes, Mr. Wakefield, and let us not forget before *you* arrived also," she adroitly added.

"True, true, but honestly, I do not think I had much to do with breaking up the lovebirds. That point goes to your mother."

Hope flinched at the dig. "Point? Is this a contest?"

"It is, Miss Dansbury. Unfortunately, the rules are unfair; the scales are tipped."

"You're not in love with Natalie, are you?"

Jonathan's eyebrows shot high. His lips turned up to form a wry smile. If he had underestimated her in any way before, he knew better than to repeat that mistake. "You are a bright young lady, Hope. It would be unwise to misjudge your ability to see through things."

Hope saw *through* things all right and overheard plenty. Like the other day when Ben told Max he had to convince Natalie of the huge mistake, she was about to make with her good-for-nothing ex-husband. Ben had fleshed out the details of how Jonathan frittered away the days doing absolutely nothing constructive and then feasted at Natalie's table at night after Natalie had put in a full day at her dress shop. Ben had finished his diatribe with how he had once loved those evenings when she invited him for dinner and how he had never taken it for granted and never expected her to go out of her way for him like that "Bastard" did. Hope felt certain that Ben's concern for Natalie was born from his still loving her; otherwise, why would Jonathan's actions even matter to him? It was all too clear. Natalie loved Ben, and she was sure Ben loved Natalie! She also had had about enough of her mother's conniving ways and felt convinced it was her job to turn things around.

"You know what, Mr. Wakefield? I believe it is time for me to even the odds."

"Anything I can do to help?" Jonathan asked, twisting the end of his thin mustache.

"Definitely. I believe you might be of great service."

***

Ben had arrived in the study thirty minutes before the appointed hour and had paced the room, nearly wearing a hole in the Oriental carpet. He knew not to expect Natalie before ten o'clock, if he should expect her at all. His early arrival meant he would suffer thirty minutes of solitary torture. Still, with everything considered, that pain would prove less than what he had endured circulating with the crowd, and this night offered no escape from discomfort. He would turn one way and catch Natalie enjoying herself in her ex-husband's company or the other way to witness every eligible man in the room fighting for his daughter's attention. Being so unstrung at a fun event in *his* home was completely unjust.

When the mantel clock finally chimed ten, he stopped and listened, but he heard no sound in the hallway or from the door latch. There was only a painstaking silence that surrounded him. He should have known Natalie would defy his order. And what if she didn't show? What would be his next plan of attack? Would he go into the crowd and quietly remind her of their meeting, or would he storm into the room unconcerned about what anyone thought and drag her back into the study? His gut twisted in agony.

"Where the hell is she!" he spat, swirling the remaining bourbon in his glass.

***

Natalie and Jonathan stood head-to-head in the corner of the room. They had decided that in approximately five minutes, Jonathan would walk to the small group and request a dance from Olivia. At that point, Natalie would move to the study to meet with Ben.

"O.K., Jonathan, but honestly, I'd like to tell him to take his orders and stuff them where the sun doesn't shine!" Natalie grumbled.

"Now, why are you acting like that, honey? Here is a perfect opportunity to be alone with your man, and you're throwing up resistance. If you want my opinion, you better make your move. There may not be too many more chances."

"What do you think he wants, Jonathan?"

Jonathan knew by instinct what Ben Walters wanted. He saw the desire that stole from the man's eyes every time he looked at Natalie.

"I do not know, honey, but whatever you do, please force him into final decisions. It is sad to see how much this has worn on you. The time has come to either end the frustration or begin the happiness."

Her head dropped. The hair of the black wig swung forward to hide her face from Jonathan's view. "It is probably the end for me." Her voice was barely above a whisper.

Jonathan lifted her chin until their gaze met. "Just remember this, honey, you will always have me. I never stopped loving you."

His confession made her feel warm inside. She held feelings of love for him too, but those feelings were far different from the ones she held for Ben Walters. They were more like the good feeling one got when sliding into a comfortable pair of slippers. His irresponsibility allowed her to think no more of him than she would a child. Though looking into his sincere face, Natalie was touched by his words.

"You are a wonderful friend, Jonathan. How many men would go along with this silly game and be such a good sport about it too? Thank you."

Jonathan knew by how she phrased it that he had no chance with her. She had changed her mind about him a long time ago. He had zero probability he would gain her favor. She was in love with Ben Walters and, for the first time since he arrived in Philadelphia, he admitted how much that hurt.

Jonathan glanced at the clock: ten o'clock, the reckoning hour. Olivia was with a group of guests at the edge of the dance floor. The setting was perfect.

"It's time," he pointed out.

"All right. Wish me luck, Jonathan." And with shaking limbs, Natalie moved toward the study doors.

***

Alone in the hall, Natalie could barely summon the courage to open the door to Ben's study. It felt like a walk to the guillotine, a final farewell. What did Ben have to tell her about Jonathan that could be so important, and why did he need her alone to say these things anyway? Her intuition told her that this meeting had everything to do with talking her out of reuniting with Jonathan and nothing to do with changing his future with Olivia.

"We've been good friends over these years, and I am only looking out for your well-being," he'd begin. If he married Olivia, as he had told her he planned, Natalie knew she could never sustain a casual friendship with him anymore. She was unsure she could remain in Philadelphia and witness him living life's best moments with another woman.

She glanced at the tall standing clock. It showed seven minutes after the hour. Natalie's hand dropped to the door latch and froze. Her heart picked up a faster pace. She turned around and caught her reflection in the large hall mirror. A stranger's face stared back at her. Gone was the strength in her stance, the spunky sparkle in her eyes. She looked drained from all hope and happiness. Why hadn't she applied more pressure in their relationship over the past two years? Why had she waited so long to goad him into that first kiss? She knew if she were given another chance, it would not be a simple nudge and bump here and there as before. If Ben ever hinted that he wanted her in his life, she would pour on the heat full blast. After all, that is what Olivia had done, and look where it got her.

Finally, Natalie pressed down on the latch and pushed the door open. A stream of light shot into the darkened area from the hallway. Quickly, she stepped into the room and closed the door behind her. It took a moment for her eyes to adjust to the meager light offered by the fireplace.

He was there.

She felt his presence.

\#

Chapter Twenty-Two

"Hello, Natalie."

Ben's deep voice drifted from across the room, stirring the butterflies in her stomach. When her eyes adjusted to the dim light, she saw that he stood behind a high-backed chair near the fireplace with a cut-glass tumbler. She uttered no reply, though her heart picked up a nervous pace as she watched him lay the item on the table and move toward her.

"Would you care to have a seat?" he offered. It is warmer by the fire."

"I'm quite comfortable where I am, thank you," she answered. "I have left Jonathan on the dance floor in the arms of Olivia. Perhaps we should make this brief.

Natalie had no idea where those words came from. Her nerves were frayed.

Ben's eyebrows drew together, forming a disconcerting expression on his face. "Your ex-husband's principles do lack greatly. No telling what he would do in a room full of people."

"You know very little about his principles, Mr. Walters," she snapped. "You've been rude to him from the very first day you met him, while Jonathan has displayed nothing less than complete courtesy to you, to Hope and your . . . your . . ."

He stood before her now with his arms at his side, fingers spread wide, and palms forward. "My what?"

"O-li-vi-a," she silently mouthed, looking at him dead on while exaggerating every syllable of her name.

"This isn't about O-li-vi-a," he returned, mimicking her actions. "It is about that jackass ex-husband of yours. Can't you see he is trifling with your emotions to get what he wants? There is nothing solid about him. He is nothing but a self-serving bastard, a drifter, a gambler, and a roving philanderer, who makes the most out of a good situation! Don't be stupid, Natalie." His voice rose with each word.

Natalie's chin jerked upward as she stepped around him and glared at him over her shoulder. "Watch whom you call STUPID, Mr. Walters. It is much like the cast iron pot calling the kettle black, don't you think? What do you think Mrs. Dansbury's motives are, anyway? Think about it. She left you high and dry seventeen years ago because another man offered her more than you could. Now he is dead, and she surprisingly finds her way back to Philadelphia to discover that you've made out quite well in life. Suddenly you are good enough! Now she thinks marriage to you might work out fine. Talk about self-serving. Really, Ben, I believe you might be the STUPID one."

Ben offered no comeback. She was right. He ran his hand through his hair and lowered it to rub the back of his neck. "Listen," he finally groaned, "I didn't call you in here to argue, Natalie."

But she had worked up a fairly good lather and wasn't willing to shut it down yet. "So then tell me, why *did* you ask me here, Ben? Perhaps we should address the subject before we are found out. We would not want anyone's pretty little nose to get out of joint, now, would we?"

"I don't give a damn about anybody else," Ben stated with raw honesty. He took hold of her bare upper arms and pulled her close. "This whole thing is about us," he stated in abject misery, then kissed her with unyielding pressure. He wanted no more talking, arguing, or reasoning and justifying. He only wanted to feel the heat of their two bodies close and her surrender.

When he sensed no resistance in her body, he walked her backward until they reached the wall, grinding his pelvis into hers until she groaned with pleasure. The bourbon had broken down his boundaries and given him the courage to do what he had denied himself for so long. Desire swelled when he felt her warmth and willingness. His tongue pushed through her closed lips, touching, probing, seeking and wanting while his fingers softly stroked the silky material of her gown. Ben's world careened. He finally admitted that he loved her, yet scars from his jilted love with Olivia had kept him at arm's length. It took Olivia's return for him to realize that Natalie was everything he had always wanted in a mate, and now he feared it was too late to turn things in his favor.

Then somewhere in the roaring thunder of the moment, Ben heard the door creak open, startling him back to reality. He pulled away from their embrace and instinctively pushed Natalie behind him.

"Father, are you in here?" It was Hope, standing in the door frame backlit by the hall. The shadows hid her facial features.

"I'm right here," he admitted, his voice thick and husky.

"I have been looking for you, and I'm so sorry, Father. I thought you were alone." Hope reached for the door latch.

"Hope it's all right," Ben called out.

"Don't be sorry, dear," Natalie added, stepping from behind Ben. "It is your father and I who are sorry. This has become a complex and sensitive matter between all of us."

Hope looked over her shoulder as if to answer, yet no words came forth. She closed the door behind her, leaving Natalie and Ben with many miserable knots in their stomach.

***

Olivia had managed to ferret out the wealthier guests or what she selected as the *"Important People of Philadelphia"* earlier in the evening and had engaged herself in their circles. One group entertained her for most of the evening with lively conversation about the social highlights of Philadelphia and the surrounding area. So interesting was the conversation that she had lost complete track of time and had never noticed Ben's prolonged absence. That was until she saw him at the entrance of his study, handing Natalie's cloak to Jonathan Wakefield. She was shocked that the Wakefields were departing so early in the evening after both had gone to such extremes with their costuming. The prizes had not yet been awarded, and surely, they knew their costumes were in the running. In addition, she wondered why they were in Ben's study since she specifically recalled Max locking the door to this room before the party. She could not understand why Ben would allow Jonathan, of all people, access to his private space. Her curiosity was piqued.

Just then, the Wakefields emerged from the study with their outerwear in place and moved toward the front portal, where Ben awaited their departure. She excused herself from her gathering and moved toward the group, but by the time she reached the door, Jonathan and Natalie had already boarded their conveyance for their ride back to Philadelphia.

"Hello, darling," Olivia greeted when she reached Ben's side. "I have been looking for you for almost an hour. Where have you been?"

"With an old friend," he answered, his grim stare fastened on the departing coach.

"I see. Well, it must have been quite a lengthy conversation," she clipped, eyeing the departing coach with disdain.

***

After Jonathan delivered Natalie safely to her doorstep, he stabled the rig and steed, then hurried back to the *Steven Matthews* to change his clothes. Hastily he donned his dark suit and brocade vest, then trod a path to *Duffy's Tavern*. The remainder of the night would not be wasted in a hotel room alone. In his opinion, the evening was still young, and there was money to be won! After all, who knew what coffers could be gained from a room full of half-drunken tars at this hour?

It wasn't long after Jonathan entered the dockside tavern that the men he had joined on a previous night called out for him to join their table again. He readily accepted their invitation, hoping to win back his losses plus some. In doing so, he failed to notice the three unsavory characters eyeing him from the table in the dark corner of the room. They were thugs who traveled from seaport city to seaport city, making their way by unloading cargo from the merchant ships. Wise men steered clear of this sort, knowing there was no level too low to stoop and nothing too horrific for them to carry out.

It was unfortunate on this night that Jonathan paid little attention to his dangerous surroundings. He was unaware how the slovenly group had eyed his dapper dress and diamond pinky ring immediately after he had entered the room and targeted him as their next prey.

Carefully the miscreants watched from their dark corner of the room, biding the moment they could make their move.

Three hours later, after Jonathan had won a sizeable booty, he called it quits and took his leave for the comfort of his bed. Upon leaving any establishment at this late hour, Jonathan always habitually slipped his hand in his coat pocket and wrapped his fingers around the handle of a small dagger he used for protection. The streets were deserted and quiet. He was always leery of the shadows, so he kept to the lighted pathways and picked up a brisk pace to safely reach the comfort of his room at the *Steven Matthews* without incident. He felt fatigued, for the entire week had held a grueling schedule with long, eventful days in preparation for the party and stressful nights at the card table. With the coin he had won here in Philadelphia and especially at the table tonight, he finally felt a few good nights' rests had been earned and looked forward to slumber.

Unfortunately, exhaustion led to poor decisions.

Ahead he saw the dark alley that cut over to Market Street, and the dark shortcut lured him into making a foolish choice. Jonathan looked over his shoulder, and when he detected no one in sight nor sounds forthcoming from any direction, he ducked into the alley at a brisk run, never noticing the large stone that jutted out from the earth at a precarious angle. It caught the toe of his shoe, throwing him off balance and down on his hands and knees.

Before he could regain footing, the thugs appeared out of thin air and were upon him. Two men held his arms while the other threw a series of punches into Jonathan's midsection, robbing his breath. When one thrust an uppercut to Jonathan's chin, the leather pouch holding his winnings flew from his brocade vest and dropped to the ground, spilling coins everywhere. One ruffian scrambled to gather the treasure while another pulled at the diamond ring on his pinky finger. Jonathan slumped forward just as the third man swung his booted foot, hitting Jonathan square in the forehead and one of his ribs. A gush of blood rushed from his nose, and he crumbled to the ground with unbearable pain.

Then a voice boomed into the darkness, startling the gang.

"What goes here?"

The streetlight silhouetted Ben Walters' hulking frame at the far end of the alley. He stood with his legs braced apart and a pistol in his right hand pointed up into the night sky. The ruffians grabbed what they could at his threatening tone and scrambled in different directions.

"Stop, I say, or your asses are mine!" Ben warned as he ran toward the melee.

The robbers never broke stride even when the lead shot from Ben's gun hit flesh. An agonizing cry was heard, yet the thugs kept their mad pace, disappearing into the darkness.

Ben hustled to the body lying face down in the alley. Even from the back, he recognized the man, his fancy clothes a dead giveaway.

"Wakefield," he ground out, turning him over. His face was a bloody pulp and swollen beyond recognition. "By damn," Ben mumbled.

He pulled Jonathan into a seated position and noticed a shiny glimmer in the cobblestones. It was Jonathan's diamond pinky ring.

"Well, they didn't get your ring, pretty boy," he said, sliding the piece into his pocket.

Ben swore that the gambler was the luckiest fool ever walking the earth. Jonathan could very well be dead now if he had not returned

Olivia and Hope to their hotel room after his party. Luckily, Ben had heard the scuffle in the alley when he left the hotel.

Ben managed to pull Jonathan's long-form to his feet. He hefted his bulk across his shoulder, carried him to the side of the building, lowered him to the cobblestones, and ran for his carriage at the end of the alley. Ben returned with the conveyance, loaded the dead weight, then quickly boarded and slapped the reins on the team and headed for help.

#

Chapter Twenty-Three

Natalie could not sleep. She had been lying in bed for hours since Jonathan returned her from Ben's party, tortured with the memory of Hope's untimely intrusion. If only the young girl would have said something or reacted in some way when she realized that Ben and she had been sharing an intimate moment. But the silence was all Hope had offered, which hurt more than anything she could have uttered.

Natalie heard the hall clock chime three times, and that is when she decided she had had enough of this torture chamber. One never knew how long the night was until they could not sleep. Her body felt sore from tossing and turning, and her head ached from the steady bombardment of ugly thoughts. She had to find relief. She slipped out of bed, wrapped herself in a dressing gown and went to the kitchen for a glass of warm milk. She hoped it would calm her nerves and encourage sleep.

Natalie lit the oil lamp by the table. A chill filled the room, so she reached for a chunk of wood and threw it atop the remaining embers in the stove. The snap and pop of the wood, as it caught fire from the bed of coals, was the only sound that filled the room. Then a knock sounded on the kitchen door, startling her so much that she nearly dropped the glass she retrieved from the sideboard. For a split second, her heart raced until she rationalized that it was probably Jonathan. He had most likely noticed her light burning and decided to drop in on his way back from some unsavory dive. After all, he had always felt free to visit no matter what hour of the day . . . or night.

She pulled back the curtain to make sure she was correct in her assumption and was shocked to see that her intruder was not Jonathan but Ben, with his arm propped up against her door jamb. She pulled her robe tight and yanked open the portal.

"My goodness, Ben," she whispered. "Please, come in."

Ben moved inside at her request, then turned and faced her with a grim expression on his face. She noticed blood on his coat, and it scared her.

Panic rose.

"Sit down, Natalie. I have some bad news."

She took a small step toward him and placed her hand on his forearm. "What happened?

"I'm here because of Wakefield."

"What is this? Were you fighting?"

"No. It's quite the opposite. Let me pour you some brandy." Ben walked over to the corner hutch and removed a cut glass decanter from the shelf. He poured both of them a healthy snifter of the amber liquid and then sat across from her at the table.

"Drink this," he insisted. Ben downed his in one swallow while Natalie sat quietly and never lifted the glass to her lips.

"Jonathan is with the doctor," he began after a moment's silence. "I had taken Olivia and Hope back to the hotel after the party and was on my way home when I came across a gang beating the ever-living hell out of him. They robbed him and would have left him for dead had it not been for my timely interruption."

Natalie lost all color in her face. "Oh, Ben," she responded in a weak voice.

"His ribs and nose are broken, and he's got a sizeable laceration on his chin," Ben continued.

Natalie dropped her head to the tabletop while the most painful sound Ben had ever heard choked from her throat.

"He's going to be all right, Natalie," Ben consoled, reaching across the table for her hand. She was taking the news much harder than he expected.

Finally, she lifted her head and moved woodenly to the door. "Thank you for all you've done," she murmured, never looking up.

Ben moved next to her and lifted her chin. "I will return in the morning. Everything will be all right, Natalie. Jonathan will heal."

Natalie nodded; her eyes were filled with sadness. "Thank you, Ben."

He wanted to take her into his arms and soothe her pain, but she had thrown a wall between them. Ben felt everything spiraling downward, and it scared the hell out of him.

***

At seven o'clock Sunday morning, Natalie left the confines of her home and walked to the doctor's office. Her hair was styled on top of her head in a tight knot, emphasizing the dark circles under her eyes from lack of sleep the night before. She wore a dark brown cloak and gown, a diverse look from her usual bright colors. The ensemble proved to extenuate her fatigue and unhappiness and erase any signs of the feisty and vivacious woman many loved. When she reached her destination, Natalie knocked on the side entrance, whereas only seconds later, Sally Finley, the doctor's wife, appeared and swung the door wide.

"Good morning, Natalie. You are certainly bright and early this morning, but I expected you under these circumstances. Please, come in."

"How is Jonathan this morning, Sally?" Natalie inquired immediately.

"He is sleeping. Harold has given him something for pain. He has been quite uncomfortable."

"May I see him?"

"Absolutely. Follow me." She led Natalie down a short corridor and into Jonathan's sleeping room. "He is resting at last. There is a chair if you care to wait," she quietly offered.

"Thank you," Natalie whispered, unable to take her gaze from Jonathan's mutilated face.

Natalie's tears poured forth. Jonathan's handsome face was nearly unrecognizable. The bridge of his nose was swollen. Dark purple and blue shaded underneath each eye while dried blood surrounded a large bandage covering his whiskered jaw. His clothing had been removed, and a clean white sheet covered him to the waist. His chest was swathed mummy-style in white bandages.

She lowered herself into the chair, never taking her gaze from him and waited for him to awaken.

***

As Ben expected, Natalie was not in her pew on Sunday morning. The knowledge that she most likely stood over Jonathan's injured body, offering him loving concern, stabbed Ben with an unholy anger. It further rankled him, knowing she had most likely insisted on nursing him back to full health once he was well enough to leave the doctor's house. Ben recalled how Natalie had generously offered her assistance to him after he had been injured in his barn fire a few years back, and like an idiot, he had rejected her offer, treating her like she was a big pain in the ass. Every time he looked back on it, he wanted to kick himself. If that opportunity ever presented itself again, he knew he'd play sick until the cows came home just to feel her hand on his forehead or anywhere else he could encourage her to touch him. The worst part was that her slimy ex-husband was not as foolish, and he'd most likely take advantage of her goodness and milk her generosity until he wove his way back into her life.

Ben had waited until Olivia and he were on the way home from church before he told her of last night's escapades. She reacted little to Ben's story, only resentment when he mentioned that he wanted to check on the man today.

"We have dinner arrangements at the Scofield's, darling. I hope you will not put your visit with Jonathan Wakefield before our friend's invitation. After all, Ben has led a reckless life and has been asking for this."

Ben did not comment. It was all too absurd.

***

The first thing Jonathan saw when his eyes opened from his rest was Natalie standing over him with a look of great concern. He didn't know how long she had been there or how long she had been holding his hand, but he felt the gentle squeeze of her fingers as soon as their gaze met.

The gesture nearly broke him down. She was so undeserving of all this trouble. It was not supposed to end like this. On the first day of his arrival in Philadelphia, he had promised himself that the deal he would strike with her would benefit her more than it would himself. He had promised himself that this time he would not let her down. Though lying in this bed, with the memory of last night's escapades, he realized he had failed her miserably once again.

"I'm sorry, honey," he softly muttered.

"Please don't say that, Jonathan. There is nothing to be sorry about. It is only important that you take your time and heal. When you feel stronger in a few days, you will move into my place so that I can closely monitor you and see to your needs."

Jonathan noticed as she spoke that her eyes filled up with tears.

"Hey, don't do this to yourself, honey. Now why are you crying?"

"Be-because you cou-could have been killed if Ben had not come along. Oh, Jonathan." The tears rolled freely down her cheeks.

Jonathan did not know what had happened past a meaty fist, a heavy boot and a lot of pain and darkness. Though he had experienced his share of barroom scuffles in his life, he felt sure that this time could have been his end had someone not come to his aid.

"Ben Walters? Did he help me?" he questioned.

"Yes, Jonathan, he did. He had just dropped Olivia off at the hotel and was going out of town when he came upon the men beating and robbing you. He shot one of them, but they all escaped."

"I see," he answered in a weak voice. "He is a good man. Yep, he is a good man."

The conversation proved too much for his weakened state. Exhaustion overtook him, and he fell back into a deep sleep. Natalie laid his hand on the mattress and returned to the chair by the window. Within minutes, she had succumbed to sleep also. The previous night's activities had taken its toll on everyone.

Natalie awoke sometime later to the murmur of male voices in the hall. It was Ben and Doc Finley discussing Jonathan's condition. She sat up straight and waited for them to enter the room.

"Miss Wakefield has been with him since the early morning hours. You may go in if you would like," she heard the doctor offer.

"Thanks, Doc, I think I will," Ben answered in a low tone. He entered the room, immediately focusing on Natalie, who looked incredibly tired and sad.

"Good morning," he whispered as soon as their gaze met.

"Good morning, Ben."

Ben glanced down at Jonathan's bruised and bristly form lying in a cloud of white sheets and felt a stab of jealousy that Natalie had been watching over his half-clothed form with such loving concern. In Ben's opinion, the gambler had done nothing to deserve this concern and attention from her.

"How is the patient?" He gestured toward the bed with a tilt of his head.

"Weak. He has gone through a lot."

"And how are you this morning?" Ben lifted her chin to look into her eyes. He saw they were filled with pain.

"I'm fine."

Ben pulled her from the chair and into his arms. "Life used to be so easy," he breathed into her hair.

"Life might have been easy for you, Ben, but it has always been an uphill battle for me."

He rubbed his hand soothingly up and down her backbone, detecting a tremor inside her. "You're a strong woman, Natalie."

"We all have our breaking point, Ben."

Ben glanced over at the bed and saw that Jonathan had at some time awakened and was taking in the whole scene.

By damn, I should have let him rot in the streets, Ben thought. *But no, I had to lug his carcass to the doctor's and save his pitiful life.*

"He is going to be fine, Natalie. Only the good die young," he coldly stated, glaring back at the smiling patient.

Natalie then pulled away from Ben's hold, detecting a change in his demeanor. She saw Jonathan had awakened and was smiling. She moved to the bedside.

"Oh, Jonathan, did we disturb you?" she asked with deep concern as she took hold of his hand.

Ben's body stiffened.

"No, certainly not. It is wonderful to arouse so many concerned friends. I am a lucky man," Jonathan answered with a toothy grin that forced his swollen eyes into tiny slits.

The gambler's comment brought a happy glow to Natalie's face while resentment swelled inside Ben. The mere idea that this fool had made her smile after he had caused so much pain gave Ben a strong desire to throw a pillow over his face and snuff the air from his lungs.

Doc Finley stuck his head in the room just then to ask Natalie if she would please step into the hall.

"Yes, certainly, I'll be right out," she agreed before returning to the men. "I'll be right outside if you need me."

"You go right ahead, honey. I have Ben here to help me if I need anything," Jonathan answered, flashing a toothy smile that forced his bruised and swollen face into an outrageous sight.

Amazed at Jonathan's continued audacity, Ben stood over him with furrowed brow and arms crossed over his chest, completely speechless.

As soon as Natalie departed, Jonathan clarified to Ben that he had something important to say. No sign of the smiling, lighthearted patient existed when Natalie was in the room. Seriousness had befallen him.

"I hear I owe you my life, Ben. Natalie painted the details of what happened last night, and it seems I am in your debt."

Ben stared down coldly at his pathetic appearance, angry that this good-for-nothing bastard, who got Natalie's attention and pity, had delivered nothing but trouble to her doorstep. He was not interested in his thank you. He was not ready to accept anything from him.

"You do not owe me anything, Wakefield. I am simply here to warn you of one thing. If I ever catch you treating Natalie badly ever again, I will kill you with my bare hands, and that's a promise."

Not trusting himself a moment longer, Ben stormed from the room, brushed past Natalie and the doctor in the hall and let the door slam behind him.

#

Chapter Twenty-Four

Jonathan had spent four days at Doc Finley's before he moved into Natalie's place. Upon his arrival, she insisted that he enjoy her comfortable bed until he fully recovered, no matter how long that took. Each morning she gave him a shave followed by a hot breakfast and a copy of the *Daily Advertiser*. Lunch was served at twelve noon, dinner at six p.m. and one of Natalie's sweet desserts and black coffee at eight. It was a life any man would find hard to resist unless you were Jonathan Wakefield. He preferred a smoky tavern, boisterous laughter, and a lively card game to quiet domesticity at Natalie's place. Simply put, life in this room felt like a veritable prison.

Jonathan reached for the hand mirror on the nightstand. He stared once again at his reflection. His skin color had undergone many changes; first black, then blue, green, and finally a sickly shade of yellow. His nose was still slightly swollen, though the laceration was barely noticeable. The only area where pain remained was in his rib cage, which hurt like hell with each move and breath he took. The doctor told him it would take some time before the ribs healed completely, and until then, he was to keep the cloth wrapped tightly around the trunk of his body so he could move around with minimal discomfort. He knew it was not long before he'd be back to normal. Full recovery was just around the corner.

Jonathan wished he felt as optimistic as Natalie's progress was concerned. Her demeanor showed every sign of defeat. She had not uttered Ben's name since that day when they were all together at the doctor's office nearly a fortnight ago. She no longer attended church services; the worst part was that the sparkle was gone from her eyes.

He decided today was the day he would change that, starting with her unneeded attention.

"Good morning, Jonathan," Natalie greeted as she entered the bedroom moments later with a towel over her shoulder and the water basin in her hands. "How did you sleep last night?" She laid the basin on the nightstand and then dipped a cloth in the warm water.

"Very well, honey, thanks to your wonderful care. In fact, I feel so much better that I thought I would shave myself this morning. I believe I have taken advantage of your good nature long enough. No reason to get dependent on this."

Natalie frowned. She wrung out the cloth. "But Jonathan, you are not well enough. Your ribs are still sore. You said so yourself. Please let me help you. Really, it is no bother." She pushed him back into the pillows and quickly laid the warm cloth across his face before he could protest. "Doesn't that feel wonderful?"

He nodded, realizing this might not be all that easy.

"Hope Dansbury stopped by the other day and asked about you," she reported as she slathered soap on his whiskers. "She told me I should let her know when you feel ready to receive guests."

Jonathan chuckled through the suds. "Receive guests? She makes me feel like the President. I have been ready for guests since I left the doc's house."

Natalie applied the blade to his face and scraped a smooth line along his jawbone. "I didn't know if you felt up to the Dansburys."

"They don't bother me." Their gaze met, and Jonathan saw that Natalie's eyebrow was raised in question. "At least Hope doesn't," he added. I would love for her to drop by."

"I'll tell her you said so," Natalie replied.

A silence fell between them. Jonathan studied her face as she concentrated on the job at hand, noticing once again the absence of her usual joy and sparkle. He had to get her back on track if it was the last thing he did. "Speaking of guests, have you heard from Ben?"

His question hit the mark. Her hand jerked at the mention of Ben's name, drawing a bead of blood along Jonathan's jawbone.

"I cut you! I am so sorry," she apologized as she pressed the towel to his skin.

"So, are you giving up?" he remarked.

"Of course not, Jonathan, I will finish. I certainly would never leave you half-shaven," she answered indignantly. Natalie turned from him and wrung out the soiled towel in the basin.

"I didn't mean my shave, and you know it."

She never looked over at him.

Jonathan grabbed the towel from her hands and wiped the remaining soap from his face. "Because Hope walked in on you and Ben? Is that why you are giving up?"

"That is certainly one reason."

"You have *more* than one reason?"

"Yes! Estelle Wilcox tells me things."

Jonathan knew that was a lie. Natalie never put any stock in the simplest thing Estelle Wilcox said, let alone something as significant as this.

"I know you better than that, honey. She has no credibility, and you have never believed anything she told you."

"Well, even if Estelle hadn't told me anything, I know now that things would have never worked out with Ben and me. I am a homewrecker, Jonathan. You should have seen the look on Hope's face when she caught us together," she stated with a quavering voice.

Jonathan could not imagine Hope carrying disdain or anger for Natalie or Ben. She was likely embarrassed and uncomfortable because she had walked in on their intimate moment.

"Do you think Hope would have come to your place if she had been angry?"

"She is a very caring child, Jonathan. I am sure she was concerned for your well-being," Natalie reasoned.

"And she didn't speak about anything else?"

"Well, yes," Natalie answered barely above a whisper.

"About what, Natalie? About Ben, her mother, the gowns you are making her?"

"No." Natalie stared down at her feet.

"No? Come on, honey, talk to me. What did she say to you?" Jonathan lifted her chin and looked directly into her eyes.

"She talked about the party and how much fun she had. She claimed it was all because of the costume I had made her, and she wanted to thank me."

Jonathan smiled. "I guess you see that as polite conversation?"

"Yes, she is a very mannerly young lady. I do not want to upset her life."

Just then, the shop bell rang. Natalie pulled her head away from his touch. "Excuse me, Jonathan. I must see my customer. I will check on you later."

"Sure, honey. Oh, by the way, if you happen to see Hope, please tell her that I am *receiving* guests now."

Natalie rolled her eyes and was gone.

As soon as Natalie left the room, Jonathan left the bed and pulled a clean suit of clothes from the armoire. He had had enough rest and recovery. It was time to get back to work.

Moments later, he stood before the mirror, tying his cravat into a neat bow. Jonathan admitted he looked good except for a telltale yellow tinge beneath his eyes and a slightly swollen nose. He had kept the tight binding around his chest for support, and surprisingly it was quite undetectable under his vest and coat. The noticeable missing item was his diamond pinky ring. He rubbed the empty digit with sad regret. The money stolen from him was insignificant, for he knew it could always be won back on another night, but the ring was another matter. It represented the life he once shared with an extraordinary woman, a woman he realized he would never have a chance with again in his life.

Jonathan brushed the sides of his hair, pulled at his cuffs, and stepped from the room. He heard female voices chattering in the shop, so he exited through the kitchen door as quietly as possible.

***

Ben had not seen Natalie since the morning after Jonathan's mishap. This past Sunday after church services, Estelle Wilcox had filled him in on every detail of Natalie's life since then. Ben did not need to hear the ugly details, but there was absolutely no stopping Estelle. She chattered non-stop about Natalie's diligent efforts to assist with Jonathan's full and rapid recovery and how lucky Natalie was, having her handsome ex-husband sequestered in her home and all to herself.

"If Natalie had a brain in her head, she would work on making him a permanent part of her life. After all, she has done it all by herself for so long. She needs a man! Don't you agree, Ben?"

Ben nearly broke his teeth to bite back his words. He offered a tolerant smile and bid the woman good day.

On Wednesday morning, Ben decided a ride into the city was necessary. He needed to find out what he could about Natalie and her good-for-nothing ex-husband. By the time he reached her street, he had still not formulated a solid reason to knock on her door, so instead, he had pulled up to the clockmaker's door across the street from her shop in hopes that she would see him and invite him over for a cup of coffee. After killing fifteen minutes inside the clockmaker's shop and another ten on his wagon seat with no sign of Natalie, he was at wits end on what to do.

"He looks terribly cold, Miss Wakefield. Don't you think you should invite him for a hot drink?" Mary suggested as she studied Mr. Walters shivering from sitting in his wagon across the street.

"This place is not a public dining room. I am a couturiere. I design and make gowns, not hot drinks for simpletons who cannot escape the cold!" she screamed with maddening force.

"I believe something is wrong. Aren't you concerned?" Mary pressed on.

"No!" And with that, Natalie stormed back to her private quarters.

Mary felt greatly troubled. Clearly, both her employer and Mr. Walters were out of sorts. She grabbed her cloak and stepped outside.

Ben's head shot up immediately when he heard the shop door open.

"Good day, Mr. Walters," Mary greeted.

"Oh, hello, Mary."

She heard the disappointment in his voice, for she knew he had hoped for Miss Wakefield instead.

"It's quite brisk today."

"Brisk. Indeed," he returned, rubbing his gloved hands together. "Is Natalie in today?"

"Why yes, she is, sir."

"Is she busy?"

"She has just walked back to her apartment. I can get her for you if you would like to step inside."

Probably waiting on that lazy gambler's hand and foot, he thought disparagingly.

Then quite unexpectantly, the front door burst open, and Natalie ran out in a panic. "Mary! I can't find Jonathan! He is gone!"

Mary's eyes darted from Mr. Walters to her employer and then back to Mr. Walters.

"He has been improving quite well, you know, Miss Wakefield. Perhaps he has gone for a walk."

Natalie gazed down the sidewalk, and that is when she remembered Ben had been parked out front. She turned and faced him.

Mary looked back and forth from one to the other. She saw Mr. Walters's hurt and the uncertainty in Miss Wakefield's eyes. The awkwardness was palpable and forced Mary to retreat inside.

"Hello, Natalie," Ben softly greeted when they were finally alone.

Natalie's lips formed a hello, though no sound came forth.

"I hoped to see you today," he said, struggling for conversation. "We should talk."

Natalie nodded, her arms hugging her body to stay warm.

"I haven't seen you in church lately," he continued.

"My schedule has been quite full nursing Jonathan back to health."

"Yes, I'm sure." The mere mention of the gambler's name furrowed Ben's brow. "How's the dressing platform working out?" He was running out of small talk.

"It is perfect. Thank you again, Ben."

"Well. . . I don't want to detain you. If I can help you with anything, do not hesitate to ask."

"Thank you, Ben. I appreciate that."

"Then I guess I will let you get back to work. I hope to speak with you soon, Natalie."

Natalie nodded, stepped back into the warmth of the shop and closed the door. As soon as he pulled away, she hung her head and wept.

***

Hope had been struggling for some time with her participation in Olivia's plan to land Ben Walters. In the beginning, she was receptive to the idea, thinking how great it would finally feel to be free of her mother's control. Olivia had promised Hope two years abroad if she agreed to convince Ben Walters that she was his daughter. Nothing sounded better than that at the time, though now, after meeting Ben and experiencing his goodness and love, she realized that her own personal freedom was not nearly as important as Ben's happiness. She had never met anyone like him. He had given her a glorious view of goodness and honesty. Ben had made her believe in herself, exposing inner strengths she had never realized she possessed. He taught her the true meaning of love.

In sharp contrast, Hope understood that her feelings for Olivia and Andrew over these years were not love but a sense of duty. Although they had given her every possible creature comfort, Olivia had also coupled that with frequent reminders that without them, she would have suffered an orphan's life, belonged to no one, and had nothing. And Hope had always been thankful for the life they had given her and exhibited that with respect and obedience for everything they expected of her. . . until now. Her love for Ben far outweighed any duty-bound pressure she felt for Olivia. She had to tell Ben the truth about her parentage. He was not in love with Olivia and was NOT her father, two excellent reasons not to marry Olivia. He was in love with

Natalie Wakefield, and Hope could not let him make a mistake that would alter his life forever.

She would start today and begin with a visit with Jonathan Wakefield.

#

Chapter Twenty-Five

As luck would have it, Hope stepped from her hotel room when Jonathan moved into the hall. Both were taken by surprise.

"Hope!"

"Hello! I certainly did not expect to see you here at the hotel. In fact, I was just on my way over to Miss Wakefield's to see if you were feeling up to a visitor today."

Jonathan smiled. "You are made of such good intentions, such thoughtful and caring ways, my dear. I am honored that you would take the time to think of me from your day. Except for this slightly misaligned nose and some remaining yellow skin, I am no worse for the wear and feel much improved, indeed. Thank you for your concern."

"Many of us were worried for your well-being. It is good to see you in such fine form."

Jonathan smiled.

"Sir, I have a matter of great importance that I would like to discuss with you. Would you have a moment to spare today?"

"Absolutely, Hope; in fact, I am available right now. Perhaps we could enjoy a cup of tea in the hotel's dining room?"

"I fear my discussion needs more privacy than what the dining room offers. Could we take a coach and ride a while?" Hope asked, noticing surprise in his expression.

"Absolutely; I'll summon a coach to the front of the hotel and wait for you on board."

In the ensuing hour, as they rode through Philadelphia within the confines of the hired coach, Hope divulged every detail of Olivia's devious scheme. She expressed her regret for participating thus far in Olivia's dishonorable act and her need to correct her wrongdoing and set things back on the right track.

"I do not want to see Ben make the wrong choice. Olivia is not the woman he loves, and if I don't stop this whole mess, I know he'll marry her. I could not live with that."

"You know, Natalie and I are not in love with each other either," Jonathan admitted.

"I hoped it wasn't for real. Although, I must admit you both play a good part."

Jonathan held up his hand, palm facing Hope, fingers spread wide. "We love each other . . . but only as friends, Hope. We are friends who know there can be nothing more than friendship. It is Ben whom Natalie loves, and you should know that we have played the smitten couple to make Ben jealous. Natalie loves him more than she has ever loved me."

"I feel so very sorry for all the pain she has gone through. What should we do?" she returned.

"Perhaps we start with the truth. You explain everything about your life and your birth parents, and I'll level with Ben and tell him the truth about Natalie and me."

"I fear that is the easy part," Hope remarked. "You do not know my mother . . . Olivia. She's a desperate woman; I will not put anything past her if she doesn't get what she wants. I feel danger is afoot, sir."

Jonathan studied Hope's pale complexion and the posture of fear and anxiety that seized her. There was no doubt that her concerns for Olivia were real. He knew enough about desperation and how it led many men and women to criminal acts.

"You are not alone, my dear. There is a small army of friends behind you. You are doing the right thing. Gather your strength; we must play it out and deal with the setbacks as they arise."

***

After returning from the ride with Hope, Jonathan realized it was time to move back into his hotel room. If he could withstand a lengthy coach ride and be no worse for the wear, then there was no reason to burden Natalie a moment longer. More importantly, his removal from her personal space was mandatory to convince Ben that he was not in love with her. It was time to move on. His only problem was convincing Natalie of that.

"Jonathan, you are not ready to be on your own. You could have a relapse. That usually happens when people return to activity before their bodies are completely healed," Natalie insisted as she stood by the armoire, clutching his coat tightly to her breast.

"I won't have any trouble, honey. I feel fine," Jonathan answered, throwing the last of his items into his valise. When he reached for his coat, Natalie hung onto the garment with all her might and jerked away.

"Don't do this, honey," he beseeched.

"Do what? Nurse you back to full recovery? Be concerned for your well-being. That is all I'm doing, Jonathan."

He stared at her. "That's not what you're doing, and you know it."

Her expression hardened. "Are you insinuating there are other reasons I want you to stay? Well, let me tell you this, I am not that desperate yet. I know you must think I am a pathetic case without a man in my life, but I'll let you know that I could have had any number of male callers. I have just never found myself attracted to any of them. Do not think I'm some charity case that needs your manly attention. I am perfectly happy with my life."

"Is that so?" Jonathan mused, taking hold of her chin and pulling her toward him. He saw a glimmer of a tear in her eyes.

"Yes, that's so."

"So happy you could just cry, huh, Natalie?"

And with that, she did.

A deluge of tears rolled down her cheeks as a painful sob choked from her throat. Jonathan wrapped his arms around her, pulled her against his chest and felt her pain.

"Don't give up your dream, honey. Think about what you are letting go and remember that this will be your last chance. If Ben marries Olivia, you will lose your chance to make your dreams come true. I believe you had better think more about your happiness than Hope's disappointment. Furthermore, have you ever thought about having a woman-to-woman talk with Hope? Who knows, she might not be as unreasonable as you believe." Jonathan held her at arm's length. He lifted her chin so he could look into her eyes. "I will be back tomorrow. Meanwhile, you give thought to what I said. If Hope Dansbury stops by the shop, talk to her."

Natalie shrugged her shoulders.

"Think about it. We will talk tomorrow at supper," Jonathan reinforced. He kissed her forehead, grabbed his gear, and quit the room, leaving Natalie with her head bowed.

Jonathan had walked only a block from Natalie's place when he spotted Ben's approaching wagon. When their gaze met, Jonathan raised his arm and shouted hello, while Ben lifted an index finger and slightly jerked his wrist in acknowledgment. Jonathan expected him to drive by, but surprisingly Ben slowed his rig and stopped before him.

"Leavin' town?" Ben bit out.

"No, I'm moving back into my room at the hotel. Natalie has nursed me back to good health, and I do not want her burdened a moment longer. I am certainly not leaving town, Ben. Got too many folks to thank, too many paybacks."

"Yeah, well, if I'm on your list of paybacks, just remember what I told you. All I want from you is for you to treat Natalie with respect. I better never catch you hurting her in any way."

"Now, Ben, why would I want to hurt Natalie? She is the best thing that's ever happened to me. In fact, I was hoping you could help me out with a little thank-you gift." Jonathan shifted the strap of the valise on his shoulder with considerable discomfort. The weight of the bag was more than what he had expected. "You know, a little something for all she's done for me. She once mentioned the beautiful jewelry box you made for your nephew's wife. She said it had a hidden compartment where you pulled open the lower drawer, moved a latch and raised a piece of wood to expose a soft velvet compartment."

"What of it?" Ben bit out, slapping the reins against his gloved palm.

"I was hoping you could make me something like that to give her. You know, to show my appreciation for all the loving attention and care she has given me."

Ben knew how much Natalie had loved that jewelry box. He had often thought of making her one in exchange for all the wonderful meals and favors she had done for him over the years but held back in fear she would misinterpret his intentions. Now, he wondered what the hell he had been so afraid of, and because of his foolish hesitation, the damn cardsharp would get to give it to her instead.

"I don't know, Wakefield. I am terribly busy."

"I will pay your price, Ben. In fact, I will pay twice your price if you will do it for me."

"The price is the price, Wakefield. Don't throw that flashy double-your-price stuff in my face. How soon do you want it?" Ben grumbled.

"Soon as you can manage to fit it in your schedule," Jonathan answered, shifting the load on his shoulder again with a grimace of pain.

Ben noticed Jonathan's discomfort and made an offer against his better judgment. "Get in. I will drop you off at the hotel. I am going that way anyhow."

Jonathan clambered aboard with his baggage without hesitation and then jovially slapped Ben on the back. "You are a good man, Ben. I really appreciate this. I truly do."

The sound that escaped from Ben's throat was comparable to that of an angry bear.

When they reached the hotel, Ben bid Jonathan a curt farewell and climbed the staircase to see if Olivia was in her room. He needed to speak with her pronto concerning the new draperies she "thought" she was having made for his Master bedroom. Yesterday, Max informed him that Martha Gingrich had stopped by the house, at Olivia's request, and took measurements for new Master bedroom draperies. That information struck a nerve so strong inside Ben that he blew! Making changes to his home without the courtesy of discussion or approval infuriated him; needless to say, changing the master bedroom drapes, which were his very favorites. Ben would not stand for her presumption of power at his home. He had been a bachelor too long, built his dynasty alone and was unwilling or foolish enough to hand it over so easily. Furious, Ben strode down the hotel corridor and rapped on her door.

Olivia answered on Ben's first sound.

"Hello, darling. What a nice surprise. Please come in," she welcomed.

"Thank you," Ben answered. He removed his gloves while he stood rigidly by the upholstered chair. "How was your day?" he asked.

"Very busy, as usual. Would you care for a glass of wine, dear?"

"No, thank you. I need to get back home. I cannot stay long."

"What about dinner, darling? Aren't you staying to dine?"

Ben slapped his gloves in the palm of his other hand. "Not tonight, Olivia. I stopped by for another reason," he bit out. He cut to the quick. "You've asked Martha Gingrich to stop by the house and measure for bedroom draperies, am I right?"

"Yes, I asked her. Do not get me wrong, darling, your home is lovely but sadly in need of a woman's touch. I thought it might be good to start with the Master suite, the most important room in the house." Olivia moved close and slipped her arms around Ben's neck, pressing her full self against him.

"I thought you'd have her working on draperies for *your* home?" Ben queried.

"I've told Russell I'm not taking the house." She stepped on tiptoes and kissed his lips.

Ben pulled her away. "Why?" he bit out.

"Why, Ben? Because it is a wasteful step. I am going to stay here at the hotel until we are married," she simply stated as if she had every right in the world.

Anger shot through him. "I do not want my bedroom changed, Olivia. Please do not assume so much where we are concerned. You might find yourself greatly disappointed."

Olivia dropped her arms and stepped back. "Ben, what are you saying?"

"I'm saying I don't want you changing things in my home without discussion." Ben walked to the door and pulled on his gloves.

"You have been a bachelor for too long, Ben. You must learn the fine art of sharing," she venomously answered.

"Share? I do not think this is about sharing, Olivia. I think this is about infringement. And another thing, who said anything about marriage?" With those words, he stepped into the hallway, closing the door in Olivia's face.

She sucked in an indignant breath and stiffened from head to toe. He had assaulted her in the first degree, and she was not willing to take treatment like that ever again.

"Ben Walters, you've pushed me too far," she hissed through clenched teeth.

#

Chapter Twenty-Six

Ben completed the jewelry box in less than a week. He wrapped it in a soft cloth and placed it on the table by his workshop door. He wanted a convenient spot for pick-up, so the gambler would not tarry long when he arrived.

The jewelry box was remarkably similar to the one he had made for his nephew's wife, except for two differences. One, it boasted a far more complex hidden compartment than the previous one, and two, where he had only placed his initials on the piece before, this one, he had painstakingly carved his first name, "Ben," and the date inside the lid. He was proud of it and wanted to ensure that, although the slick gambler was giving it, Natalie would always remember whose hands had made it.

An unexpected rap sounded on Ben's workshop door. He had not heard footsteps on the porch and was surprised by the sudden intrusion. Surprise turned into a groan of despair when the door creaked open, and Jonathan's head popped in, displaying his trademark wide-toothed grin.

"Ooo-wee, it's colder than a witch's tit out there," Jonathan announced as he stepped inside and moved to the warm fireplace.

Ben remained by the workbench in disgruntled silence. The annoying cardsharp grated on him so much that he could not even look at him when he spoke.

"I finished the jewelry box. It is there by the door," Ben barked, pointing to the object with one arm while he cleared his workbench with the other.

"Thank you, Ben," Jonathan answered, enthusiastically moving toward the item.

Jonathan removed the cloth and lifted it from its resting place to examine the handiwork. It was clear that Ben had truly outdone himself this time. The darkly stained wood had been lacquered to smooth perfection, the box's corners expertly dovetailed, and each drawer was neatly lined with rich red velvet.

"Why it's damn near perfect! Genuinely nice, Ben, but I didn't expect less. Natalie is going to love this."

Ben never looked up. He offered no reply.

"I really didn't think you'd put so much of yourself into it, Ben," Jonathan taunted, shooting Ben a side-eyed glance. The gambler returned the jewelry box to the table and covered it again with the soft cloth, tucking each corner under and positioning it at just the right angle. "You have done a fine job, yes indeed. Ben, you have surprised me. I know I am not one of your favorite people, and because of that, I highly expected something slap-dash. You know, something half-assed."

That was it! Ben blew!

"*HALF-ASSED!* The only thing *HALF-ASSED* in this workshop is you, Wakefield, and, for the life of me, I cannot figure out what

Natalie sees in you. The fact that she has made that mistake with you not only once in her life but twice has me concerned for her sanity."

Ben picked up a hammer lying on his workbench just as Jonathan reached out and tapped him on his shoulder.

"What?" Ben yelled.

Jonathan's touch fueled Ben's anger. He threw the hammer down with such force that it slid the full length of the workbench and then crashed to the floor with a loud clank.

"Do you *really* think she loves *me*?" Jonathan asked in an incredulous tone, seemingly unruffled by Ben's action.

Ben squeezed his eyelids shut and breathed in a hefty volume of air. "Don't you have a card game waiting on you, Wakefield?"

With that, Jonathan finally lost his lighthearted attitude and spoke out with more force than any punch he could have thrust into Ben's gut.

"I think Natalie loves you more than she has ever loved me, you fool. And you know what else I think? I think she is out of her mind. She has given you years of devotion and care. She has welcomed you time and again into her home for her delicious meals. She has given you hours of enjoyable conversation and years of friendship, and tell me what you have given her in exchange except for a lot of resistance. Then to top it off, that pitiful excuse for a woman, Olivia Dansbury, blows back into town years after she's kicked you in the head, wiggles her skinny rump, and you're back for more. Tell me something, Ben. Have I treated her any worse than you? I might be half-assed, Ben, but you . . . you're a FULL-ASS!"

Ben grabbed the front of Jonathan's coat and drew his clenched fist back for a punch.

"Go ahead; it's already been broken once," Jonathan pushed. "Throw the punch, but I guarantee you one thing, Walters, it's not going to make you feel any better because you know I'm right."

Ben held the pose and stared him down for a frozen moment, finally releasing his grip on Jonathan's coat. He turned from the cardsharp's accusing eyes and walked to the end of his workbench, bent down and picked the hammer off the floor and pounded the tool into the workbench with one powerful swing, putting a permanent indentation in the top of the wood surface. A silent moment passed between them.

"I never thought she needed anything. She is so damn self-sufficient," Ben finally uttered, his head bowed in resignation.

"Why would you hold that against her? Are you threatened by that?" Jonathan asked with calm directness.

Ben lifted his head to glare at him but never answered.

"She is talented, beautiful, intelligent, aggressive and hard-working. She is also a very faithful woman. She looks indestructible, but the truth is Natalie is a very lonely lady," Jonathan declared.

"Not so lonely since you've been back in town," Ben quipped.

Jonathan ignored his dig. "I have ruined many years of Natalie's life, and I'm not proud of that. She worked very hard through our years of marriage, and I gambled away a lot of that hard work. She had been in the flower of her youth: young, desirable, and married to a bum who knew nothing but the game of chance."

Ben opened his mouth to comment, but Jonathan was on a roll and would not be stopped.

"I will admit, when I came to Philadelphia a few weeks back, I was down on my luck, busted. I needed Natalie's help. My first day in town was when you and I met at Natalie's shop. It had been easy for me to detect the attraction between you two. Easier yet to realize Natalie's broken heart over your interest in Olivia Dansbury. It was an opportunity that I could not afford to pass up. I needed money and had convinced her that if she would help me with a loan, I would help her by acting as the ex-husband to win back her heart. I had hoped it would make you jealous. I was correct on that one, by damn," he quipped with a wink and a click of his tongue. "I had also hoped you'd forget that worthless woman from Massachusetts."

"You mean you and Natalie are not in love?" Ben cut in with honest surprise.

"I love her, but not the way you think. Natalie deserves to be number one, and as much as I hate to admit it, number one in my life is gambling and always will be. She loves *you*, Walters, and she has loved you for a long time."

Ben moved silently around the workshop absorbing the gambler's declarations. For all the ugly feelings he'd harbored for this man over the past weeks, he displayed a surprising honesty and sensitivity that Ben hadn't realized the good-for-nothing gambler possessed.

"She has no idea how you feel," Jonathan explained.

"Natalie thinks you love Olivia, and she doesn't want to hurt Hope anymore than she thinks she has already. She feels like a homewrecker."

231

"I have only known my daughter for a few short weeks. Yet, there is no home to wreck. Doesn't Natalie know that?" Ben answered.

"No, you half-wit, she does not. Listen up; Hope is coming here today with something important to tell you. Think carefully about everything she says and hear her out before you make any hasty decisions."

"How the hell do you know any of this?"

Jonathan gave him a wicked smile. "Cause I'm on the inner circle, didn't you know?"

Ben ran a hand through his hair. "Argh, we're in the midst of a hell of a mess," Ben groaned, feeling anger and disquiet at the situation.

"I believe you are the one in a hell of a mess, Walters. Me, well, besides offering sound advice, I am just here to help Natalie to the best of my ability!" The gambler slapped Ben on the shoulder and then moved toward the door. "Before I leave, I think I will see if Max has any of that delicious cider left. I am mighty thirsty, indeed," he finished with a smile as he closed the shop door behind him, deliberately forgetting the jewelry box on the table.

Ben glared at the closed door with one eye squinted, teeth gritted, and fists clenched.

***

When Ben entered the kitchen, there was no sign of Hope, just Jonathan and Max conversing at the kitchen table.

"The day is passing. Shouldn't she be here by now?" Ben questioned as soon as his gaze fell on the gambler.

"Yes, I told Max I believe I will mosey into town and see what's detained her. Maybe the little gal met up with a snag."

"Tell Ethan to saddle my steed, Max," Ben ordered. "I'm going with you, Wakefield."

"But what if she shows up here? Then what? Stay here. There is no reason to tag along, Ben."

"Like hell I will," he roared, reaching for his coat and pushing past Jonathan. "I am going! You are crazy if you think I'm going to stay here and let you report back!" Ben slammed the door behind him.

Jonathan grinned at Max. "Looks like you will have to hold down the fort, Max. I believe Ben has made up his mind."

"It does look that way, Jonathan. Yep, looks like you got yourself a sidekick."

***

When Natalie's last customer finally departed from her shop, she walked back the hallway to her apartment, sighing with disappointment when she perused her now empty bedroom. Jonathan had moved out. She should have felt relief getting her bed back along with the privacy of her bedroom, but instead, she felt sad and abandoned. She now realized how much Jonathan had helped her with the heartbreak and pain she had suffered these past weeks. Tonight would be a sad return to loneliness.

A knock sounded on her door when she reached the kitchen. She prayed Jonathan reconsidered his decision to return to Steven Matthews. She truly hoped he had returned for a few more days, so she could fill her alone hours caring for him. Surprise washed over her when she opened the door and found Hope shivering in the early evening air.

"Hope! Come in, my dear," Natalie offered. "Here, give me your wrap." Natalie pulled a chair from the table, and Hope accepted the proffered seat. "I am so sorry, but Jonathan is no longer here," Natalie continued. "He has moved back to the hotel against my better judgment. I have never gotten through that man's thick skull to talk any sense into him. He is a rambler and a gambler, and a single-minded hardhead. I will never change him," she prattled on.

"It is not Mr. Wakefield I have come to see. If you don't mind, I'd like to share a few moments with you. Can you spare the time?"

"Why, yes, I have the time. Would you like a cup of tea?"

"That would be very nice if it's not too much trouble."

"No trouble at all," Natalie sang, putting the teapot on the stove and grabbing mugs from the corner hutch. "Is there a special gown you had in mind?" Natalie asked, anxious to know why the young woman was visiting.

"No, ma'am. Thank you again for the beautiful costume."

Natalie heard a strain in the young girl's voice. She glanced over and noticed Hope staring at her folded hands resting on the tabletop. It was clear that something was heavy on her mind, so Natalie placed the mugs on the table and sat until the water heated.

"Now, what is troubling you?"

Hope looked directly into her eyes and began, "I came to inform you of things you should know about me, Olivia, and Ben."

Natalie felt uneasiness. "Hope, you do not owe me any explanations. It is I who owes you. I am ashamed of my actions."

"Ashamed of what? Ashamed of loving Ben? Ashamed of showing him affection, something Olivia has never done?"

Natalie was shocked at the tone with which the young girl spoke of her mother.

"Listen to me, Miss Wakefield; I hold you in the highest regard. You are straightforward when you need to be and soft and understanding when life calls for it. You have made a good life for yourself against many obstacles, and I admire that about you. I know you have sacrificed plenty and are willing to sacrifice again not to hurt people, but I will not let you do that. I am here to tell you the truth."

"What truth, dear?" Natalie asked with honest puzzlement.

Hope reached across the table and took Natalie's hand into hers. "The truth is, Ben is not----"

But the remainder of Hope's confession was halted when the kitchen door flew open and smashed against the back wall. Hope screamed just before the intruding, masked figure could clamp his gloved hand across her mouth.

"Make a sound, and I'll kill her," the intruder warned Natalie while holding a knife to Hope's throat. "Get back the hall, both of you."

"What is this? Let her go! I will give you whatever you want," Natalie pleaded.

"I said move!"

And Natalie obeyed without hesitation, knowing the dangerous monster meant every threat. She berated herself for failing to lock the door after Hope's arrival.

"Get in the bedroom and shut up," the cad demanded, his eyes shifting nervously. "One foolish move, and I swear I'll cut her from ear to ear."

"What do you want?" Natalie begged.

"Pick up that scarf and gag her mouth." He drew Hope closer to him and breathed his stale breath into the side of her face. "Your mother is gonna be surprised to find out that she got two for the price of one. You shouldn't have been here, little girl. Looks like your unlucky day."

#

Chapter Twenty-Seven

Hope realized her mother had lost her mind, for the idea that she had hired a man to carry out such a heinous act was unfathomable. After Andrew's death, Olivia often acted unstable and made irrational decisions, but Hope had always considered it part of her grieving process. She had never dreamed that Olivia would continue making outrageous demands and running her life with noticeable irrationality and desperation.

Now, Hope saw that Olivia's behavior was not a temporary thing. It was a condition of self-absorption that had become a permanent part of her personality and created a dangerous crack in her behavior. A trickle of fear and overwhelming anger washed over Hope as she realized what that meant for her friend Natalie and herself.

She glanced down and noticed a small pair of shears on Natalie's vanity. Unfortunately, the thug held a knife to her throat, which made it difficult to reach without incident. Instead, she remained still and hoped for one careless move on his part. If that occurred, she would be ready to take action.

"Take that scarf and gag her mouth. Tight! I don't want any sounds," the villain ordered Natalie.

Natalie did exactly as she was told. She placed the scarf in Hope's mouth and tied it securely. Their gaze met for a fraction of a second, and Natalie winked at her with a warning. Hope braced herself for whatever move Natalie was about to make.

"There, it's done," Natalie claimed as she stepped away.

"Get on the bed," the villain growled.

The room was small and full of furnishings: a bed, a dressing screen, a standing mirror and a chifforobe. There was little room to move.

"You'll need to step back so I can pass," Natalie quipped to the man, casting another warning look at Hope.

He moved the knife from Hope's throat to beneath her breast and dragged her backward, but it proved careless. When Hope shifted her weight, he was thrown off balance by a small box Natalie had slid behind him when she secured Hope's gag. It caused him to stumble, lose his stronghold on Hope and drop the knife.

Hope's adrenaline surged that instant. She stretched her upper body, grabbed the shears from the table, swung her arm around and thrust the blade of the shears into his neck. The man weakened and finally collapsed to the floor with a solid clunk. His facial muscles contorted with agony, a grotesque gurgle sounded from his throat, and he finally lay still.

***

After checking numerous locales with no sign of Olivia or Hope, Ben and Jonathan decided to check Natalie's property. Strong foreboding washed over both men when they arrived at her property and noticed the kitchen door standing ajar. They moved silently, alarmed to discover an overturned kitchen chair and the table pushed out of position. Hearing a scuffle and crash from Natalie's bedroom, both men rushed toward the sound, entering the room just as the hulking intruder hit the floor.

Ben rushed to Natalie's side and took her in his arms.

"Are you hurt?" he asked, tilting her face to meet his.

"No, Ben, just shaken," she breathed.

"Over here," Jonathan called out. "He got Hope. She has been stabbed, and she is losing blood fast."

"Oh, dear!" Natalie grabbed a quilt and threw it across the bed. "Put her right here," she implored.

Ben and Jonathan gently lifted the young girl from the floor and carried her to the prepared bed. Blood flowed from a wound under her breast.

"That bastard," Ben said between clenched teeth. "Go get Doc and tell him to get down here, Wakefield, while we try to stem this bleeding."

Without question, Jonathan bolted from the room to do Ben's bidding. Meanwhile, Natalie split open Hope's gown at the bloodied area to examine the wound.

"Get me a basin of warm water, Ben, and also a clean sheet from the armoire," she demanded.

Hope's lips quivered, her voice barely a whisper. "I am so sorry. I never thought it would come to this."

"Please do not talk, Hope. You are very weak," Natalie beseeched.

Ben returned with the requested items and laid them next to where Natalie sat on the bed, then reached for Hope's hand. He felt her return a feeble squeeze.

"Olivia lied," Hope whispered between dry lips, tears streaming down her face. "I am not your daughter, Ben. Please do not hate me. You do not deserve the things she's done to you."

"You are in shock. You need to stay calm until the doctor arrives, Hope. Everything is going to be all right. Please rest; save your energy," Ben pleaded.

Ben did not like her using his given name. She had called him father for weeks, and he had grown quite used to hearing the paternal address. 'Ben' was so distant, so cold.

"You do not understand. Olivia is an extremely dangerous woman. Miss Wakefield, tell him. Tell him he is not my father. Make him believe it. He loves you, and you love him and . . . tell him that I am not his *daughter!*"

Then her eyelids dropped, and she lay still.

"Hope! Hope!" Ben whispered close to her face.

She did not respond. Her breathing was shallow.

***

Olivia hurried back to her hotel room and nervously paced while waiting for news from her hired man. She thought he should have been done with the deed and back by now. And where was Hope? Then a rap sounded on her door, and she yanked it open, thinking it was him, before asking for the person's identity. She was taken aback to find Jonathan Wakefield accompanied by an official-looking gentleman.

"Good evening, Mrs. Dansbury; my name is Sheriff Giles."

Olivia's heart picked up at a fast pace. She felt panic. Her expression turned desperate.

"Mr. Wakefield has reported an unpleasant incident that took place at his ex-wife's home this evening, and I have good reason to believe that you are involved in this matter. I am here to take you in for questioning. Kindly get your wrap."

Olivia's eyes grew wide. "Are you insane? I will certainly NOT get my wrap." Olivia cast a venomous look at Jonathan. "Sheriff, if this man is your source of information, you are being misled. He is nothing but a lying, cheating gambler."

"I'm sorry, Mrs. Dansbury, but you will have to come along with me," the sheriff enforced.

"What are you taking me in for? What has happened? This is unlawful. You cannot take me in without proof. Explain yourself."

"We have reason to believe you were involved in a conspiracy to commit murder." The sheriff reached for her arm, though Olivia viciously yanked away from him and backed out of his reach.

"Unhand me!" She moved deeper into the room, sidling beside a large tapestry bag by the bed.

Both men felt imminent danger.

"Mrs. Dansbury, I suggest you move away from that bag before anyone gets hurt," the sheriff warned.

Jonathan did not give her the benefit of the doubt. He dove toward the bed, pulled the bag away from her and tossed it to the opposite side of the room. When the bag hit the floor, the hard clunk that sounded assured him that a firearm lay inside. He grabbed her wrist and pulled her down on the mattress.

"You fool!" he ground out. "You'd risk anyone's life to get what you want, wouldn't you?"

She struggled to pull away, but the Sheriff restrained her other arm, making her escape impossible.

"My husband is an attorney. He is one of the most powerful men in the States. You will not get away with this," she screamed in a crazed voice.

"You're coming with us right now, Mrs. Dansbury," the sheriff demanded as he pulled her to her feet. "Grab her cloak, Mr. Wakefield."

Jonathan retrieved her outerwear, draped it over her shoulders and whispered one last warning. "I don't think your husband can help you much from the grave, Olivia. You better come up with a better trick than that."

Olivia jerked her head to look away.

"Your daughter has been seriously injured by the man you allegedly hired to kill Natalie Wakefield. Would you care to stop by the doctor's office first to check on her condition before we proceed to the jailhouse?" the sheriff asked.

Olivia's eyes were fixed on a spot on the far wall. She showed no remorse at the news of her daughter's condition and gave no reply to the question he asked. The trio left the room in silence.

***

Ben joined Natalie at her kitchen table for what seemed an eternity while the doctor sutured Hope. The night had turned bizarre, yet he knew that amidst the chaos and absurd happenings, a sanctuary of peace and love kept calling him closer, offering happiness and fulfillment. A haven of love and giving offered to him by this loving woman regardless of his continuous rude rebuff or thoughtless conduct. She was a constant light that welcomed him closer, always ready to listen and understand, always entranced by his simplest words.

Ben studied her closely. Even in her disheveled and shattered state, an infinite beauty shone through. He had turned away from her goodness and loving ways time and again, all because of another woman he had thought he loved, a woman who had managed to play him for a fool not only once in his life but twice.

After a long silence, Natalie explained more of the evening's experience. "That horrible man told us that he was hired by Olivia. I guess she felt very desperate, Ben. She thought I stood in the way of her future." Natalie sniffed and then wiped a tear from her cheek.

Ben reached across the table and took her hand in his. "You did stand in the way of things; Natalie and Olivia knew it better than anyone, even me."

Natalie's head lifted; her tear-filled eyes studied his and saw his honesty.

"It took me too long to admit what you mean to me. I have been such a fool." Ben squeezed her hand. "I love you."

"You do?" she asked in an incredulous tone.

"Yes, I do." Ben walked around the table and took her into his arms. "I need you in my life."

Moments later, the doctor entered, buttoning the front of a clean white shirt. "Miss Dansbury is stable. The knife blade missed her vital organs. My main concern is for the blood the young lady has lost. She will need plenty of rest and recuperation. I am hoping one of you can arrange a close watch over her for the first forty- eight hours.

"I will do it."

"She can stay with me."

Natalie and Ben answered simultaneously. They stared silently at each other for a moment before Natalie firmly pointed out what she felt was the clear logic for the situation.

"She is a single young woman, Ben. You could not possibly see to her needs."

"She is my daughter and my responsibility. She will stay at my place, and I will hire a woman for Hope's personal needs."

"Why on God's green earth would you do something like that? I took good care of Jonathan during his recuperation and can easily care for Hope."

"Don't remind me."

Natalie cut him off before he could bellyache about the care and attention she gave Jonathan. She faced the doctor. "Wouldn't you say my offer is far more suitable for the young woman? Furthermore, we really should not move her, should we?"

"Wait a minute, please," Ben said in a strong and unyielding voice that got Natalie's attention. "We are not going to fight over this. When Hope stabilizes, I am transporting her in my coach to my home, where a competent nurse will see her until she is well. You are a terribly busy woman, Natalie. I do not expect you to play nursemaid to Hope and keep your business running efficiently. It is unfortunate that others are too blind to realize that their free-loading, lengthy stay at your home might drain you of your energies, and I, for one, will not let that happen again. I am concerned for your well-being and would not think of having it any other way."

"Fine," the doctor replied. "I see there will be no need to worry about Miss Dansbury's care. I will return in a few hours to give her one last check before bedtime, then again in the early a.m. Why don't you all get a good night's sleep?" The doctor gathered his belongings and bid farewell.

Ben turned to Natalie when the door closed. "I would like to stay the night. If you could find me some blankets, I will make a bed in the fitting room on the platform."

Ben was assertive with his request. He wanted to stay close to Hope for the first few hours, but most of all, he needed to be near Natalie. He would not chance to lose her to Jonathan Wakefield tonight or any night in the future. Tonight, he would show her how much she means to him.

#

Chapter Twenty-Eight

A cold shiver raced along Natalie's spine when her gaze fell upon Hope's inert, pale form lying death-like in her bed. She quietly moved to the bedside and checked for the rise and fall of the young woman's chest. Hope's breathing was very shallow. She bent down to kiss her forehead.

"Fight, my dear. You are important to many people. People who love you very much."

Natalie grabbed blankets and pillows from the trunk at the foot of her bed before closing the bedroom door behind her. When she entered the sitting room with the goods, she found Ben bare-chested, hanging his shirt on the dressing screen in the corner.

"Here, give me those things," he insisted, reaching for the items with outstretched muscular arms. "I could have gotten these, Natalie. You have certainly had enough today."

He moved around the platform, straightening and stretching the blankets in his half-dressed glory, having no idea how his nakedness affected her. She stood transfixed, watching his every move.

"Where can I find a clean towel and a bar of soap," he asked as he plumped up the pillows. "I'd like to wash up before I turn in."

His presence among her female accouterments was particularly unsettling. It was a scene she had only before dreamed of, and the reality of him here in all his manly glory took every ounce of her self-control to restrain from rushing into his strong arms and feeling the security of his embrace. She needed that more tonight than ever before.

"I'll fetch a basin of warm water and lay out all you need in the kitchen," she softly answered.

Ben scratched a spot above his left nipple, then slid down to rub his side. "I can get the soap and towel, Natalie; just tell me where."

"No, please give me a minute. I will get it," she insisted. "I will lay out everything you need in the kitchen. I am on my way."

A few minutes later, Ben entered the kitchen and saw the bathing supplies waiting as promised. He braced his hands on the table and bowed his head over the basin. With closed eyes, he thought about the many evenings spent in this room enjoying Natalie's conversation, her delicious meals and her caring ways. Though tonight he felt things beyond that; a strong pull aroused a hunger to know all of her. Ben dipped the linen into the warm water and then pressed it against his face, inhaling one deep, strong breath. Beneath the cloth, he heard water splashing from the other room; Natalie's soft hum drifting down the hallway, urging him on. He realized the promising opportunity that might await him, so he hustled through the remainder of his bath with hopeful spirits.

When Natalie completed her toilette, she returned to the kitchen and found the empty basin, folded linen and the cake of her lilac soap stacked neatly on a chair by the stove. Ben was nowhere in sight. She felt disappointed that he had retired without saying goodnight. After all, it had been such an emotional day, and it seemed fitting that he would bid her a restful night after such horrendous events.

Natalie sighed, tightened the belt on her robe then moved to her bedroom to make one last check on Hope. The young girl was as before: a still, pale form. Natalie bent down and kissed her forehead.

"Sleep well, my dear."

When she turned from the bed, she was startled by the sight of Ben standing shirtless in the doorway. A quiver worked its way down her body as she drank in the sight of his manly physique. His damp hair had been finger combed away from his face, and he wore an expression that spoke volumes. It ignited a heat within her that threatened to burn out of control, for she clearly read his bold intentions as he moved toward her. He was a beautiful man that rendered her weak with desire. She wanted to pinch herself, for in the past few years, sights like this were never witnessed but in her dreams.

"You take good care of people, Natalie," he stated in a husky tone, his eyes burning with desire.

"Only those I care about, and I care greatly for Hope. I want to make her as comfortable as possible," Natalie whispered, struggling to keep her voice steady as Ben's gaze washed over her with a heat that made her toes curl. Her heart raced as she moved toward Ben.

"Speaking of comfort, you had promised to lay out everything I needed, but I believe you have forgotten something."

"I am not equipped with manly provisions, Ben. I apologize that I could not be more accommodating."

He slid his arm around her waist and drew her so close she could feel his erection. "You're equipped with everything I need, madam."

Natalie's hands gripped his biceps. She tilted her head back, and their gaze locked. "Really?"

"Absolutely everything," he answered, then kissed her lips tenderly. Natalie's grip tightened on his upper arms when his tongue slipped inside, and a moan escaped her lips. Her world was spinning.

He gently pulled away and looked at her with a fire burning in his eyes. "I thought you might want to tuck me into bed."

He took her by the hand and led her down the hall to the fitting room. She saw he had prepared a love nest on the platform made with comforters and soft pillows. It was a sensual scene with a backdrop of mirrors and a single lighted candle beside the makeshift bed.

"Do you take me for an easy, woman?" she asked, taking in the scene before her. She watched Ben unbutton his breeches. He let them slide to the floor, then lowered himself to the comforters, pulling her to his side.

"I take you for a beautiful woman. I take you for a desirable woman, but *easy* never entered my mind," he answered with candor.

Natalie lay down next to him and ran her hand across the soft carpet of hair on his chest. "Are you saying I'm difficult?"

"Very difficult."

His strong hand slid down her body on the outside of her robe and came to rest on her right buttocks.

"With you, Ben, I never want to be difficult. What can I do to convince you?" Natalie coyly inquired while staring at the whiskers on his chin. She ran her fingers over the stubbly surface.

The simple gesture fueled Ben's fire. Then he took her hand and moved it to his hardened manhood. "I can only think of one thing at this moment."

Cyn Garrett

"Mmmmmm," She softly stroked his warm flesh.

Ben groaned with pleasure, running his hands down her arm. He felt her soft body through the fabric of her robe. "It isn't healthy to wear clothing to bed. It restricts your breathing," he whispered against her lips.

Ben untied the sash at her waist, pushed the fabric down over her shoulders, and then pulled the gown away from her form. Together they found the natural curves of their bodies and molded themselves as one, entwining silken limbs against rugged muscle, a perfect fit. When they finally nestled within the warmth of the comforters, Ben reached for her left hand and ceremoniously slid a circle of yarn around the third finger.

"I love you. I want you to know this before we go any further," he said with conviction.

Natalie stared at the yarn ring in wonder. "Ben, what is this?"

"This is my promise to you. It is my official mark of ownership. Tomorrow, I want to buy you a betrothal ring. I hope you will accept."

"Ben," she whispered in complete astonishment. Natalie touched the yarn around her finger. "I know I should act coy, make you wait for an answer, but I cannot. I have hoped for this for so long."

"I have been such a fool," he breathed, running his hands down her curves, not wanting to miss a spot. She was beautifully formed, soft, and womanly. Her breasts felt warm against his chest, and when she began to do amazing things with her fingers, touching him in the most sensitive areas and bringing him to heights of pure pleasure, he wondered what had taken him this long to realize how much he needed her, how much he wanted her for his wife. He had allowed himself to fantasize on a few occasions about her, but that dream had always

250

been squelched with the fear that she did not need him or any other man in her life. Now, he knew he had been a fool to believe it. She needed this part of her life just like any other woman. Most of all, he had realized over these past weeks how much he preferred her self-sufficiency over Olivia's spoiled behavior.

Ben's lips slid down her throat. He kissed the upper swell of her breast, then hungrily moved to capture the darkened crest. She arched in his arms and purred like a kitten.

"This better not be a dream," she breathed. "I have had my fill of dreams."

Ben placed soft kisses on her belly. "Have I been part of your dreams?" he asked.

"Yes, and part of my nightmares." Her breath caught as he slid lower to continue his path of kisses.

"What exactly did I do in your dreams?"

"Oh, you took off your clothes and . . ."

"And what?"

"Then I think you kissed me," she said, barely able to breathe.

"Mmmm, where did I kiss you?

"Everywhere."

"Here? Is this where I kissed you?"

"Oooooooo, I believe that's the exact spot."

Ben glanced up to find she was lying in complete abandon. She looked beautiful. Slowly he slid his body up the length of her outstretched form and then, unable to wait a moment more, pushed inside her while gazing down at her beautiful face. "You have me now, sweetheart. You have all of me and forever."

Natalie revealed this long-awaited moment. She touched the yarn ring with her thumb and let their lovemaking spiral them to the clouds. Then at the same moment, as if it were perfectly timed, they cried out together, "I love you."

***

Natalie and Ben awakened early the next morning to a persistent rap on the kitchen door. Ben hastily pulled on his breeches while Natalie slipped into her robe and tied the sash tight. She asked Ben to stay out of sight until she got rid of the intruder, but with everything that had happened in the past twenty-four hours, Ben was not convinced to stay too far behind. He positioned himself to the rear of the closed kitchen door just in case Natalie needed assistance.

"Who is it?" Natalie called out before unlatching the door.

"It's me, honey. Let me in."

"Oh, hello, Jonathan," she greeted, hurriedly opening the door and welcoming him. "Have a seat, and I'll make coffee."

"I couldn't sleep very well last night worrying about Hope. Sorry if I am early."

"Early! Hell, that is an understatement. Why the night's not even over yet, Wakefield," Ben blustered as he walked from behind the door into plain view.

"Sorry Honey, I didn't know you had company." Jonathan apologized, ignoring Ben's biting comment. He quickly glanced at Ben's bare-chested, disheveled condition, felt a swift blow to his heart, then continued without missing a beat. "Glad you stayed on with Natalie, Ben. She certainly did not need to shoulder everything alone." He turned back to Natalie. "Mind if I check on Hope?"

Ben harrumphed.

"No, go right ahead. Ben, please fetch me some wood out back," Natalie requested, giving him a nervous smile. Jonathan's arrival had changed Ben's mood, and the tension was palpable.

Ben stood up to do her bidding, but in the process, he collided with Jonathan making his way toward the bedroom.

"Excuse me, Ben," Jonathan politely exclaimed.

"You know what, Wakefield? I have realized there isn't enough room for both of us in Natalie's home, much less this town," Ben roared.

"Ben! What is wrong with you?" Natalie cried. Her nerves were spent over this tension between them, and she had had enough after all that had transpired. "Why are you so hostile? What do you have against Jonathan? He has never done anything to you."

Ben strode to Natalie in two giant steps. "He has held you in his arms. He has shared your bed. He has felt your loving touch. The thought of that tears me apart. Do not say he's never done anything to me."

Natalie put her hands on his chest. "Ben, please."

Then Jonathan came back in a serious tone, a stronger voice than Ben had ever heard him use. "Yeah, but she has never looked at me the way she looks at you, Walters. She has given me her friendship, but I've never had her adoration."

253

The room fell silent as the two men stared each other down.

Jonathan broke first. "If you'll excuse me, I'd like to check on Hope." He pushed past Ben and strode down the hallway.

Ben watched him until he disappeared into Natalie's bedroom. The fact was that Jonathan's words humbled him. There was truth in what he said, making Ben feel foolish for his accusations. Deep down, Ben knew that he owed Jonathan Wakefield a lot. After all, if it had not been for the part Jonathan played, Ben knew he'd probably be tangled in a hell of a mess with Olivia. He truly felt humbled. He turned to Natalie, controlling his feelings and spoke in a softer tone.

"I'm sorry for that," he said, running his hand down her arm. "I should be going. I have a lot to accomplish today."

"Ben, you haven't had any breakfast. Please stay and eat something," Natalie begged.

"No, really, I should be going. I must check with the sheriff and let Max know what happened." He ran his hand along the backside of her neck, rubbing his thumb on her skin in a tender caress. "This predicament could tie me up for a few days, Natalie. I want to care for as much as possible without involving you. You have already handled more of this mess than what is fair, and I feel guilty as hell that-----"

She pressed her fingers against his lips. "I understand, Ben."

Ben gathered her into his arms and kissed her lips, delivering a thousand sensations of desire and promise.

"I love you, Natalie. I will sort this out as soon as possible. I promise," he whispered, pulling from her embrace and moving to the fitting room.

Kiss Me Once

He finished dressing, gathered the remains of his personal items, then left without another word.

#

Chapter Twenty-Nine

Jonathan had grown very fond of Hope Dansbury over the past weeks. As he stood by her still form, he wondered what it would have been like to live out the role of a father, how it would have felt for a son or a daughter to call him Pa. He quickly pushed the thought aside, realizing he would have failed. Jonathan knew if he had spawned children, they would have probably taught their friends card tricks before they turned five.

Hope's eyes opened. "Hello," she whispered.

Jonathan reached for her hand and squeezed her fingertips.

"Hello, Hope. We have been very worried about you."

She smiled and lightly returned the squeeze.

"You were very brave. All of us owe you a lot for saving Natalie's life," Jonathan declared.

Hope did not answer. She knew she was the one indebted. None of them owed her a thing. They had given her so much friendship and love, something she knew little of in her life, and in return, she had given them deceit.

"Are you in a lot of pain?" Jonathan asked.

"A little."

"May I get you something?"

"Is Miss Wakefield here?"

"Yes, she will be incredibly happy to see you awake. I will get her," Jonathan said, returning her hand to the covers.

"Does she hate me? Hope asked.

Jonathan frowned. "Hate you? I would venture to say she loves you and admires you."

"He's right, you know," Natalie voiced from the doorway.

"Miss Wakefield," Hope whispered, her lips quivering. Natalie moved to the bedside. "Hello, dear. The doctor says you will need plenty of tender, loving care. We intend to see to that."

"I have deceived so many people. So many fine people," the young woman shamefully admitted.

"Hope, you must not worry about this right now. You have been gravely injured and need all your strength for recovery. Please relax and let me help you with anything you may need."

"Where is Ben?" Hope asked.

"He's taking care of the loose ends."

"And my mother, where is she?"

Natalie glanced at Jonathan with uncertainty. "She's with the sheriff, Hope," she answered, knowing this subject could not be avoided.

Hope squeezed her eyes shut and nodded. "Andrew spoiled her," she began in a tormented voice. Even though he left her a wealthy woman, she could not handle life as a widow. She needed a man around to escort her to her so-called "important events". She did not love Ben. He merely fit Olivia's criteria for a husband: an eligible, wealthy man with high community standing." Hope lifted her head and looked directly at Natalie. "She feared you. You were the one thing that stood in her way. I never thought she would go so far as to hire a man to kill you. I am ashamed and feel so guilty."

"It is not your fault, Hope. I do not blame you. Please rest now. Your body needs sleep. Someone will be close by if you need anything." Natalie ran her fingers lightly over Hope's eyes. "Close your eyes and sleep."

Hope closed her eyes. Natalie and Jonathan quietly left the room, but when the door closed, Hope's eyes reopened. Misery consumed her as she thought about how much she was to blame for everything. She had allowed her mother to deceive honest and loving folk continuously, people who had become the closest friends she had ever known. The pain bore down with such relentless pressure that tears welled and burst forth in a mad flood down her cheeks. She felt entirely ashamed and alone.

***

Max pulled the door open the minute Ben's foot hit the stoop. "Is everything alright?" he cried.

"Hope's been stabbed, Olivia's in jail, and I'm going to marry Natalie Wakefield." He pushed past the older man to climb the stairs two at a time. "Go down to the workshop and get the jewelry box I made. It is wrapped in a tan cloth on the table by the window. I am in a hurry," he shouted and slammed the bedroom door behind him.

Max shook his head in confusion, grabbed his coat and shot into action.

Thirty minutes later, Ben entered the kitchen, freshly shaven and sporting a clean set of clothes. Max stood by the stove, stirring a large kettle.

"Sorry, Max, I didn't mean to be curt," Ben offered. "I have a lot to do today and not enough hours to accomplish it all." Ben eyed the jewelry box on the kitchen table. "Thanks a lot for getting this for me."

"Nice job," Max remarked. He watched Ben open the lid and inspect its interior.

"You gonna fill me in on what happened, or what?" Max probed.

"Yeah, sit down a minute, Max. I'll tell you everything."

After Ben explained the horror of what happened at Natalie's the night before, Max felt a strong need to ride into town and check on his young friend. He had to go, even if he could only stand by her bedside for a short while.

Hope, and he had grown close over the past months. Through their short friendship, he learned how Olivia had orchestrated Hope's entire life and how she had never made decisions for fear of disappointing her parents. Max knew she could not harm a soul, and he needed to let her know she had his full support and eternal friendship through this difficult time. One hour later, he found himself in Natalie's kitchen.

"May I see her, please, madam? I won't stay long, I promise."

"Naturally, Max, follow me; she is in my bedroom. Natalie peeked in to see if Hope was awake. "Go ahead. I think she is awake," Natalie whispered, pushing the door open.

Max stepped inside and took a seat by the bedside. Hope was staring at the bedroom ceiling. He reached for her hand.

"Good morning, young lady."

She offered no response. Nothing moved, not a finger, her lips, or even a pulsebeat in her throat. The tips of her eyelashes were wet with tears.

"No one blames you, dear. You are not responsible for your mother's actions. You did the honorable thing by coming to Natalie and confessing the truth. It took a lot of strength to do that, Hope."

A moment passed, and then finally, Hope rolled her head to face Max. "I have never known people like you, Ben and Miss Wakefield. Even Jonathan Wakefield. You have given me my happiest days. I do not deserve your friendship." Her voice was barely above a whisper.

"You have our friendship and our love, Hope. This is not easy for you, and we understand that."

Hope smiled weakly. "There were so many times I wanted to tell you the truth. I guess I did not have enough nerve. Each day our friendship grew deeper, and it became increasingly more difficult to confess. I did not want to lose you, any of you." Tears streamed down her face. "If Miss Wakefield had been killed, I would never have been able to live with myself."

"But that did not happen, dear. You saved her life instead," Max praised.

"I had to tell the sheriff the truth. The strange part is that I also feel a lot of pain for Olivia. She is the only mother I have ever known. She has done a terrible thing, Max, but . . . I do not know what I'm trying to say. This is very painful." She burst into tears.

"Time will heal, Hope. An old man knows this much about life. Time will heal."

***

Ben rode back into Philadelphia, stopping first at the sheriff's office. For Hope's sake, he was compelled to find out about Olivia's charges.

"Good day, Mr. Walters," the young sheriff greeted from behind a large wooden desk.

"Sheriff Giles," Ben greeted, pulling off a pair of leather gloves and slapping them on his thighs. "Where do things stand?"

"I stopped by Miss Wakefield's home today and spoke with Miss Dansbury. She gave me a full account of her mother's intentions. Olivia Dansbury had allegedly hired the man to kill Natalie Wakefield."

Ben was surprised that Hope felt well enough to speak with the sheriff. He knew the law had little patience when uncovering facts about a case and would do whatever was necessary to unearth them.

"Hope Dansbury was strong enough for your interview?" Ben inquired.

"I merely stopped by to assure her that her mother was not mistreated. Miss Dansbury was the one who willingly offered the information. I did not need to ask further questions. She told me everything."

"And Olivia Dansbury?" Ben inquired.

"She has not answered any questions. I understand her deceased husband was a prominent attorney in Massachusetts. He schooled her

261

well. She would not budge. She just asked me to contact Russell Gray, her lawyer, and said he would clear her name."

Ben headed directly to the Steven Matthews Hotel from the sheriff's office. Not so much for Olivia's possessions, but he wanted to gather Hope's belongings for safekeeping. Kirk Mathews was in the front vestibule when Ben arrived and hustled over to him with a look of grave concern.

"Ben, how is Hope? I heard about the incident at Natalie's last night. Is she going to be alright?"

Ben explained the details to Kirk, assuring him that Hope was in stable condition and under Natalie's tender care, but advised the young man to stay clear until Hope had a chance to regain her strength and better appreciate his company.

"I would like to gather Olivia and Hope's personal items and take them with me today, Kirk. Could I have the key to their room?"

"Yes, of course," Kirk answered.

Kirk inserted the key into the hole, turned and pushed the door wide. "Do you need some help, Ben?"

The full impact of this mission suddenly hit him. It wasn't a simple matter of grabbing a few gowns. It had not even dawned on him that there would be many undergarments and private womanly effects for both women that needed to be handled.

"Could you send a maid? Women know more about these things than us men," Ben stammered.

"We men know a little about them," Kirk chuckled, stabbing Ben in the side with his elbow.

"Send a maid," Ben growled.

Kirk chuckled. "A trifle protective, aren't you?"

"Where you're concerned, it's more than a trifle."

Chapter Thirty

Two days had passed since the skirmish at Natalie's home. Since then, she had seen nothing more of Ben, putting her at wit's end.

Hope had shown remarkable improvement, enjoying the friends who had stopped by to visit. Her most frequent visitor, Kirk Matthews brought flowers, books and a delectable dessert from the hotel's kitchen today. Their growing friendship only seemed to fuel Natalie's insecurities about her relationship with Ben. She worried that he might have changed his mind when he visited Olivia in jail. Perhaps she convinced him she was totally innocent and needed his help more now than ever. Maybe what had happened in Natalie's bedroom the other night was only the result of an emotionally charged event. She worriedly rubbed the yarn ring on her finger and stared out the window.

The bell tinkled on her shop door, severing her thoughts. She looked up to find Jonathan dressed in a new suit of clothes. He looked dashing. His hair was freshly trimmed, and she could smell his tangy cologne as he drew closer.

"Hi, Honey," he greeted. "Are you busy, or could you spare a moment?" he asked as he lowered to the stool beside her.

"I just finished this gown. Would you like a cup of tea or a bite to eat, Jonathan?"

"No, thank you. I cannot stay long. I have an appointment with the minister at three o'clock."

"Confessing your sins?" she teased.

Jonathan chuckled. "I'm sure the man doesn't have all day, and I need at least that long to confess all my sins." Jonathan reached for her hand and enclosed it in his. "I want to apologize. I will not be able to follow through with the Christmas choir arrangements I have promised. A family emergency has arisen, and I am leaving for Carolina tomorrow morning."

Natalie's grip tightened. She knew there was no family emergency. He did not even have a family down south.

"Before I leave, I want to express my thanks for everything you have done for me in these past weeks and for all of the years of marriage we shared. I am going to miss you, honey." Jonathan reached into his coat pocket and pulled out a leather pouch filled with coins. He clanked it down on her desktop. "Here's the money you loaned me, with interest."

"Jon----"

He cut her off before she could protest. "I'm never going to give "Her" up, Natalie. Lady Luck's been my mistress for too many years. Please take this. I have won a lot of money here in Philadelphia. I am giving you only a small repayment for everything you've done for me in the past."

"We had a deal, Jonathan. You didn't renege on your half, and I will not renege on mine." She picked up the pouch and dropped it on his lap.

"Ouch! Watch where you throw that thing." He lifted the sack and dramatically rubbed his groin.

"You are such a baby, Jonathan. That did not hurt."

"How would you know? You are not a man!" He slammed the pouch down on the desktop. "You are keeping this, Natalie. I worked damned hard for this money, and you will not tell me what to do with it. I owe you a hell of a lot more than what is in this damn little sack.

Now, I want you to close your shop, take a nice long bath, put on your prettiest gown and be ready by six o'clock. Ben is sending his coach for you and Hope. He has a special arrangement for Hope's travel comfort, so do not worry about the details. All of us: You, Hope, Kirk, and I are invited to Ben's for dinner this evening." He said this with more authority than he had ever used on Natalie.

"Ben?"

"Yes, Ben"

"Well."

"You better be ready, little lady; that's all I can say." Jonathan moved toward the door. "And maybe you ought to wear that peach-colored gown Ben likes so much," he whispered, closing the door behind him.

*****

Max observed the approaching coach from the dining room window. Tonight was a special event and, as far as he was concerned, the most important dinner party Ben had ever thrown. In honor of that, Max had chosen his favorite recipes for the guests. He had also made sure the atmosphere was perfect too. Candles, sparkling wine goblets and a warm and welcoming fire. He watched as Ben was first to alight from the conveyance, looking dashing and happier than ever. He stood by the carriage steps while two stable hands lifted Hope into a chair and carried her carefully into the manse. Ben assisted Natalie with great care while his remaining gentlemen guests were left to their own capabilities. Together they moved to the front door in lively fellowship and excitement. They chorused a round of hellos to Max, handing over their wraps before moving into the sitting room.

"You certainly look very dapper this evening, Max," Kirk commented.

Ben agreed. "Actually, Max, I can't say when I've seen you look better."

"There was another day that I looked better, sir." Max glibly added.

"Oh yes, and what day was that?"

"My wedding day, sir. I was a younger man then and cut a fine figure. Though I can honestly say my spirits almost duplicated those, I held that day. Tonight will be a night to remember."

"I feel the same, Max. It's a gay and grand collection of friends."

"Sir, I might add my appreciation for inviting me to share a place at your table with these special people."

Ben grabbed Max's shoulders in a strong grip. "You're one of the most special guests this evening, Max."

"Thank you, sir."

The crowd gathered in the sitting room to share a small tray of hors d'oeuvres and Max's homemade wine. Hope sat in the soft upholstered chair by the fireplace, looking beautiful despite her serious injury. Natalie stood by her side, mothering her every move.

"If you feel the slightest discomfort, dear, please let me know. We can take you upstairs to the bedroom." Natalie insisted.

"I would not miss this evening for the world. I feel wonderful."

"Well, you certainly look wonderful," Kirk commented, squatting before her. Kirk smiled with warmth and touched the rim of his glass to hers.

Hope blushed.

"She does look wonderful, doesn't she?" Natalie added.

Kirk looked up at Natalie. "She is also a brave heroine, I hear. You, ladies, were quite the daring duo. The story is rich. Two exceedingly beautiful women conquer the bad guy with a well-placed object to trip over and a tiny pair of scissors. Kirk reached for Natalie's hand and kissed her fingertips.

"Watch your step; she's taken," Ben warned as he removed Natalie's hand from Kirk's grip and turned her toward him. "You look exceptionally beautiful tonight. Have I ever told you that this gown you are wearing is my favorite?"

"Only with your eyes," Natalie answered. Their gaze was locked in a passionate promise.

Jonathan severed the moment with his overly loud enthusiasm. He threw his arms up and turned in a complete circle while admiring the room.

"This is some fine place you have, Ben. I did not have a chance to tell you on the night of your party, but wow, yes, this is sooooome place!"

Jonathan moved next to Ben and rested his arm on his host's broad shoulders in a posture of friendship.

With a slight turn of his head, Ben frowned at the appendage.

Natalie hiccupped, whether from the wine or nerves.

Max saved the day and announced that dinner was now served in the dining room.

When the crowd entered the room, they saw small name cards placed at each table setting defining the seating arrangement, all of which was engineered by Ben. Ben was at the head with Natalie to his left and Max to Natalie's other side. Kirk sat across from Natalie, Hope beside Kirk and, surprisingly enough, at the far end of the table in what was considered another place of honor, Jonathan. Lively banter flowed throughout the meal, and just before the dessert course was served, Ben stood from his chair and addressed the group with a wine glass in hand.

"I am a rich man to have such fine friends." Thank you for coming this evening. Before the final course is served, I would like to express my feelings to each of you. Perhaps the most appropriate place to begin is with the man who has given me his undying devotion and service for the past five years. This man has shared his wisdom to help me see life as it should be. He has clarified my troubles and helped me face them with strength. My confidante, my friend, Max Seigel." Ben lifted his wineglass to his lips, and the guests followed suit. Max Seigel's smile stretched from ear to ear.

Ben's gaze then moved to Hope. "I know that from every bad experience in life, something good is always learned and gained. Perhaps I should thank Olivia for bringing you into my life. You are what every man dreams of having for a daughter, and if you do not mind, I would like to consider you just that. Hope, there is always a place for you here in my home."

Her eyes filled with tears. "I love you. . . Father." A lively applause broke out.

"Does that mean you're going to stay?" Kirk interjected. "I hope so because I much prefer that to a long-distance courtship,"

Hope smiled.

"If you intend to call on my daughter, Kirk, there will be a few rules and regulations," Ben retorted.

"Only a father for a few months, and look how he's acting!" Kirk replied, bringing laughter from the dinner guests.

When the laughter died down, Ben continued on a more serious note. He walked to the sideboard, lifted a cloth-covered object, and returned it to the table.

"Recently, I met a man who has shown me the true power of jealousy. I must honestly say that I have never felt such a wide range of feelings for one person." Ben locked his gaze on Jonathan. He realized that this was his one chance to tell Wakefield *his* true feelings in *his* home, serving *his* food and standing at the head of *his* table. If he did not say it now, he knew he'd never have a chance like this again.

"Before I even met you, Wakefield, I decided I didn't like you."

One could hear a pin drop.

"Natalie never told me much about you except for the fact that she had been married to a man who chose cards over her. I never understood that. I hated you. I did not know why, wasn't inclined to worry why, until I finally faced the fact that I loved Natalie and wanted no part of any other man in her life."

Jonathan's eyebrow shot up in surprise.

"It took your clever game to make me see it," Ben admitted.

He pulled the cloth off to reveal the jewelry box, and a chorus of appreciative sighs sounded around the table.

"I had agreed to make this for you to give Natalie, but all the while I was making it, I knew I couldn't let you give it to her."

Jonathan chuckled and finally cut in. "So, I guess you want to swing a deal, huh? Bet you want to give it to her instead, so she will give *you* all the credit for making the gift and the idea. I don't know if I can give you that edge."

"I don't blame you," Ben answered with a touch of humor. "I owe you a lot and would hate to take your thunder."

The crowd genuinely enjoyed their playful banter. They watched enthusiastically as Ben lifted the jewelry box lid and then turned it in Jonathan's direction.

"I thought that if I returned your cherished possession, I might win over your generosity."

Nestled in the middle compartment rested Jonathan's diamond pinky ring.

Jonathan was stupefied. He could not speak.

"The thugs must have dropped the ring in their haste to escape. I saw the glimmer of the diamond in the street when I bent down to help you that night." Ben removed the ring from its resting place and extended it to Jonathan.

Jonathan slid the ring back on his pinky finger tilting his hand back and forth till the stone caught the light. A wide smile grew on his lips. He reached for Ben's hand, shook it, pulled him into his embrace, and hugged him with force.

"Thank you, Ben. Thank you very much."

"Thought you might want it back, though heaven knows why. Too flashy for my taste," Ben sarcastically added.

"I do not believe our tastes are that different, my friend. Remember, we both chose Natalie," Jonathan pointed out.

Ben frowned at the reference. "By darn, Wakefield, thank you for your efforts, but you make it damn near intolerable!"

The guests around the table fell silent.

"Your rude reminders about the life you and Natalie once shared are uncalled for."

"Ben!" Natalie cut in. "Jonathan was merely drawing parallels. All he meant was that you fell in love with the same woman for the same reasons, right Jonathan?"

"Right, Honey."

He leaned back, balancing himself on the back legs of his chair, his arms folded across his chest and a big, toothy grin covering his face.

"I should be the jealous one, Ben. You are the one she loves. But let's get to the point. I guess you want to ask if you could give her the jewelry box instead of me, huh?"

Ben gave him a cold stare.

Jonathan lowered the chair until all four legs rested on the floor. He propped his forearms on the table before him and dropped his head. Then in a soft voice, he began.

"You want to give her the jewelry box because you designed and built it with your hands. You want to say it came from your heart because you have loved her more than any other woman. You want her to know that this is only the beginning of all the things you will make her and give her in the years to come and that even the jewelry boxes you have made in the past do not compare to this one because this one was made with love, and there lies the difference. Am I right, Ben Walters? Is this what you want to say?" Jonathan lifted his head and looked Ben straight in the eyes.

"Yeah, that's what I want to say," Ben answered, looking straight at Natalie. He realized once again that his archrival was a better man than he gave him credit for.

"Then how about if you let Max serve us some dessert so we can get out of here? I believe you might want to be alone when you tell her those things. You know, no need for your guests to be privy to your private life," Jonathan joked.

The guests snickered.

"Yeah, no need for that," Ben grumbled. Then after a moment of thought, Ben smiled too. "Max, bring on the dessert." He let out a bellow of laughter, then in front of his guests, he leaned down and

Cyn Garrett

gave Natalie a kiss that commanded the applause of everyone in the room.

The coach traveled back to the city with only Jonathan and Kirk aboard. The evening had drained Hope's strength, so she took refuge in the comfort of the bedroom Max prepared especially for her.

Although Olivia had behaved in a reprehensible way, Hope wrestled with the feelings she still held for her mother. Olivia had given her a good life and had loved her the only way she had known. The future would not be easy.

Hope's satisfaction came knowing that Ben's life would finally be filled with happiness. After all the years of living alone, he could now share it with a woman who knew how to give love, and, with these pleasant thoughts, she fell into a deep, peaceful slumber.

Downstairs two lovebirds sat sipping brandy by the fire.

"You're still wearing the yarn ring; I see," Ben commented, lifting Natalie's slender finger.

She rolled her head toward him on the upholstered chair and smiled. "Still wearing it."

"It's a pitiful sight." Ben reached for the jewelry box that rested on the small footstool before him and placed it on her lap. "This is not some ordinary jewelry box, you know? There is a secret compartment within."

Natalie placed her brandy snifter on the table and sat up straight. "I guess you want me to figure it out."

"You'll never do it," Ben simply answered. "If you could, then I guess it would not be secret. Open the lid and pull the velvet away from the back section."

274

Beneath, Natalie noticed a small brass hook lying flush with the unit's wall. She pushed it open and pulled the piece away.

"Aha! You are very clever," Ben uttered.

Surprisingly, Natalie was able to figure out the majority of it herself. Ben enjoyed watching her excitement. Though nothing compared to the look on her face when she opened the secret drawer and discovered the ring lying within. A wide gold band encrusted with rubies and diamonds winked back at her.

"Ben!" she breathed.

He removed the box from her lap and the yarn from her finger. Plucking the ring from its resting place, Ben pulled her from the chair and moved them closer to the flickering firelight.

"Will you marry me," he asked.

"What took you so long," Natalie answered in a quivering voice.

Ben slid the ring onto Natalie's finger. "It is all your fault, you know. If you had goaded me into that kiss years ago, we would now be married."

"That's all it would have taken?" she asked.

Ben pulled her against his hard body. Just before his lips claimed hers, he whispered, "Yep, all you had to do was kiss me once."

#

Printed in the USA
CPSIA information can be obtained
at www.ICGtesting.com
LVHW020607190923
758536LV00005B/223